HERACLITEAN FIRE

Sketches from a Life before Nature

ERWIN CHARGAFF

A Warner/Murray Curtin Book

A Warner Communications Company

This Jack, joke, poor potsherd, patch, matchwood,
  immortal diamond,
        Is immortal diamond.

                G.M. HOPKINS, *That Nature is a*
                Heraclitean Fire and of the
                comfort of the Resurrection

                For
                V., T., B.

Warner Books Edition

Copyright © 1978 Erwin Chargaff

Reprinted by arrangement with The Rockefeller University Press,
1230 York Avenue,
New York, N.Y. 10021.

Warner Books, Inc., 75 Rockefeller Plaza, New York, N.Y. 10019

Cover design by Dennis Wheeler

First printing: October 1980

10 9 8 7 6 5 4 3 2 1

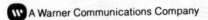 A Warner Communications Company

Printed in the United States of America

Library of Congress Cataloging in Publication Data

Chargaff, Erwin.
  Heraclitean fire.

  Reprint of the 1978 ed. published by the Rockefeller
University Press, New York.
  Bibliography: p.
  Includes index.
  1. Chargaff, Erwin.   2. Biochemists—United States
—Biography.   I. Title.
[QP511.8.C45A33 1980] 574.19′2′0924 [B] 80-14253
ISBN 0-446-97659-8 (U.S.A.)
ISBN 0-446-97783-7 (Canada)

CONTENTS

I

II

CONTINUED

III

THE SUN AND THE DEATH

A FEVER OF
REASON

La jeunesse est une ivresse continuelle:
c'est la fièvre de la raison.

LA ROCHEFOUCAULD

White Blood, Red Snow

THESE PAGES were written just about thirty years after the atomic bombs fell on Hiroshima and Nagasaki. I was forty years old in 1945, poorly paid, and still an assistant professor at Columbia University; I had already published nearly ninety papers; I had a good laboratory and a few gifted young collaborators; and I was getting ready to begin the study of the nucleic acids. A yearly grant of $6,000 from the Markle Foundation was the seal of my earthly success.

It is difficult to describe the effect that the triumph of nuclear physics had on me. (I have recently seen a film made by the Japanese at that time, and all the horror was revived, if "revive" is the correct word in front of mega-death.) It was an early evening in August, 1945 — was it the sixth? — my wife, my son, and I were spending the summer in Maine, in South Brooksville, and we had gone on an after-dinner walk where Penobscot Bay could be seen in all its sunset loveliness. We met a man who told us that he had heard something on the radio about a new kind of bomb which had been dropped in Japan. Next day, the *New York Times* had all the details. But the details have never stopped coming in since that day.

The double horror of two Japanese city names grew for me into another kind of double horror: an estranging awareness of what the United States was capable of, the country that five years before had given me its citizenship; a nauseating terror at the direction in which the natural sciences were going. Never far from an apocalyptic vision of the world, I saw the end of the essence of mankind; an end brought nearer, or even made possible, by the profession to which I belonged. In my view, all natural sciences were as one; and if one science could no longer plead innocence, none could. The time had long gone when you could say that you had become a scientist because you wanted to learn more about nature. You would immediately be asked: "Why do you want to know more about nature? Do we not know enough?" — and you would be lured into the expected answer: "No, we don't know enough; but when we do, we shall improve, we shall exploit nature. We shall be the masters of the universe." And even if you did not give this silly answer, you felt inwardly that the evil do-gooders might get away with such talk, were it not for death, the great eraser of stupidities. For had not Bacon assured me that knowledge was power, and Nietzsche — or rather his misinterpreters, his sister and the other exploiters of the silenced great man — that this was what I had wanted all my life? Of course, they were completely wrong, as far as I am concerned; and there is more wisdom in one of Tolstoy's folk tales than in the entire *Novum Organum* (with *Zarathustra* added without regret).

In 1945, therefore, I proved a sentimental fool; and Mr. Truman could safely have classified me among the whimpering idiots whom he did not wish admitted to the presidential office. For I felt that no man has the right to decree so much suffering, and that science, in providing and sharpening the knife and in upholding the arm, had incurred a guilt of which it will never get rid. It was at that time that the nexus between science and murder became clear to me. For several years after the somber event, between 1947 and 1952, I tried desperately to find a position in what then appeared to me as bucolic Switzerland, but I had no success.

That this was not the first, and not the greatest, slaughter of the innocent in our times dawned on me only later and very gradually. The governments of the world, both friend and enemy, had very successfully, and for multiple reasons of their own, concealed all knowledge of the German extermination factories. Such names as Auschwitz, Belsen, Chelmno, and the rest of that infernal ABC of suffocation and incineration, down to Westerbork and Yanov, fell only slowly on my consciousness, like blood drops from hell.

In the first years of this century, the great Léon Bloy looked at science — and what a tiny giant it then was! — and this is what he wrote[1]: *La science pour aller vite, la science pour jouir, la science pour tuer!* In the meantime we have gone faster, we have enjoyed less, and we have killed more. The Nazi experiment in eugenics — "the elimination of racially inferior elements" — was the outgrowth of the same kind of mechanistic thinking that, in an outwardly very different form, contributed to what most people would consider the glories of modern science. The diabolical dialectics of progress change causes into symptoms, symptoms into causes; the distinction between torturer and victim becomes merely a function of the plane of vision. Humanity has not learned — if I were a true scientist, i.e., an optimist, I should insert here the adverb "yet" — how to call a halt to this dizzying tumble into the geometrical progression of disasters which we call progress.

This was not the kind of science envisioned by me when I made my choice; we shall come to that later. At that time, I had certainly not understood that science was to grow into a machine for solving all kinds of problems which, in being solved scientifically, would give rise to even greater problems, and so on. The year 1945 changed my entire attitude toward science or, at any rate, the kind of science that surrounded me. Even when I was young, my inclinations were always in favor of critical scepticism — as shown by some of the reviews I wrote very early: one on the chemistry of the tubercle bacillus,[2] the other on lipoproteins[3] — but even I was not prepared for the orgy of exaggeration and empty promise that was soon to engulf biology. (When the so-called think tanks began to replace the thought processes of human beings, I called them the aseptic tanks.)

The Advantage of Being Uncomfortable

WHEN I WAS YOUNGER and people sometimes still told me the truth, I was often called a misfit; and all I could do was to nod sadly and affirmatively. For it is a fact that, with only a few glorious exceptions, I have not fitted well into the country and the society in which I had to live; into the language in which I had to converse; yes, even into the century into which I was born. This has been the fate of many people throughout history; our inhuman century, so full of enormous wars, unprecedented devastations, heart-rending dislocations, has added more than its share to the sum of human misery. But not everybody is born with a stone in the shoe.

However, there accrue to the outsider great benefits, too; there is some comfort in being uncomfortable. If one is left alone in the sense of solitude, one is also left alone in the sense of bother. Having never in my life received a call from another university—and this, probably more than my sedentary habits or the rightly undefinable charm of Columbia University, explains why I remained there for forty years—has spared me the upheaval of frequent moving. Never having filled a post at any of the professional societies to which I belong has protected me from having to make those vapid speeches with which our statesmen, scientific or otherwise, are expected to hypnotize the populace. If I have never belonged to the house of peers that goes by the name of "study section," I cannot complain, for "peer review" has been decent to me and I have not lacked scientific support; at least until the time when age, remoteness, estrangement, and perhaps even wisdom, built an armor of ice around me.

Nevertheless, if at one time or another I have brushed a few colleagues the wrong way, I must apologize: I had not realized that they were covered with fur.

The Outsider on the Inside

THE ESSAY FROM WHICH the present account arose was originally written by invitation and formed the prefatory chapter of a volume of the *Annual Review of Biochemistry*, in which scientific advances are reported periodically. I really do not know why I was asked. This perplexity should not be considered an instance of arrogant humility; I cannot serve as an example for younger scientists to follow. What I can teach cannot be learned. I have never been a "100 percent scientist." My reading has always been shamefully nonprofessional. I do not own an attaché case, and therefore cannot carry it home at night, full of journals and papers to read. I like long vacations, and a catalogue of my activities in general would be a scandal in the ears of the apostles of cost-effectiveness. I do not play the recorder, nor do I like to attend NATO workshops on a Greek island or a Sicilian mountain top; this shows that I am not even a molecular biologist. In fact, the list of what I have not got makes up the American Dream. Readers, if any, will conclude rightly that the *Gradus ad Parnassum* will have to be learned at somebody else's feet.

To sum up, I have always tried to maintain my amateur status.[4] I am not even sure that I comply with my own definition of a good teacher: he learned much, he taught more. Of one thing I am certain: a good teacher can only have dissident pupils, and in this respect I may have done some good.

I have often referred to myself as an outsider on the inside of science. The keepers of the flame may say correctly that they have no use for such outsiders. Well, they don't, but science does. Every activity of the human mind has, throughout history, given rise to criticism within its own ranks; and some—philosophy, for instance—consist to a large extent of criticism of previous efforts and their conceptual basis. Only science has, in our times, become complacent; it slumbers beatifically in euphoric orthodoxy, disregarding contemptuously the few timid voices of apprehension. These may, however, be the heralds of storms to come.

Our scientific mass society regards the outsider with little tenderness. Nowhere, however, is the penalty on even the mildest case of nonconformity higher than in the United States. I have lived in this country for forty-six years or so, and most of my scientific work and nearly all my teaching have taken place here. Whether some of my scientific observations are worth anything remains to be seen. But whatever the future decides — and I am afraid it will have other worries — I cannot but find it remarkable that almost all the recognition my work received has come from Europe. A major exception occurred, however, at the very end of my scientific career: the National Medal of Science given me in 1975.

A Bad Night for a Child to Be Out

I STARTED with this account in the middle of my life, and it is now time for me to go back. I was born on August 11, 1905, in Czernowitz, at that time a provincial capital of the Austrian monarchy. Having been born in 1905 meant that I was too young for the First and too old for the Second World War: a fact that was not without influence on my future life.

I had a peaceful and happy childhood, growing up in the last glow of a calm, sunlit period that was soon to end. I was the first child; a sister came five years later, and when the new bundle was shown to me I looked at it with dull surprise. Reading in other people's biographies about the many loves, hatreds, complexes, and multiple disorders of their young lives, I can only feel ashamed about the complete absence of comparable complaints in my own impassive case. I loved my parents and they loved me; they were good to me and helped me when I needed them; had I had a chance, I should have been good to them. But they were dead before I could be of much help.

I have always thought with great pity of my wonderful parents; they had a harder life than I have had. My father, Hermann Chargaff (1870–1934), had inherited modest wealth and a small private bank from his father. He had studied medicine at the University of Vienna, but had to give it up owing to my grandfather's early death. My mother's name was Rosa Silberstein. She was born in 1878 and died, only God knows where and when, having been deported into nothingness from Vienna in 1943.* She lives, a gentle and merciful figure, in the memories of my childhood, embodying for me, more than anyone else I ever met, what the Latin language calls, out of its very heart, *misericordia*.

I can still see her standing before me, in the beautiful dress of the early century, widehatted, longfrocked — was it "the liquefaction of her clothes" or of my dreaming child eyes? — a young and graceful and sad figure. When some time ago I saw Visconti's film *Death in Venice*, I experienced a melancholy leap of remembrance, a dreamlike recognition of the unrecognizable: there was my young mother in several hazily trembling replicas, walking on a misty beach, floating behind a screen of tears.

My father, as I remember him as a relatively young man, had, in double contrast to me, a jovial temperament and a big moustache. He retained both characteristics throughout his life, but he was of rather fragile health. The rough and cruel years that began with the outbreak of the First World War were more than he could bear. He was, in many respects, a typical old-fashioned Austrian, brought up in gentler times, and he did not have the strength to cope with war, inflation, impoverishment. He was a good violinist, but an injury to a hand prevented him from playing during the later part of his life. I can recall his library very vividly. It was housed in a huge, tastelessly orna-

* An Austrian scoundrel-physician and a heartless American consul combined forces to prevent her from joining me in New York before the war broke out.

mented bookcase with glass doors. The centerpiece consisted of a voluminous encyclopedia, *Meyer's Grosses Konversationslexikon*, in twenty-four volumes. A ridiculously polymathic child, I derived much of my premature erudition from this solid compilation. Then there were the so-called classics—Goethe, Schiller, Lessing, and also Shakespeare, in the bad Dingelstedt translation, I believe—heavily gilded folios, resplendent with illustrations in the worst taste of the *Gründerzeit*. But there were also the good and reticent Cotta editions of the German poets, a few of which—Kleist, E.T.A. Hoffmann, Platen, Chamisso—have stayed with me all my life. These, and my father's watch, comprised my inheritance.

The frequent misspelling of my family name under which I suffered even as a youth showed me early how rare, or even unique, the name is. During my time of frequent and wide-ranging travel I must have consulted hundreds of telephone directories, but I never found this name. My father's father was Isaak Don Chargaf (1848–1903)—this was the spelling of the surname in a document I once saw—and one of the many dubious family legends reported that my ancestors always had "Don" as their second forename. Whether this points to their having come from Spain, I do not know; nor whether the double consonant at the end of the name was the product of a sort of Germanization, a pre-Darwinian allusion to my primordial forebear. I must add that I have never been particularly interested in genealogy, having come to the conclusion that, if one tries hard enough, one can always trace back one's ancestry to Aeneas, William the Conqueror, Lucas Cranach the Elder, or, in the alternative case, to Rabbi Katzenellenbogen.

When I was born, my parents were well off and I grew up in what, in the present abominable sociologico-economic jargon, would be called an upper middle-class family. In subsequent years, the capital of my father's small bank vanished, mostly owing to the misplaced trust my father had put in employees and customers; he liquidated the firm in 1910 and had to seek employment. According to one of the numerous highly untrustworthy family legends, some of the embezzled or otherwise defalcated money ended up in the United States, contributing to the early glory of Hollywood. I could have wished it a better use.

These were the last peaceful years of a century that will surely be remembered in history, if there will still be history, as the century of mass slaughter. It is true, I missed the Boer War and the Russian-Japanese War; but from the time I was seven years old my life has been accompanied, an incessant bourdon, as it were, by reports from battlefields, by daily body counts, by tales of slaughter. The first film I ever saw, a newsreel in 1912, showed a troop train in the Balkan War, and the engine came at me with frightening speed, accelerated by the hammering of the pianist. Later, when I was older, science seemed a refuge from the horrors, but these have caught up with me.

My memories of the city of my birth are dim. Colors keep coming back to me: black and rose; the bright costumes of the Ruthenian peasants who came to the market; the park of the Episcopal palace — never again has anything been so green in my life. And then the garden behind our house: there was a tiny grotto in it, and all the dangers of medieval chivalry were relived shiveringly in the dead-serious world of a dreamy child. Rather dull to reality, I lived in a world of my own making; and if it was not as well-furnished as Mörike's Orplid or the dream world of the Brontë children, I had to build it all by myself, for I had few friends.

I can still hear my mother's voice when the three-year-old ventured to climb a tiny hill in the garden. *Erwinchen*, she called, *du bist kein Hochtourist*! And so I never became much of a mountain climber. As reports have it, I was very late in starting to talk: a deficiency for which I have surely made up since.

The larger cities of the Habsburg monarchy all carried a strong family resemblance, which, despite the vicissitudes of recent history, they still retain. When a few years ago I visited

Zagreb in the Croatian part of Yugoslavia, there was my birthplace again. The same eclectic style—a sort of fiscal renaissance—of the centrally placed, solid city theater, the university, the courthouse, usually called *Justizpalast*, the *Gymnasium*, the *Volksgarten*. I suppose similar tears of melancholy recognition fill the eyes of some Americans when they come upon a Hotdog Emporium or a Hamburger Haven in Yokohama. But the Austrian coffeehouses spread a better kind of civilization.

And then came 1914. We were spending the summer in Zoppot on the Baltic Sea. One afternoon at the end of June, we were watching the younger sons of Emperor Wilhelm II playing tennis; an adjutant came and whispered something into the imperial ears. They threw down their rackets and went away: the Austrian Archduke Franz Ferdinand had been assassinated. The nineteenth century had come to an end: the lamps that went out all over Europe during that summer have never been lit again.

When the summer was over and we were due to return, there was no home any more: Czernowitz was about to be occupied by the Russian army. We went to Vienna, a city that in many respects I have always considered as my home town. At any rate, it is in Vienna that my father is buried, it was from Vienna that my mother was taken away.

Experimental Station for the End of the World

THE AUSTRO-HUNGARIAN monarchy, whose evening glow I barely experienced, was a unique institution. The nuptial skills of the Habsburgs, immortalized in a celebrated hexameter,* really had as little to do with

---

* *Bella gerant alii, tu, felix Austria, nube!* (Let others conduct wars; you, lucky Austria, marry!). Matrimony was, in fact, the continuation of warfare by other means.

it as the well-known Viennese *Gemütlichkeit*, which is often a thin crust over a truly bestial ferocity. Prince Metternich—the Kissinger of the nineteenth century, only better-looking—was no more responsible for it than were Haydn or Mozart or Schubert, Stifter or Nestroy or Trakl. The empire, much more humanized by its subjugated Slavic components than by its Germanic, let alone its Hungarian, masters, was actually held together by the patina it had acquired, more or less accidentally, through many centuries. When first I opened my eyes and saw it, the monarchy was in an extremely unstable equilibrium. A passage from one of Heinrich von Kleist's letters (November 16, 1800) comes to mind. He had been passing through an arched gateway: "Why, I thought, does the vault not collapse, though entirely without support? It stands, I replied, because all the stones want to fall down at the same time." The Antonine repose of the late monarchy was fictitious; but like all genuine fiction it lived a life of its own. I suppose it had to break up; its disappearance did not make for a better world.

A description of what it meant to live during the dying years of the Austrian monarchy, and especially in Vienna, has often been attempted, seldom successfully. The odor exhaled by all official buildings, a mixture of wilted roses and fermenting urine, cannot be duplicated, except in dreams; the combination of easy-going *Schlamperei*, sycophantic good-naturedness, and ferocious brutality was probably as unique as was the instinctive search for the middle way, the willingness to propose and accept a compromise, as long as it was advantageous to the party proposing it. I suspect, however, that every *bas-empire* will develop similar channels of blissful decrepitude. Child though I was, I soon became a not unobserving spectator, for my eyes had been opened early.

While rummaging through my uncle's books one day in 1915 or 1916, I came across a recent issue of *Die Fackel* (The Torch), a periodical edited and at that time written entirely by Karl Kraus. An avid extracurricular reader even then, I tried to understand, though it was not easy. Besides, the text was full of white patches: the censor had done his work. For Karl Kraus, the greatest satirical and polemical writer of our times, was a fearless critic of the war and of the society that had given rise to it. He was the deepest influence on my formative years; his ethical teachings and his view of mankind, of language, of poetry, have never left my heart. He made me resentful of platitudes, he taught me to take care of words as if they were little children, to weigh the consequences of what I said as if I were testifying under oath. For my growing years he became a sort of portable Last Judgment. This apocalyptic writer — the title of this chapter comes from one of his descriptions of Austria — was truly my only teacher; and when, many years later, I dedicated a collection of essays[5] to his memory, I acquitted myself of a small share of a grateful debt. Several people who noticed the dedication asked me whether it was to a former high-school teacher of mine. I said yes.

The teachings of Karl Kraus derived mainly from his relation to the spoken and written word. This was, at any rate, what influenced me most in my youth, for we take from others what is in us. He considered language as the mirror of the human soul, and its misuse as a forerunner of black and evil deeds. A grammatical haruspex, as it were, he read the barbarous and bloody times to come in the entrails of the daily press. The press, in turn, repaid its greatest enemy by a conspiracy of silence that lasted his entire lifetime. Hundreds of masterly essays, miracles of style and thought, many books, several plays, seven volumes of poetry, three collections of aphorisms: all this the press tried to bury in an unnamed pauper's grave. Paradoxically, this form of burial ends with the life of the victim, owing to the operation of mysterious forces that are only inadequately expressed by the old adage *Veritas praevalebit*. The conspiracy of which I have spoken, this instinctive automatic consensus, was, of course, not a Viennese specialty. I have seen similar successful camarilla operations in action against one of the greatest literary critics of our time, Frank R. Leavis; and, much later in my life, in brief periods of temporary megalomania, I believe I felt myself the same evil breath.

Once in my early life I experienced Austria in its expiring glory, and that was in 1916 when the eighty-six-year-old Emperor Franz Joseph died and was laid to rest with all the pomp of the Spanish baroque. The spectacle impressed me deeply, though it may only have been a Makart copy of a Greco original. The riderless black horses tripped their way through my dreams for quite some time.

A much more momentous event, which I remember vividly, occurred one year later. I am thinking, of course, of the Russian revolution. I was twelve at that time, and must already have been a regular reader of the leading newspaper, *Neue Freie Presse*, whose trite editorials accompanied the bloody war and the disastrous collapse of Austria-Hungary. I remember reading about Kerensky, and later about Lenin and also about Trotsky, with whose sons my wife used to play as a small girl in pre-war Vienna. For various reasons, the words Winter Palace and Brest-Litovsk stand out in my memory. I followed the day-by-day descriptions of the conference that was to take Russia out of the war with a great deal of stupid interest. Did I know that I was witnessing the most epochal event of this century, or was I more interested in my Boy Scout uniform and the privilege thereby conferred on me to salute the Austrian generals, on leave from one of the frequent army debacles? Really, I do not know.

I received most of my education in one of the excellent *Gymnasiums* which Vienna at that time possessed, the *Maximiliansgymnasium* in the ninth district. The instruction was limited in scope, but of very high quality. In particular, I loved the classical languages and was very good at them. I had excellent teachers whose names I have not forgotten: Latin, Lackenbacher; Greek, Nathansky; German, Zellweker; history, Valentin Pollak; mathematics, Manlik. These were the principal subjects, in addition to some philosophy, a little physics, and a ridiculous quantity of "natural history." Of chemistry and the rest of the natural sciences there was nothing. I was one of those horrible types who enjoy school; I had a good memory and learned easily.

The Vienna theater, and especially the *Burgtheater*, had been great in the nineteenth century, but I saw no more than the last glow of a glorious period. Yet, I remember my first *Iphigenie* with Hedwig Bleibtreu. But music was still great. Unforgettable evenings in the *Hofoper*, later called *Staatsoper*, with Jeritza as Tosca, Mayr as Leporello, with Richard Strauss conducting Mozart or his own works, with Franz Schalk conducting *Fidelio*; and later the terrible battles with the "Stieglitz gang," a semilicensed claque which tyrannized the queues for standing room. Unforgettable afternoons with the Rosé Quartet or with the Philharmonic Symphony conducted by Nikisch, Weingartner, or Bruno Walter. Such names as Schönberg, Webern, Berg, I barely heard mentioned. The audience went, reluctantly, up to Gustav Mahler and stopped there.

Altogether, the stratification of cultural life was truly remarkable; except, perhaps, for literature, we lived much more in the past than in the present. On my way to school I passed every day the house in the Berggasse where, at the entrance door, a plaque announced the office of "Dr. S. Freud." This meant nothing to me: I had not heard the name of the man who had discovered entire continents of the soul that, arguably, might better have been left undiscovered. That great work was done around me in many disciplines, in philosophy and linguistics, in the history of art and economics, in mathematics, escaped me almost entirely. Although I had some contact with the Vienna Circle of philosophers — I attended, for instance, one of Schlick's courses — the name of Wittgenstein became known to me only when I lived in New York.

The flavor of life in Vienna at that time can be gathered from a few novels, such as Robert Musil's *Der Mann ohne Eigenschaften*

(The Man Without Qualities) or Joseph Roth's *Radetzkymarsch* (Radetzky March), and from the prose poems of Peter Altenberg. The intellectual history of Austria has been summarized in an excellent book by my friend Albert Fuchs, written shortly before he died at an early age.[6]

The Forest and Its Trees

THE LITERARY childhood disease of my generation was represented by an excessive admiration for the juvenile adventure stories of Karl May. In my case, this affliction passed very early. Even as a child I was an unremitting reader, and by the time I entered the upper classes of the *Gymnasium* I must have devoured most of the classical literature of the Western world. Although German is, next to Russian, perhaps the best language for translations, many of those must have been awful, if I am to judge from a recent inspection of three of the books through which I fought my way, in stupid bliss, when I was twelve. I still have them, and there they stand, these great falsifiers of all that the poet felt and expressed, and they call themselves *Die göttliche Komödie*, *Der rasende Roland*, and *Das befreite Jerusalem*. But the same was undoubtedly also true of *Krieg und Frieden* or *Gullivers Reisen*, and innumerable other translations from many languages which contributed to my premature introduction to the literary past and present. Only French I never read in translation. Much later, when I had learned several other languages, I became aware of the extent to which almost all translations betray the spirit of the writer. Reading Ronsard or Goethe or Blake in translation amounts to listening to a transcription of the B Minor Mass for the ocarina. So far as the German language is concerned, there are, however, two great exceptions: the Luther Bible (in its early editions) and the translation of part of Shakespeare by A.W. Schlegel. These books have grown into the very heart and mind of everybody whose mother tongue is German. But my real reading began, I believe, in 1920, when my mother gave me as a present Goethe's complete works in the sixteen volumes of the beautiful Insel edition. They still stand, much-read since, on my shelves, although the postwar buckram and glue gave up their service a long time ago.

In addition to Karl Kraus, whom I have already mentioned, two other writers, both Scandinavian, greatly influenced my growing years: Knut Hamsun and Søren Kierkegaard. The first novel of Hamsun that I read was *Mysterier*, and the tongue-tied sincerity, the exuberant reticence, the radical conservatism, the dialectical lyricism of this remarkable and widely misunderstood writer accompanied me while I grew up. For various reasons, Hamsun has never occupied the same high rank among English readers as he has with my generation in Austria and Germany. As for America, I can, however, well understand why the erstwhile trolley conductor in Chicago, one of the early defectors from the American Dream, commanded little sympathy.

To an even greater dialectician of the soul, to Kierkegaard, I came by a more devious route. When I was fifteen or sixteen years old, something I had read in *Die Fackel* drew my attention to a not widely known literary-philosophical periodical published in, of all places, Innsbruck. *Der Brenner* appeared at irregular intervals under the editorship of one of those great, self-effacing maieutic helpers of great literature, Ludwig von Ficker. It was a most unconventional journal and, perhaps, the best of its kind. The great Austrian poet Georg Trakl was first published there, and so was the profound and not easily explored philosopher Ferdinand Ebner. One of the regular contributors was Theodor Haecker, next to Bernanos the most impressive polemical writer and essayist of modern Catholicism. It was an essay of Haecker's that directed me to Kierkegaard, and I read, with more enthusiasm than understanding, first *Enten-Eller* (Either-Or) and then *Frygt og Baeven* (Fear and Trembling), both in a pedantically denaturing translation.

Reading, as I still sometimes do, though now with the meager help of a Danish dictionary, Kierkegaard's passionately engaged prose—in his Diary, his Sermons or, at its reddest heat, in *Øjeblikket* (The Moment)—I cannot but regret that a trite wet blanket of uncommitted rationality is now covering the entire world. Where do dreamy young people find the little hole through which to escape, if only for a short night, this frightening world: in hashish, in Hesse? A hundred years ago, they would have laughed with Offenbach, Nestroy, even Labiche; now it is at best Woody Allen.

It will become clear that since my childhood I have had a magical relationship to language. I have always been an ardent lover of words, in the sense both of *Worte* and of *Wörter*, of *paroles* and of *mots*; and, for this reason and many others, I regret the trend that has made of linguistics a mock science, a sort of molecular philology, in which the precision of the trappings conceals the emptiness of the core—just as in molecular biology. They prattle about *l'écriture* and "the degree zero of writing"; but it seems to me that nobody writes any more, and those who claim to do so have begun to resemble Pavlovian dogs, except that they salivate even without the ringing of a bell.

Language, that most mysterious gift of humanity, is usually singled out as the one faculty that distinguishes man from animal. I could think of other less flattering differences; but at any rate it *is* true that language separates man from man, that it is the most faithful mirror of growth and decline. For instance, it has often occurred to me that as inconspicuous an event as the disappearance from English usage of the nominative pronoun of the second person singular, i.e., of "thou," may have represented a greater upheaval for those concerned than many more famous revolutions. God, lovers, and letter-carriers are addressed in the same manner; the majesty of intimacy has given place to a polite remoteness; the indispensable ritual of changing from *vous* to *tu* has become the victim of a grammatical egalitarianism that has corroded the poetic core of the language.

Its lyrical labyrinths have been filled up and made useful for all purposes. After this happened, only the greatest of poets have been able to break through the utility barriers of a tired vocabulary.

There must, of course, have been reasons why this happened, but I am not eager to give, or ask for, an explanation. My long life in the midst of the explanatory sciences has made me tired of explanations. They are, except in the most trivial instances, a placebo for our reason, dulling us to the mysteries surrounding us, without which we could not live. Great as is my admiration for the modern concept of "biological information," I do not, for instance, believe that it is some form of genetic change — the loss of a few purines from English DNA — that has caused the disappearance of the invaluable pronoun.

For this reason, and for many others, I look with great diffidence on the struggles between the various schools of modern linguistics: between what one could call molecular or Cartesian linguistics on the one hand and behaviorist linguistics on the other. Those who assume that the ability to form syntactic structures is born with us are probably correct. Does this mean that there are certain regions in our DNA that "program" us for the ability or, better, for the compulsion? I doubt it. Life is the continual intervention of the inexplicable. It is likely that we could learn more about the initiation of language from following the creation of a lyrical poem than from studying sentence structures.* If the abrupt throwing of bridges above the dark abyss of the onset of human life, if the explosive formation of associations, in which sense and sound become undistinguishable, make the great poet or the great wit, then the young child is probably both.

Although I have often said that, were I given a second life of learning, I should take up the study of language, I must say

---

* One could spend a few very profitable hours in following, for instance, the multiple layers of meaning, rhythm, and expression through which one of Hölderlin's hymnic poems developed.

that I have always learned more about language from great writers than from textbooks. Unfortunately, few poets have spoken about words, since they very rightly did not consider them as tools. But there exist a few passages of great interest. The third act of the Second Part of *Faust*, the magical resurrection of Helen of Troy —*Bewundert viel und viel gescholten, Helena* — is, perhaps, the greatest transsubstantiation of mythical antiquity into a modern language. On August 25, 1827, a young writer, Carl Iken, sent Goethe a long letter about this work, and Goethe answered one month later. From these two remarkable letters, not widely known, I have learned much about created language. Another of the rare instances of deep insight into the creative processes in which language is implicated may be seen in the profound essays that Karl Kraus included in his book *Die Sprache*.

It is not accidental that in following the numerous hypotheses on the origin of language, which have been put forward in the last 200 years or so, one is constantly reminded of the more recent, and equally fruitless, discussions on the origin of life. The substitution of the experimentally provable "could-have-been" for the experimentally inaccessible "has-been" is an old trick of pseudo-scientific prestidigitation that usually ends in calling "life" what is not life and "language" what is not language. The attempt to define the undefinable, to achieve a retrogression into the origin of origins, will always end in the banal recognition that the experimental sciences are not historical ones and that they are even less philosophical than is present-day philosophy. Goethe, so often maligned by idiots in his capacity of thinker about nature, has said it once for all. *Das schönste Glück des denkenden Menschen ist, das Erforschliche erforscht zu haben und das Unerforschliche ruhig zu verehren.**

* (It is the highest bliss for the thinking man to have explored what can be explored and quietly to worship what cannot.) Even in this simple instance, there appears the predicament of the translator-traitor. All languages are equally rich, but not in convertible currency.

In the evening and at night, my friend Albert Fuchs and I often walked through the beautiful streets of Vienna, and we talked endlessly about writing: what made a text genuine, what caused a poem to be good. We distinguished between *Aussage* (statement) and *Ausdruck* (expression), and we concluded that only the genius could "express," whereas any talent could "state." Something of this distinction has remained with me, and I would still say that only what is "stated" can be translated, but not what is "expressed." That is why Thomas Mann is eminently translatable and Stifter or Rimbaud are not.

Having learned from Karl Kraus how heavy words can be, I have always lamented my enforced separation from the language in which my mother spoke to me when I was a child. I have never let myself be torn away from the German language, nor have I ever declared war on it; but there is an unavoidable estrangement. This is not compensated by my having learned, in the meantime, many languages, one of which, French, I spoke better when I was four than I do now. (*Fräuleins* from Fribourg or Neuchâtel saw to it.) There exist mysterious links between language and the human brain; and the heartless and brutal way in which language is used in our times, as if it were only a power tool in public relations, a shortcut from sly producer to gullible consumer, has always seemed to me the most threatening portent of incipient bestialization. It is frightening to observe that a progressive aphasia, not organically determined, appears to overtake large numbers of people who seem to be unable to express themselves except by hoarse barks and (undeleted) expletives. The gift of tongues, not explainable on the basis of natural selection, is the true attribute of *Menschwerdung* (hominization); and it is only fitting that it be revoked shortly before the tails begin to grow.

The World in One Voice

WHEN THE CONSEQUENCES of the war — truncation, famine, inflation — began to be felt less severely, Vienna and its appendix, the Austrian republic, settled down to pushing tourism. Foreigners who were able to pay* got a thick slice of the well-known Viennese *Gemütlichkeit* thrown at them; a commodity that in earlier times had not been much in evidence with respect to other types of foreigners, for instance, poor Bohemian tailors or Polish cooks. But now festivals were organized everywhere. The entire cultural past of Austria — and it was a great past — was mobilized to catch the boobies. Publicity vultures, disguised as melodious pigeons, descended on the whole world; and merchants of genius, such as Max Reinhardt, succeeded in making the *Salzburger Festspiele* into a permanent institution, so that even after more than fifty years the bell still tolls for Everyman in Hofmannsthal's pale adaptation.

Deification usually begins soon after the body has been thrown into the pauper's pit in the cemetery. In the case of Mozart, it took Austria a little longer; but when I was young he was the pivot of the Austrian obsession with *Fremdenverkehr* (foreign tourism). This had the welcome consequence that his truly indispensable works were very often performed and very well.

Otherwise, the frantic effort of playing minstrel to the world led to the production of a great deal of rubbish. Especially, the theater declined, except for occasional visits by actors or troupes from other towns. Berlin and, perhaps, Munich had more to offer.

But my friends and I were little concerned with all this, for we had found elsewhere the theater of our souls: at that time

---

* Such a term as *kaufkräftige Ausländer* (foreigners able to purchase) embodied the oozing of what was then called *valuta* from all pores of the moderately amused victim. Ironically, the Austrian shilling is at present much more a "valuta" than the U.S. dollar.

Karl Kraus gave frequent recitals, and between 1920 and 1928 I must have attended most of them. Since they are all listed in *Die Fackel*, I see that, for instance, seventeen readings were held in Vienna in 1921 and eighteen in 1927. Even the program leaflets for those evenings or afternoons were unusual and interesting, consisting mostly of one large sheet of paper, about 11 × 8.5 inches, carrying, on both sides, all sorts of text: program and notes, poems, manifestoes, letters of rebuke or approval, announcements of forthcoming events, solicitations on behalf of charities.* For many years, Kraus donated the receipts from all his lectures to war victims, to Russian children during the famine, and to similar causes.

The recitals covered an unimaginable range of texts. Very often he would read from his own writings: poems, short satirical or polemical pieces — the celebrated *Glossen*, an art form completely original with him — sometimes longer essays or a few scenes from his *Last Days of Mankind*, a gigantic work that cannot be classified, although outwardly it looks like a drama. Sometimes he would insert a section devoted to poems of the seventeenth or eighteenth century, many of which he had rediscovered. This is the period when, with such names as Gryphius, Hofmannswaldau, Günther, Claudius, Goecking, Klopstock, Bürger, Hölty, and Goethe, German lyrical poetry reached a rank that has seldom been equaled in other languages. At other times, he read an entire play, by Büchner or by Wedekind, by Raimund, Niebergall, or Gerhart Hauptmann. But most of all he liked to read Shakespeare, Nestroy, and Offenbach. Of many of Shakespeare's plays he had prepared stage editions. Two volumes of these have been published; the continuation was cut off by the death of Kraus in 1936 at the age of sixty-two.

---

* When, after the deportation of my mother from Vienna, her apartment was looted by the natives, not only most of the books and papers of my youth were lost, but also an irreplaceable collection of more than a hundred of these programs.

Having mentioned, in the company of Shakespeare, a name that cannot be familiar to most readers, I should perhaps say that Johann Nestroy (1801–1862), playwright and actor, is one of those marvels of wit, satire, and linguistic imagination that embarrass the literary critic because of difficulties of understanding and classification. He was, in many respects, a second Molière, though much less translatable and, to my taste, much funnier. That his fame never went beyond the boundaries of his native Vienna has to do with several facts: the Vienna of Franz Joseph was not the Paris of Louis XIV; Nestroy's language, sparkling with the reflections of a vigorous dialect, was not the classical language of a newly founded *Académie*; in a period of blissful hebetude, as it pervaded Europe before 1914, it is the comic spirit that suffers first. In any event, Karl Kraus had much to do with the resurrection of his celebrity. This started with an essay, *Nestroy and Posterity*, which he read in 1912 at an event commemorating the fiftieth anniversary of Nestroy's death.

The readings of Kraus sometimes followed each other in a feverish tempo, and this was in addition to a truly monumental literary productivity of the highest rank. For instance, within three weeks in 1925 there were four recitals, three devoted to his own works, one to *King Lear*; and again, in 1927, within three weeks: Nestroy's *The Confused Magician* and three works by Offenbach—*Bluebeard*, *The Grand Duchess of Gerolstein*, and *Parisian Life*.

I know of few instances of this combination of very great literary and theatrical gifts; Dickens is the only one who comes to mind. In his youth, Karl Kraus had wanted to become an actor. At 19 he had made an unsuccessful debut in a semiprofessional performance of Schiller's *Die Räuber*, in which he played the evil brother Franz Moor. On the same occasion, a minor part was acted by Max Reinhardt.

The readings usually took place in small concert or lecture halls, approximately the size of Carnegie Recital Hall in New

York. Several hundred people attended and the rooms were always full, often sold out. The audience was preponderantly young, hysterically enthusiastic, and given to noisy ovations, which obviously gave great pleasure to Kraus, whose existence and activity were otherwise deliberately ignored by the press and the officialdom of his home town. In this respect, Kraus joined the other great Viennese figures of his day: Freud, Schönberg, Musil. Musil, incidentally, was a not unmalicious observer of the enthusiasm that on occasion could detonate noisily during the recitals. He notes in his diary around 1937: "Long before there were dictators, our time gave rise to a spiritual dictator worship. See [Stefan] George, but also Kraus and Freud, Adler and Jung. . . . "

In addition to this young contingent in the audience, there were many older, no less devoted, habitual listeners, many of them persons of great distinction. I remember, for instance, one handsome couple whom I saw at most sessions, sitting in one of the first rows and applauding vigorously. Only much later did I find out that this was the composer Alban Berg and his wife. And there were many others. It was almost the only opportunity for registering one's cultural and, therefore, political protest against the prostitution of everything that had made Austria great; a sellout in which all of official Austria participated: political parties, the press, art, the theater, the universities. As I try to recall the features of Europe's Hippocratic face, getting ready to die, as I bring back to mind the objects of our protest, their similarity to what I see now in the United States becomes frightening.

The setting of the lectures: a small bare table and a chair, a bit off-center on the platform. Kraus enters rapidly from the side, carrying several books, with markers sticking out, or a sheaf of papers. He is slightly under middle size and one shoulder is a little higher than the other. The first impression is of an exceedingly shy aloofness. The burst of applause that greets him is usually not acknowledged. The reading begins, but not without a ceremonial and careful wiping and changing of eye glasses and frequent blowing of the nose. The latter activity, occurring sometimes at moments of greatest excitement, is one of the tools of *Verfremdung*, of which Kraus was an early master.* The illusion that is created must be broken into by the realization that this is a created illusion. No use having a dream if you do not know that you are dreaming.

He reads seated at the table, with strong accentuation of the grammatical and logical structure, so that even the most complex sentences—and the German language is rich in possibilities—become clear as one listens, as if one were viewing a labyrinth from high up. Sometimes a hand is thrown up high in the air or an invective punctuated by sharp raps on the table. At certain emphatic moments he stands up, the paper grasped by two fists, and the voice becomes staccato and trenchant, a deep falsetto of impending doom. (Some people laughed; but quite enough doom has occurred in the meanwhile, and the compound interest is not yet paid in.)

At other times, there will be rapid cascades of the most astonishing, revealing, and frightening wordplay. The English language has only the name of pun for it; the fact that this is taken to be a cheap aberration only shows how old our English has become. For wordplay is thoughtplay; and play can be a dead-serious business, the rhythmic awareness of the unimagined possibilities of an ever-renewing, dying, and resurgent nature. To find one's way back to the clear and undefiled spring from which language flows is granted a few. Rabelais was one of those, and so were Lichtenberg and Kraus. It is Lichtenberg of whom Goethe once said: "Where he makes a joke, there hides a

---

* *Verfremdung* cannot be translated as *estrangement* or *alienation*. In his Stockholm lecture of 1939, *On Experimental Theater*, Brecht writes: "*Verfremdung* of an event or of a character simply means that the event or the character is deprived of its matter-of-factness, its familiarity, its plausibility, and is made into an object of surprise and curiosity." In some respects surrealism, at any rate in the paintings of Magritte and Delvaux, is the art of *Verfremdung*.

problem." This was equally true of Kraus, who was probably the wittiest writer in the German language. The syntactic cataract of his periods, delivered in a specially pointed voice, was an ambush, hiding associations of a shockingly unexpected immediacy.

And what a voice his was! To describe it I should have to use some of the sonorous adjectives with which the German baroque writers, drunk with the expressive abundance of their language, embellished their paeans: *freveltrotzig*, *grimmbewehrt*, *zornblind*, but also *holdselig*, *liebreich*, *lustreizend*. (The English language now is too desiccated to welcome onomatopoeia born of the inner core of the sound and meaning of words. Translation would involve a long and dull paraphrase. Let it be enough to say that the first group of words thunders of compounded hatred, anger, wrath, whereas the second series whispers of loveliness and bliss and charm.)

On other occasions, when light operas were presented or when singing was required by the frequent musical interludes of the Nestroy plays, the audience was entertained in a different way. Kraus, who had a deep understanding of certain kinds of music, had a pleasant, though untrained, tenor voice. He delivered the music in a parlando style whose intellectual lucidity made it impossible to raise the question of technical sufficiency. (The excellent pianists who accompanied him were usually hidden behind a screen.) For many of these songs, arias, or chansons he wrote additional stanzas that were very funny and usually bore on problems of the day. This technique, which he also employed in his own plays, is, incidentally, not the only way in which Kraus had a lasting influence on Bertolt Brecht, whom he held in the highest esteem. His reading of Brecht's poem *Die Liebenden* was an unforgettable experience. It is not an accident that Kraus and Brecht, the two most intense German writers of this century, had great respect for each other.

Why have I written all this? Mainly to bear witness to my good fortune in having had such a teacher.

No Hercules, No Crossroads

MY GENERATION in Central Europe will always be marked as the children of the Great Inflation. The extent to which the value of money was wiped out in Austria and Germany can hardly be imagined, although as I write this the beginnings of a similar process become noticeable, at any rate in the capitalist countries. Savings and pensions disappeared into the darkening sky that was to unload itself finally in the thunderstorm which the Hitler regime represented for Central and Western Europe. When an insurance policy that my father had taken out in 1902 was redeemed twenty years later it amounted to the price of one trolley ticket. When, in the summer of 1923, before entering the University, I made my *Maturareise* through Germany, one had to eat with the utmost celerity because prices often went up during the meal. My parents were not exceptional in being completely impoverished.

I was eighteen and the world was before me, as the silly saying goes. Actually, the world never is before anyone, nor does it ever look darker than when one is eighteen. The future scientist should be able to tell stories of his early past, how he always knew that he wanted to be a chemist or a lepidopterist; how he could be nothing else, having blown himself up at six years of age in his basement laboratory or having captured, in tender years, a butterfly of such splendor and rarity as to make Mr. Nabokov blanch with envy. I can offer nothing of the sort. Being gifted for many things, I was gifted for nothing. Indolent, shy, and sensitive, I had laid my traps where no game would ever pass.

It was quite clear to everybody that I should have to enter the University and acquire a doctor's degree. This had the advantage of postponing the unpleasant decision about my future by four years or so, and also of equipping me with the indispensable prefix to my name without which a middle-class Austrian of my generation would have felt naked. Quite different from more advanced civilizations, where this appellative is reserved for medical businessmen, in Vienna the doctor's title became a fundamental part of one's *persona*, and it has stuck to me even down to the current New York telephone directory; this particular form of amputation would have been much too painful.

There remained the decision in which faculty to register. Decisions usually are not made as a consequence of profound deliberations, but by much more casual routes which then are subjected to a post-factum rationalization. This was certainly my case. There were four, later five, faculties at the University: philosophy, law, medicine, theology, and later political science. In addition, there was the *Technische Hochschule* with its several branches of engineering, but here, unless you worked long years for the Dr.-Ing., you got only the degree of "Ingenieur," much less useful for impressing hotel concierges, barbers, tailors. I rejected medicine, since I felt it to be incompatible with my temperament, and law, partly for the same reason, partly because I did not want to become a businessman. Teaching in any form also appeared repulsive to me. I was not irresistibly attracted by anything else, so I chose chemistry for essentially frivolous reasons: 1) chemistry was one of the subjects I knew least about, never having studied it before; 2) in the Vienna of 1923 the only natural science offering some hope of employment was chemistry; 3) like almost all Viennese, I had a rich uncle, but unlike most other uncles he owned alcohol refineries and similar things in Poland, and there were vague promises of future splendor. But even before I had started on my dissertation, the uncle was dead and the alcoholic hopes had evaporated in the hot summer of 1926.

I had conceived a harebrained scheme: I would register simultaneously at two universities—my good grades exempted me from almost all tuition—and study chemistry at the Institute of Technology, at the same time following courses at the University in the history of literature and in English philology.

In this way, I hoped, I could acquire, in parallel, both a chemical engineer's degree and a Dr.phil. The arrangement worked for one year, but then began to give signs of breaking down, owing to difficult logistics; therefore, I transferred the study of chemistry to the University, from which I received the Dr.phil. in chemistry in 1928.

I do not believe that the University of Vienna in my time, 1923 to 1928, could still have been called outstanding. The collapse of the Austro-Hungarian Empire; the turmoil of the 1918 revolution, though it was not much of a revolution; the dreadful economic disorganization of the postwar years; the sudden restriction of the pool of talents to a few small Alpine provinces—all this tended to produce a brotherhood of chummy incompetents. The faculty of medicine still formed an exception, and there also were a few very bright lights in other departments. But on the whole the aspect was dismal. It must be admitted, even under the best of circumstances, there is something bizarre about the modern university, that caravanserai of disconnected specialties, in which the patrimony of the West is being dispensed in innumerable tiny vials of many different colors to hordes of mostly reluctant recipients. This grotesque feature is reinforced in the United States, where the concentration of the "campus" establishes even more clearly the character of a spiritual hotel. The European universities functioned—in my time, at any rate—more as offices for the issuing of various licenses.

As I had begun the study of chemistry almost without any knowledge of what I was getting into, I could not help falling under the spell of the novelty and the coherence of a mature and fully developed exact science. True, it may have been the sort of attraction exerted by a football game; but there it was, and I disliked it much less than I had expected. The shock of getting into very strange territory was probably lessened by the old-fashioned type of instruction we were getting, especially in the introductory lectures. The revolution in chemical theory, which marked the twenties, passed me by nearly unnoticed, and I have never been good at "electron pushing." The only intrusion of modernism took place in the infrequent colloquia, and I listened to lectures by many of the great in physics and chemistry. But not a single American journal was kept in the chemistry library; when I once inquired about the *Journal of the American Chemical Society*, I was informed that nothing worthwhile was being published there.

Looking back — and when you get old this is all you can do — I must say that I have not learned much from my teachers. In the strictest sense of the word I have had none. During almost my entire life I have myself been much more of a teacher than a pupil; and even this, in the complete moral and intellectual collapse of our time, may not amount to much. The sciences are extremely pedigree-conscious, and the road to the top of Mount Olympus is paved with letters of recommendation, friendly whispers at meetings, telephone calls at night. From all this I have never been able to benefit. I am, to an unusual extent, my own product. In contrast, I remember having been at a scientific meeting together with four prominent colleagues, each of whom could rightly claim to have been the favorite pupil of Meyerhof.

Thus, I have not been the pupil, favorite or otherwise, of any of the great establishment figures of the past, unable to exploit this glory from my own cradle to the master's grave and beyond. This I have never regretted. If there is such a thing as a great scientist — I have met in my life perhaps one or two to whom I should have granted this attribute — that greatness can certainly not be transferred by what is commonly called teaching. What the disciples learn are mannerisms, tricks of the trade, ways to make a career, or perhaps, in the rarest cases, a critical view of the meaning of scientific evidence and its interpretation. A real teacher can teach through his example — this is what the ducklings get from their mothers — or, most infrequently, through the intensity and the originality of his view or vision of nature.

Who, then, were my *professors*? The Institute of Physical

Chemistry was directed by old Wegscheider (he certainly was then much younger than I am as I write this), a very typical Austrian *Hofrat*, courteous and grouchy-benign, unemphatic, but not uninsidious. I could not say that he succeeded in making physical chemistry sound as interesting and important as it deserved. Only a few years later, when I lived in Berlin, I realized what could have been made of it. The Professor of Organic Chemistry was E. Späth. He was a good organic chemist and a great authority on alkaloids, but not exactly inspiring as a lofty example. The narrow slit through which the scientist, if he wants to be successful, must view nature constricts, if this goes on for a long time, his entire character; and, more often than not, he ends by becoming what the German language so appositely calls a *Fachidiot* (professional idiot). It was not easy to be accepted by Späth as a doctoral candidate; it also cost a lot of money (graduate students had to pay for all chemicals and apparatus required in the course of their work), and so I did not even try. I must, however, say that Späth treated me decently throughout my studies; and in the final examinations, the *Rigorosum*, which came after the completion of the dissertation, when he examined me for two hours in organic chemistry, he gave me a *summa cum laude*.

I was very anxious to be able to support myself soon, and it was clear that I had to choose a thesis sponsor whose problems were known to require neither much time nor much money. My choice fell on Fritz Feigl, who at that time was a *Privatdozent* in Späth's institute. He looked much more like an Italian tenor than a scientist, and was a very decent man. His interests were divided between politics — he was an active social-democrat — and the chemistry of metal-organic complexes. The first contributed indirectly to his economic well-being, the second to the development of the technique of spot tests on which he wrote a well-known treatise. Our heartless centrifugal century propelled this typical Viennese all the way to Rio de Janeiro, where he lived from 1939 and where he died after a long, active, and, I hope, reasonably happy life.

My dissertation, completed at the end of 1927, dealt with organic silver complexes and with the action of iodine on azides. My first two scientific publications described part of my work.[7, 8] The most interesting portion, namely, the discovery that organic sulfhydryl derivatives catalyzed the oxidation of sodium azide by iodine, was not published at that time. Many years later, I fell back on this reaction as a device for the demonstration, by paper chromatography, of sulfur-containing amino acids.[9]

In the early summer of 1928 I received my Dr.phil. degree from the University of Vienna. The great decision was about to be made, as usual, on insufficient grounds and in an aleatory fashion. Actually, this decision was never made; I floated from one thing to the next.

Il Gran Rifiuto

THE DECISION, of course, was to determine what I was going to do. There were almost no suitable positions to be found in Austria. Truncated by the loss of the war, in many respects well-deserved, this megalocephalic dwarf had inherited most of the German-speaking system of advanced education erected in the course of centuries by the large monarchy. The production of academically trained people continued at a high rate, but there was no place for them to go; they had to be exported. Most went, partly for linguistic reasons, to Germany, where the outlook for employment in industry, let alone in a university, was far from good. A few went to the successor countries of the monarchy: Czechoslovakia, Hungary, Poland.

The year in which it fell to me to decide on my future, 1928, was an ominous year. Black clouds had begun to gather everywhere. America was getting ready to elect "The Great Engineer" as its next president. The postwar boom, in which even Central Europe had participated after the stabilization of its currencies, had dissipated itself. The beasts of the abyss, held both on leash and in reserve by the German industry, were beginning to dream the noble dream of the night of the long knives. They were soon to be let loose to begin drawing blood. The workers were confused and poorly led. One year earlier, in 1927, I could witness the first huge street riots in Vienna; they were suppressed in a most cruel and bloody manner by the icy monsignor who led the Austrian cabinet, truly an exponent of the *ecclesia militans*. Thus, I was sensitized early against such slogans as "law and order." All that they produce in the end is a *Chile con sangre*. But to be entirely just, I should mention that, listening to the parliamentary twaddle and verbal tricks with which the social democrats of the world claimed to fight the growth of fascism, I jotted down, at that time, one of my first aphorisms: "Austrian social democracy: in case of rain, the revolution will take place in the hall."

Somehow, I wanted to get away from it all, at least for some time: into another country, into another language. But the whole was governed by a sort of fairy-tale logic: I would take the first thing that offered itself, whether industry, research, or teaching. As if, in the tale, the boy were told to go out in the street and follow the first animal he met. The first animal that came along in that Brothers Grimm world of mine was called "research"; and so I have stayed with it all my life. It has always been my habit to float passively where the currents would take me. Whenever the currents stopped, I got stuck. That it was research that was first pulled out of the pack of cards probably suited my unacknowledged preferences; I have always longed for a remote ivory tower (with air-conditioning and running cold and hot water). But, all jokes left aside, in at least one respect getting into research in 1928 was quite different from what it has been during, say, the last twenty years. I have recently tried to describe this change of atmosphere[10] and I do not want to repeat myself here. Perhaps the most important difference is that, when I got in, the selection of apprentices still operated.through a sort of pledge of eternal poverty. (That at the same time some of the sorcerers who administered the pledge were quite well off failed to strike our young and inexperienced eyes.)

What I did not realize for a long time was the enormous pull of the vortex into which I let myself be carried. By the time I was twenty-three, I was wont to distinguish strictly between what one did with one's head and what one considered as one's profession. Chemistry was my profession and I hoped it would feed and sustain me; and not only me, for I was getting ready to marry Miss Vera Broido, whom I had met at the University. But at the same time I thought of myself as a writer. I had written a great deal; a little of it had been published; more would have been but for my timidity and lack of contacts. Had I not left Vienna, tearing myself away from the German language and, even more (what a tremendous "more" this is!), had not the entire world collapsed into the most bloody barbarism under the leadership of that very same German language, there might have been one more mediocre German writer. The spiritual economy of the world being obscure to me, I cannot gauge the loss or gain. In any event, the pull that science exerts even on a critical and questioning mind proved immensely stronger than I had expected; and this is what, in greater words, the title of this section means to express.

Bluebird of Happiness

THIS IS HOW it all came about. I was in the middle of learning Danish—there was a rumor that Sörensen had an opening at the Carlsberg Laboratories in Copenhagen—and had just begun to master its most disagreeable phonetic specialty, the glottal stop, that timid death rattle of an expiring introvert, when a more solid rumor reached me. S. Fränkel, one of the physiological chemistry professors at the Medical School, had just returned from a lecture tour in the United States and brought back the news that Treat B. Johnson of Yale University had a research fellowship available for a young man willing to assist Rudolph J. Anderson in his work on the lipids of tubercle bacilli. I knew English quite well at that time, having acquired a stilted form of upper-class English with the help of two Cambridge spinsters who ran a small school in Vienna. But I knew nearly nothing of the United States, and what I knew was not conducive to learning more. As a child I had read Cooper, Poe, and Mark Twain in mostly very bad translations, and also Whitman's poems with little enthusiasm. Some of Dreiser's and Sinclair Lewis's books I had read in the original without being over-whelmed by their literary quality. The maudlin films out of Hollywood made me sick, although I made an exception for Greta Garbo. But I loved Charlie Chaplin, Buster Keaton, and Harold Lloyd: out of that threatening continent, somber and dehumanized, there seemed to arise a wind of the freedom of the absurd.

In any event, I applied for the job and, to my great discom-fiture, was accepted. The "Milton Campbell Research Fellow-ship in Organic Chemistry" paid $2,000 per year, in ten monthly instalments. (This was about one-sixth of what a Sterling Profes-sor, holder of an elite professorship at Yale, earned. Despite the lapse of nearly 50 years, the span between the income of a beginning "post-doc" and that of a very full professor has remained about the same.) I was to start in autumn. As I knew nothing about lipids, a short stay in Fränkel's laboratory was supposed to make me know and love them, but it accomplished neither. As the time of my departure grew nearer, so grew my fears. I was afraid of going to a country that was younger than most of Vienna's toilets. Others would try to console me, telling me that I should be surprised and that America would turn out much better than I expected. But I remained doubtful, adapting to that Promised Land an immortal saying of one of Vienna's wits, Anton Kuh: "*Wie der kleine Moritz sich Amerika vorstellt, so ist es*." (As little Maurice imagines America to be, so it is).*

The giant liner *Leviathan* brought me to New York. No sooner had I approached the Land of the Free than I found myself in jail. A remarkably gruff immigration officer took a look at my passport, in which my name was embellished with a doctor's title, as for reasons outlined before it had to be; then he looked at the "student's visa," which a far-from-charming American consul in Vienna had handed me as if it were the Holy Grail. The officer's face reflected painful and somber cerebration, and out of the side of his thin mouth came the words "Ellis Island."

Imprisoned in that noteworthy American concentration camp, I had an excellent view of the Statue of Liberty. I thought that this conjunction of jail and monument was not accidental; it had the purpose of teaching some of the detained immigrants the advantages of dialectical thinking. But the view, early in the morning, of the fog-shrouded seascape was enchanting, and the plaintive sounds of the foghorns and the cries of the sea gulls were a melancholy accompaniment to an America that would never be.

One or two days later I was brought before a tribunal presided over by a very big black lady who was assisted by two somnolent, uniformed, elderly gentlemen wearing what looked to me like Salvation Army fatigues. The verdict—immediate deportation—was prompt, for the case was clear: I was revealed as a double impostor. If I was a doctor, I could not be a student; if I was a student, how could I be a doctor? I stammered something about Faust, despite multiple doctorates, having

---

* "Little Maurice," an important figure in the Austrian jocular universe, is an awfully obtuse boy, the typical "terrible simplifier"; and therefore he is often right when the sages falter in their complicated constructions.

been an eternal student. I might as well have tried playing pinochle with a Martian. The whole thing could have been a scene from Jarry's *Ubu Roi*. I was taken back to my quarters, which were really sixteenths, sent a telegram to Yale University, whose counsel intervened in Washington, and was set free after a few days. Whether sternness was overcome by reasonable argument or by something more potent, I have never been able to ascertain. I may, in fact, have been some sort of a test case, for I belonged to the early crop of post-doc's who at that time began to flock to the United States in ever-increasing numbers.

In New Haven, Treat B. Johnson, Sterling Professor of Chemistry and, hence, six times as powerful as my insignificant ego, met me at the railway station. He was a decent and kind man, very much a remnant of an older and better America, whose last traces were then still visible, and he tried to lighten my first painful days on this excessively new continent. Later, when I became interested in the nucleic acids, I realized how important his work on the chemistry of purines and pyrimidines had been. Johnson took me to his own house as a guest for a few days. In my room, there was a sort of embroidered panel on the wall. It showed a blue bird and underneath it said: "May the bluebird of happiness find an eternal resting place in your home." I was moved by the trust that America sets in bluebirds. Where I came from, birds were of the utmost grayness.

Of Root and Destiny

I HAVE OFTEN thought about the meaning of the word "rootlessness." When I first heard or read about somebody being a rootless person I could not understand it, and I said to myself: "But a man is not a plant." The truth, however, is that a man *is* a plant. The legend of the giant Antaeus who lost his strength when lifted from the earth is profound. We wither when deprived of a soil into which we can drive roots, were they ever so metaphorical. The slogan "blood and soil" has been discredited forever by the Nazis, whose leadership consisted of rootless hysterics, very much *fin-de-siècle*, masquerading as ancient Teutons; they produced plenty of blood-drenched soil in their vain attempt to achieve racial identity. All this would be better forgotten, but it can never be. Leaving aside the blood, whose phantom purity I do not venerate — there is, after all, little DNA in blood, except in the leucocytes — I asked myself about the metaphysical roots in the allegorical soil.

I came to the conclusion that my generation represented the prototype of rootlessness. A really pious person is rooted in his or her religion. There may be many of them, but I have never met one, although I have encountered numerous unquestioning followers of inherited religious rites. No doubt the strength of custom can function as a substitute root. An equally or even more effective surrogate is nationalism or its less aggressive twin, patriotism. And for many of my contemporaries, science — or, if you want, orthodontics or bookkeeping — turned into the makeshift that kept them alive. In Tolstoy's tales, however, or in those of Knut Hamsun or Willa Cather, I seemed to encounter people who were different. Were they only fictional?

It is ridiculous to say, but it is true, that my parents were rooted in the Austrian monarchy. Religion played almost no role, society very little; family ties had become loose, except for the immediate microfamily: father, mother, sister, and I. Literature and music were late-evening ornaments of a pale variety — but there was the ancient dual monarchy, and my parents conformed to the stereotype of an Austrian of the last century. This was shattered by the First World War, and we all became professional refugees, with substitute homes, substitute nationalities, and later even with a substitute language. In some ways I was luckier than those to whom it happened at a more advanced age, for when I woke up to the world, it was a world without illusion; but it was also a world in which few could feel at home. If I, even as a child, could have dreamed of roots, they would have consisted of my parents, who were soon to vanish; above all, it would have been the language in which my mother had spoken to me. But my mother tongue was burned together with my mother. When this was gone, nothing remained.

I grew up into a savage, dangerous, shiftless, paranoiac world. By the time I was twenty-three and setting out for America, I looked upon myself as a foundling left at the gates of the city of Sodom. All was now to remain behind: I was sailing into a new world. How would it receive me, and, more importantly, how should I receive it? The arrival proved a great shock. In trying to recall here my first and, therefore, decisive impressions, I know that I am engaging in a treacherous undertaking.

A man coming from Sodom to Gomorrah will see many things that are similar and others that are different; and if he is given to apocalyptic fits—a metaphysical form of apoplexy—he will conclude that there may be only one Paradise, but that there surely are many Hells. If, in addition, he has a penchant for the symbolic treatment of everyday events, much that he encounters will remind him of the future, as it were; of a future that he is afraid to face. When, moreover, the Gomorrans ask him, right after his arrival, how he likes Gomorrah and whether he is happy to have left Sodom, he falls silent. What can he say? He does not want to be called an incorrigible Sodomite.

People who have retained the power of positive thinking have often told me that I exaggerate. Maybe so; but whose is the tape, whose is the measure? Perhaps a tiny corner of the gene that propelled Ezechiel has come my way; or is it plain dyspepsia? If I had a stronger belief in doctors, I should ask them. As it is, they would have been ready to prescribe tranquilizers for St. John of Patmos; and he was better without them.

Never will the man from Sodom gain a firm foothold in Gomorrah, never will he be at home again in Sodom. Of course, he cannot read the future, that most implacable of tenses, but he has read the book of Genesis, and he remembers that it was the same fire storm that destroyed both Sodom and Gomorrah.

*   *

I had not come to America as an immigrant. But even to a curious visitor, the shock of seeing New York and hearing its weird voices and noises was indescribably severe. The neurasthenic pulse of a city that never went to sleep because it never was awake; the grotesque ceremonial of Prohibition, when everybody one met seemed to be "sent by Joe"; the primitive sophistication of an uneducated and conceited intelligentsia; the incredible dirtiness of all that was not incredibly shiny and mock-luxurious; the shameless hypocrisy of all institutions and the boyish grin with which the discovery of deception was acknowledged and defused; the bought dithyrambs accompanying political or commercial careers that soon after ended in oblivion or in jail; the confusion of language and the devaluation of all grammatical forms, especially the superlative; the gigantic make-believe as the national gospel, rendering all future belief impossible: all this was bound to overwhelm a young man who, believing to have left Europe behind, found a super-Europe. How far it all seemed from James Fenimore Cooper or Chateaubriand! This was, of course, naive on my part: Did I expect to find crocodiles swimming in the Hudson or Sioux on the warpath shooting at me in the avenues of Manhattan? It was only much later that I discovered that everything that I had thought I should find did exist, but always in unexpected disguises.

When I first came to America in 1928, I used to walk many hours through the disconsolate streets, which at that time still were fairly safe, looking for a human face. What I saw frightened me: the new world seemed to have given rise to a new sort of physiognomy, sometimes empty, mostly sad and listless or distorted into a ghastly smile. "Sunny boy!" they crooned in the first talking film I then saw; but wherever I looked — in the streets and the subway, in speakeasies and theaters, in lecture halls and churches — people seemed inexpressibly unhappy, as if they were trying to say something for which they had no words. Everywhere I perceived driven runners, hurrying desperately through an unswept and cracking Chirico landscape, hiding hopelessly from a fate for which they had only the name of indigence or poverty, though more metaphysical anxieties doubtless also played a role. Whenever on my cheerless wanderings I heard something that sounded like human laughter, I looked around me and what I saw were only black faces. This bliss of primary, almost primeval, gaiety, the last remnant of what people were in previous centuries, has in the meantime also vanished. In the midst of so much canned and mechanically magnified hilarity of grin and smirk, America has become a very grim country.

Looking at an old, tired, black woman, walking in the mourning veil of her skin, I realized that I was now in a country where the poor wore their poverty in their faces. Alyosha Karamazov or Prince Myshkin were far away. It was then that I became convinced that the greatest of all revolutions was still to come, one which would liberate mankind from the fetters of mechanistic thinking into which it had permitted itself to be lured by songs about progress, by hymns about science. I am equally convinced now that this ought to happen, but am much less confident that it will. Millennial dreams have faded, and the aged chiliast realizes that thousand-year empires sometimes last less long than a three-minute egg.

Readers of these pages will, perhaps, perceive how much of a consolation the wonderful English language has become for me. I am not establishing a hierarchy: all languages are the best, I used to say. But few have proved so sturdy in all richness, so concise and flexible. Few languages have survived so much brutal misuse without going under, as French is in danger of doing. We are not the masters, we are the slaves of our languages. In my case, English has been a lenient and understanding master, and I prize the day that has brought me near the language of Shakespeare and Donne, of Pope and Swift, of Gibbon and Blake. One of the last of man-made, handmade marvels, the *Oxford English Dictionary*, has been a silent friend. Now, dictionaries are made by computers, and nondiscriminating, never-tiring light beams scan the junk for codification.

There exists a rather meaningless, but venerable, statement, attributed to many ancient sages, among them Heraclitus. It says: "A man's character is his destiny." (Heraclitus actually used the word *ethos*, not "character.") It all depends upon the definitions of character and of destiny. Was Schubert's typhus fever part of his character? Uprootedness was certainly a factor in the fates of my generation, but was rootlessness part of our characters? Playing metaphysical Scrabble has never been among my pastimes. Inability or disinclination to form roots — imposed or avoidable, beneficial or deplorable — may have marked my life. But character, destiny? As I used to say in merrier times: "Destiny comes later, but first he must fall into the pit."

Sunrise in New Haven

THE POSTDOCTORAL position that I assumed at Yale University in October, 1928, caused my first prolonged absence from home. Now that people all over the world have become so much more mobile — they spend a large portion of their lives on senseless locomotion, going to and fro — it is difficult to convey what this then meant to me. Mine had been a very sedentary family. I believe my father did not own a passport until late in life, and I must have inherited his desire to stay in one place. That this wish was not granted to me, nor to countless others, is not astonishing, in view of our so excessively migratory century.

The great friendliness with which I was received by nearly everybody at Yale University made the pain of separation less acute, but it persisted for a long time. In a way, it has never ended, although I should find it difficult to say from what I feel torn away. I used to say of myself that I was born with a stone in my shoe; this stone's name is homelessness. I cannot define it; just as Dante succeeded so much better in describing Hell than Paradise: he had lived in the first and forgotten the second.

Rudolph J. Anderson looked very much like a British army officer in reluctantly civilian clothes. Born in Sweden, but brought up in New Orleans, he represented a peculiar mixture of national and cultural characteristics. He was an excellent experimental chemist, and it was from him that I learned the respect for matter, the care for quantity even in essentially qualitative investigations, the reverence for accuracy in observation and description. If every research scientist needs a teacher, he was that in my case; and yet I hesitate to call him so, for I do not believe that my future course was influenced by him. A teacher is one who can show you the way to yourself; and this no one has done for me.

I worked two years with Anderson, remaining in the Yale chemistry department from 1928 to 1930. He had come to Yale not long before to set up a program of research on the chemical composition of tubercle bacilli and other acid-fast microorganisms. My stay was productive: I published seven papers with Anderson, the most interesting of which dealt with the discovery of the peculiar branched-chain fatty acids, tuberculostearic and phthioic acids,[11, 12] and with the complex lipopolysaccharides of the tubercle bacillus.[13] In this connection, I also got to know a very remarkable lady, Florence Sabin of The Rockefeller Institute, who did important cytological work on the effect on tissues of the substances which we had isolated from tubercle bacilli. In addition, I found the time to pursue entirely independent studies on iodine cyanide,[14] organic iodine compounds,[15] and also on the carotenoid pigments of the timothy bacillus.[16] In the course of the work on pigments, I came across M.S. Tswett's forgotten studies on chromatographic separation (1906) and was able to make use of them some time before the massive application of these procedures by Richard Kuhn and his collaborators in Heidelberg.

When July, 1929, came around, I returned to Vienna for the summer. I had saved enough from my $2,000 to pay also for my fiancée's passage to the United States, and I went over to bring her back with me. We could not marry in Vienna: my visa did not permit me to bring a wife along. She had to travel under her maiden name as a temporary visitor, and we thus occupied two chastely distant cabins on the *Berengaria*. Before leaving Vienna I had bought two tickets for the opera, and we celebrated our departure by hearing *Die Zauberflöte*. The cry *Zurück!* repelling the prince Tamino from all entrances to Sarastro's castle of light sounded to me like a mixed chorus of U.S. immigration inspectors. This time it was, however, Vera who had to spend two or three days on Ellis Island—for reasons of symmetry, I suppose—whereas I stepped on the shores of freedom entirely undetained.

In any event, in September, 1929, we got married in New York. Two disrespectable-looking gentlemen, who made themselves available at the entrance to City Hall, testified to our identities. I owe a debt of eternal gratitude to those two bums.

When my second year with Anderson was finished, another one of those halfhearted decisions, which consisted mostly in deciding not to decide, had to be made. I did not want to stay in the United States. I wrote to Paul Karrer in Zurich; he offered to take me if I brought my own salary with me. I wrote to the Bach Institute in Moscow, which, if I remember correctly, never answered. (Twenty-seven years later, when I was in Moscow attending a symposium of the Russian Academy of Sciences, a Russian colleague with whom I spoke remembered, however, the fact of my ancient inquiry.)

We felt dreadfully unhappy in America and we longed for

Europe. We had just enough money for a couple of months and for the return tickets. Despite the lure of an assistant professorship of chemistry at Duke University, at that time devoted excessively to tobacco research, I left the United States in the summer of 1930 for Europe: the rare case of a rat returning to the sinking ship.

We did not imagine how soon we should have to return.

Late Evening in Berlin

ON MY RETURN to Vienna, I discovered that the economic situation had worsened seriously during the two years I had been absent. Even as obtuse an economical thinker as I am should have been warned by the collapse of the New York stock market that I had witnessed from nearby. Instead of entombing myself in Durham, North Carolina, to devote my life to the study of all the properties of the tobacco plant, I decided to try my luck in Berlin, which had always been the place where desperate Viennese threatened to go, in order to enjoy, for once, the comforts of cleanliness, order, and punctuality (together with very bad food).

At the time when I went to Berlin in September, 1930, for what I hoped would be an extended stay, the worms had long been eating away at the foundations of the Weimar Republic. But to my inexperienced eyes this bland edifice was in no greater danger of collapsing than was the rest of the progress-drunk, profit-greedy, naively cynical Western world. I was mistaken. Only two and one-half years later, in April, 1933, the express train took us, my wife and me, to Paris; and forty years were to elapse before I should see Berlin again. It was, indeed, a very different city.

Reminiscing about those distant days, I used to say that my stay at the University of Berlin—October, 1930, until April, 1933—was perhaps the happiest time of my life. How could I say that, people asked. What was there so special about a city and a country that were about to tumble into the deepest abyss ever to engulf a civilized people? I should like to analyze the elements that made life in Berlin so pleasant to me then.

I came to a city of growing unemployment and an ever-sharpening economic crisis. The few Viennese acquaintances who had preceded me worked in various Kaiser Wilhelm institutes. They were of no help except for advising me to write abstracts for the *Chemisches Zentralblatt;* the monthly income would not have paid for one night's lodging. I had no letters of recommendation and should, in any event, have been too clumsy to make use of them. But I found, miraculously, a good position almost without delay. This was due to a combination of sheer accident and the fact that I had just come from two years as a postdoc in the United States. At the Institute of Hygiene of the University, which at the same time was also the Department of Bacteriology, I had met Professor Julius Hirsch, a most friendly and benign man, who was familiar with the work I had done at Yale University in Rudolph Anderson's laboratory. Was it the charm of my youthful unblown personality, or my knowledge of tubercle bacilli? In any event, Hirsch took me down immediately to the chief, Geheimrat Martin Hahn (of Buchner and Hahn fame), and in a few minutes I was installed as *Voluntärassistent*. (Later I became *ordentlicher Assistent* in charge of chemistry.)

Equal rapidity presided over the provision of a stipend. I was sent to see the president of the *Deutsche Forschungsgemeinschaft*, Exzellenz Schmidt-Ott, an eminent Arabist, if I remember right. The great man asked me many questions, few having to do with science, and I went away anointed and appointed. The informality and swiftness of decision-making, the openness to new ideas, the absence of shabbiness, the largeness of views: all this could not help but impress a shy young man who had only recently come away from nagging, malevolent, and immobile Vienna, where even the bedbugs followed the ancient Spanish court ceremonial, and from the hierarchical and caste-conscious provincialism of Yale. Martin Hahn treated me during our entire association with an incredible benevolence. I was given an apartment in the Institute—a few steps away from the *Reichstag* whose flames were soon to illuminate the onset of the Third Reich. I was entirely independent in my research and even began to have collaborators.

Germany was in a deep economic crisis, which at that time was not yet borne with as much docility as it seems to be in our brain-washed and tranquilized era. There was great unrest in Berlin, and at the same time the most brilliant cultural life that I have ever experienced. The Berlin Philharmonic under Furtwängler; the Kroll Oper under Klemperer, with such splendid performances as that of Offenbach's *Perichole* in the adaptation of Karl Kraus; the first and deeply impressive showing of *Mahagonny* by Brecht and Weill. But there was a film of unreality over everything; there was an immense sadness in people's eyes: the nineteenth century was impacted on the twenty-first. The miserable prostitution of Friedrichstrasse, the shame-faced and shameless poverty of Alexanderplatz, subject of Döblin's excellent novel, clashed with the bombast and the luxury of the West side. It was at this time that I began to understand that our world had become too complicated for human beings, that the main motive of our times would be the flight, the blind running away from an intolerable daily day, into madness, violence, destruction.

Work went on in many directions. Two of the most substantial pieces—a study of the lipids of the *Bacillus Calmette-Guérin* (BCG)[17] and a detailed investigation of the fat and the phosphatide fractions of diphtheria bacteria[18]—were designed for my *Habilitationsschrift*, the treatise whose submission precedes the appointment as *Privatdozent*. At the medical school to which my Institute belonged, this title, i.e., the right to give lectures, was limited to holders of the Dr.med. degree. Therefore, Martin Hahn arranged for me to become *Privatdozent* at the Berlin

Institute of Technology. At the end of January, 1933, the Black Plague had assumed the government of Germany, and one week later I could have been seen trotting absurdly to Charlottenburg with a careful parcel, in order to deposit my *magnum opus* in the *Technische Hochschule*. By the time the appointment was taken up I was, however, far from Berlin, having left for Paris long before. I could have stayed on for a while, protected by my Austrian passport, but one look at the style and the physiognomy of the new powers was enough. I wish I could have remained so light-footed in later predicaments.

I should like, however, to glance back once more on the city in which I first breathed the air of independent research. I found myself in what must have appeared to a young and inexperienced chemist as the very empyrean of science. The Institute in which I had my laboratory formed part of a complex of rather ugly large buildings faced with red brick that bordered on Dorotheenstrasse and Neue Wilhelmstrasse. (I revisited these streets, sentimentally, in 1973; the buildings still stood, dirtier-looking, but the street names now remember Clara Zetkin and Karl Liebknecht.) Several University institutes were housed there, and many of the names connected with them sounded familiar. There was Nernst in physics. He had his official apartment, as did I on a minute scale, in one of the tracts, and from my window I could observe the meticulous care with which he supervised the daily washing of his large car in the courtyard. The days of the Third Law of Thermodynamics were far away, and I remember a ridiculous lecture given by 68-year-old Nernst about some kind of electrical piano which he had constructed. Cacophonous samples accompanied the display.

There were Trendelenburg and Krayer in pharmacology, Bodenstein and Marckwald in physical chemistry. Not far away were the chemical laboratories with Schlenk, Leuchs, and Ernst Bergmann. Steudel was in physiological chemistry. But the list of names has barely begun; and for one who had passed the stiff final *Rigorosum* only two years before, many of these names were of a nightmarish hue. At that time, the Kaiser Wilhelm Institutes in green and pleasant Dahlem lived through their greatest period: physics with von Laue and Einstein; biology with Correns and Hartmann; physical chemistry with Haber, Polanyi, Freundlich; cell physiology with Warburg; and there were a few more small principalities, with Neuberg, Herzog, Hess, and others. I met most of these men and many of their collaborators, for the freemasonry of science was never wider open than at that time, and never again would I have the feeling of belonging to a worthy and reasonable community of scholars. It is absurd to say — but I cannot help it — as I look back on those days, I get the the impression that the last rays of the setting sun of the civilized nineteenth century were falling on my head. And this in 1931 or 1932, when the "long knives" had begun growing at a frightening speed.

The Haber and Warburg colloquia were of particular distinction. Fritz Haber had a marvelously Socratic skill of drawing the best out of speaker and audience. Many of the talks were way over my head. But how great was my relief when Haber got up at the end and declared: "I haven't understood a word." And then, turning to his paladins, "Herr Polanyi," or "Herr Weiss, could you perhaps explain to me what it was all about?" There followed a brilliant dialogue, or rather a polylogue, through which everything seemed to be clear, even to me. But when I went home opaqueness had reassembled.

Otto Warburg's seminars were of a different character. It fell to me to give one, and, as is usual, my extempore talk was prepared carefully. My wife and I walked for hours in the *Tiergarten*, rehearsing my improvisations. All went well, despite the formal atmosphere. The great man sat in the first row and seemed to be arrogantly asleep. But when I had finished, he asked most intelligent questions. I realized that geniuses learn by a form of osmosis; a gift entirely denied to me.

At about the same time, I heard Max Planck give a far-from-impromptu lecture. Painstakingly and painfully, the old man read from an abstruse manuscript. This served me as a warning that, for the scientist, philosophy is one of the hazards of old age. Soon after, there came the somber days of January, 1933. The last lights went out, and in the dark streets I could hear the tramp of marching boots. The evening was at an end, and it was followed by a long, blood-guilty night.

The End of the Beginning

THAT I COULD so easily transfer my activities to Paris was due to another piece of work I had done. Geheimrat Hahn was one of the court experts in the well-known "Lübeck case," in which several physicians were prosecuted for being responsible for the death of a large number of babies who, instead of BCG vaccine, had been fed cultures of virulent tubercle bacilli. Hahn asked me to undertake the chemical portion of his report, and I believe that my studies contributed materially to an understanding of what had really happened. This work was published,[19] and Albert Calmette, deputy director of the Institut Pasteur, who naturally was happy about the proof that his BCG preparations were not responsible for the catastrophe, read my paper. In March, 1933, I received an entirely unsolicited letter from him, inviting me to come to the Institut Pasteur. In the middle of April we were in Paris.

Calmette was a charming, good-hearted, and very intelligent man in his early seventies. He was extremely hard of hearing, a deplorable fact that he wished to be ignored, which made conversation difficult. The tuberculosis section which he headed occupied a separate, at that time modern, building and was the only part of the Pasteur Institute in which up-to-date work could be done. The main building of the Institute, on the other side of rue Dutot, was beyond description.* Its director was Emile Roux, an extemely frugal, mummified octagenarian, who, I was told, had done some distinguished work forty years earlier. Salaries were very low; and without the help of The Rockefeller Foundation I should myself soon have looked like the director. I was informed by my colleagues that requests for more money were useless, but that after the third intervention with Dr. Roux he saw to it that one received the *Légion d'honneur* as a consolation prize. Unfortunately, at the end of 1933, after only my second visit to him, Roux died, preceded by Calmette; and so I have remained entirely undecorated with the *petit ruban*. Although the principal building of the Institute, in my time, lacked toilets, it contained a rather tasteless crypt — in a peculiar, Second Empire-Byzantine style — devoted to Louis Pasteur. There I participated in the death vigil, first for Calmette, then for Roux, being assigned, as a junior member, the period from three to four in the morning.

I did some work at the Institut Pasteur, not very much, on bacterial pigments and polysaccharides. The working conditions were, compared with Yale and Berlin, far from inviting, although the French colleagues were, on the whole, extremely friendly and helpful. Especially the heart-warming accents of the *langue d'oc*, to be heard frequently at the Institute, enveloped the embarrassed newcomer in a linguistic halo of welcome and Mediterranean gaiety. But I still remember with unquenched sorrow what happened to me when I needed a thermometer to determine melting points. None was to be found, and I consulted Calmette. "*Un thermomètre?*" he exclaimed incredulously, "*alors il faut aller chez Monsieur Thurneyssen.*" Monsieur Thurneyssen, it turned out, was an old craftsman, looking like Nostradamus, who had a shop in which he made, by hand, the most

---

* It is not even necessary for me to attempt an account of that labyrinth of torture chambers of rabbits, guinea pigs, and mice. This has been done, with masterful maliciousness, in one of the greatest French novels of this century, Céline's *Voyage au bout de la nuit* (pages 275–9 of the Pléiade edition).

beautiful instruments. I recited my request and was told to return in a few weeks. When the appointed time, and a little more, had elapsed, I was handed an incredibly elegant master-piece of the instrument-maker's art. Blown out of very thin glass, the thermometer, with its hand-engraved scale and orna-mentally curlicued ciphers, seemed to call for a vitrine rather than a laboratory bench. On the first attempt to insert the tender masterwork in a stopper, it disintegrated, and I believe I took my next melting point in New York a few months later.

We had a charming small apartment in a new building on the southern edge of the 15th arrondissement, and we walked endlessly through the ancient streets of Paris. The region of Montparnasse was the social and cultural center of the emigra-tion; in such coffeehouses as *La Coupole* and *Le Dôme* one heard more German and Russian than French. The wonderful city of Paris lived at that time, perhaps, its last genuine moments, before losing its French tears and its French laughter, becoming Teutonized, Americanized, Pompidolized. But the shadows began to fall, and the Institut Pasteur got an insignificant director who wore a skull cap. Foreigners began to be called *métèques*, which, despite its noble Greek derivation, was not meant to be friendly. I knew I had to go, and with the help of Harry Sobotka of The Mount Sinai Hospital of New York, we left Paris at the end of 1934 and sailed again, to our own amazement, to America.

But that is another story, and the following chapters will relate it. In any event, after much searching, it turned out in 1935 that Hans Clarke had a little job for me at Columbia University.

The Silence of the Heavens

I CAME TO BIOCHEMISTRY through chemistry; I came to chemistry, partly by the labyrinthine routes that I have related, and partly through the youthfully romantic notion that the natural sciences had something to do with nature. What I liked about chemistry was its clarity surrounded by darkness; what attracted me, slowly and hesitatingly, to biology was its darkness surrounded by the brightness of the givenness of nature, the holiness of life. And so I have always oscillated between the brightness of reality and the darkness of the unknowable. When Pascal speaks of God in hiding, *Deus absconditus*, we hear not only the profound existential thinker, but also the great searcher for the reality of the world. I consider this unquenchable resonance as the greatest gift that can be bestowed on a naturalist.

When I look back on my early way in science, on the problems I studied, on the papers I published—and even more, perhaps, on those things that never got into print—I notice a freedom of movement, a lack of guild-imposed narrowness, whose existence in my youth I myself, as I write this, had almost forgotten. The world of science was open before us to a degree that has become inconceivable now, when pages and pages of application papers must justify the plan of investigating, "in depth," the thirty-fifth foot of the centipede; and one is judged by a jury of one's peers who are all centipedists or molecular podiatrists. I would say that most of the great scientists of the past could not have arisen, that, in fact, most sciences could not have been founded, if the present utility-drunk and goal-directed attitude had prevailed.

It is clear that to meditate on the whole of nature, or even on the whole of living nature, is not a road that the natural sciences could long have traveled. This is the way of the poet, the philosopher, the seer. A division of labor had to take place. But the overfragmentation of the vision of nature—or actually its complete disappearance among the majority of scientists — has created a Humpty-Dumpty world that must become increasingly unmanageable as more and tinier pieces are broken off, "for closer inspection," from the continuum of nature. The consequence of the excessive specialization, which often brings us news that nobody cares to hear, has been that in revisiting a field with which one had been very familiar, say, ten or twenty years earlier, one feels like an intruder in one's own bathroom, with twenty-four grim experts sharing the tub.

Profounder men than I have failed to diagnose, let alone cure, the disease that has infected us all, and I should say that the ostensible goals have obliterated the real origins of our search. Without a firm center we flounder. The wonderful, inconceivably intricate tapestry is being taken apart strand by strand; each thread is being pulled out, torn up, and analyzed; and at the end even the memory of the design is lost and can no longer be recalled. What has become of an enterprise that started as an exploration of the *gesta Dei per naturam*?

To follow the acts of God by way of nature is itself an act that can never be completed. Kepler knew this and so did many others, but it is now being forgotten. In general, it is hoped that our road will lead to understanding; mostly it leads only to explanations. The difference between these two terms is also being forgotten: a sleight of hand that I have considered in a recent essay.[20, 21] Einstein is somewhere quoted as having said: "The ununderstandable about nature is that it is understandable." I think he should have said: "that it is explainable." These are two very different things, for we understand very little about nature. Even the most exact of our exact sciences float above axiomatic abysses that cannot be explored. It is true, when one's reason runs a fever, one believes, as in a dream, that this understanding can be grasped; but when one wakes up and the fever is gone, all one is left with are litanies of shallowness.

In our time, so-called laws of nature are being fabricated on the assembly line. But how often is the regularity of these "laws of nature" only the reflection of the regularity of the method employed in their formulation! Lately, many tricks have been discovered about nature; but these tricks seem to have been specially produced by nature for the imbeciles to find out; and there is no Maimonides to guide them out of their confusion. In other words, science is still faced with the age-old predicament, the lack of ultimate verification. It is written in the *Analects* of Confucius (XII, 19): "The Master said, Heaven does not speak."

MORE FOOLISH AND
MORE WISE

En vieillissant, on devient plus fou et plus sage.

LA ROCHEFOUCAULD

In Praise of Broken Edges

A FEW YEARS AGO, I reviewed a scientific autobiography, a shallow bestseller. In my article I had something to say about this species of books, and this I should like to repeat here, if for no other reason, as a warning to myself.

This is then a scientific autobiography; and to the extent that it is nothing else, it belongs to a most awkward literary genre. If the difficulties facing a man trying to record his life are great — and few have overcome them successfully — they are compounded in the case of scientists, of whom many lead monotonous and uneventful lives and who, besides, often do not know how to write. Though I have no profound knowledge of this field, most scientific autobiographies that I have seen give me the impression of having been written for the remainder tables of the bookstores, reaching them almost before they are published. There are, of course, exceptions; but even Darwin and his circle come to life much more convincingly in Mrs. Raverat's charming recollections of a Cambridge childhood than in his own autobiography, remarkable a book though it is. When Darwin, hypochondriacally wrapped in his shivering plaid, wrote his memoirs, he was in the last years of his life. This touches on another characteristic facet: scientists write their life's history usually after they have retired from active life, in the solemn moment when they feel that they have not much else to say. This is what makes these books so sad to read: the eagerness has gone; the beaverness remains. . . .

There may also be profounder reasons for the general triteness of scientific autobiographies. *Timon of Athens* could not have been written, *Les demoiselles d'Avignon* not have been painted, had Shakespeare and Picasso not existed. But of how many scientific achievements can this be claimed? One could almost say that, with very few exceptions, it is not the men that make science; it is science that makes the men. What A does today, B or C or D could surely do tomorrow.

I wrote this in 1968, and I have not changed my mind. What I should have added, however, had I had the space, was that if A, B, C, or D had discovered the same fact of nature, worthy of trumpet sounds, this did not mean that they were identical human beings. What makes Cardano's or Cellini's life stories worth reading — not to speak of the great Augustinus in the twilight of shattered antiquity — is that they had a life and a story to tell. Out of these withered pages there looks at us a human face, there beats a human heart. But what most scientists choose to describe — apart from the trivial day-to-day of laboratory work — deals, at best, with how they felt in Stockholm, retreating crabwise, but as highly decorated crabs, from where the King gracefully stood; or they report their sensations when donning the scarlet gown or tipping the academic cap on the occasion of their twentieth honorary doctorate. Their dull books mostly are accounts of a career, not of a life.

It could, of course, be argued that one's career is one's life; but even in the peak years of bourgeois society, say around 1850, this was not entirely true, although the thick brown sauce of work ethic and golden rule concealed successfully all motions of the heart and the mind. If the leading German novel of that dismal time carried the unalluring title of *Debit and Credit*, Russian literature dug more deeply and came back with *Crime and Punishment,* just as Büchner's *Force and Matter* was redeemed by *Fear and Trembling,* written by a very private man in Copenhagen. It is given to few people to express their genius, or at least their talent, in their life, and I have not been one of those. It is probable that, had I been granted this opportunity, I should not have known what to do. In any event, all this is idle speculation, for in our epoch, and probably since the French Revolution, what goes as art and literature and science is only an artificial, youthful-looking, blooming skin stretched tight over a crumbling skeleton. When Hölderlin fled into madness and Rimbaud into Ethiopia, they knew what they were doing.

Is our life, as we look back on it, a continuum? After all,

there is only one way to be born and so many to die. Of course, I am told, wholly we are born and wholly we die; but how about the interval, which in my case is excessively long? Even the claim of totality that I just made is not entirely uncontradicted. There rises, for instance, an ancient Roman face out of the classical dust and it intones an immortal poem: *Non omnis moriar*. This may apply to you, Horace, but we have forgotten what you knew, and what we know you would have disdained to learn. And once I have you here, I may also point out that our monuments, in contrast to yours, can hardly be more perennial than steel, since that is what they are made of. They stand on many pedestals, but the same name is written on all which is Oblivion. Brecht knew it very well. *Von diesen Städten wird bleiben: der durch sie hindurchging, der Wind!* (Of these cities will remain what passed through them: the wind!)

If we could not forget, we could not remember; just as only the trembling balance can weigh. There are nights with a rose tint, there are days black with clouds, a groan from a deathbed, a hand on my hair, a voice out of the pyre of forgottenness. The ashes do speak, but it is a broken murmur. Brief reflections of brightness, as from a shattered mirror, play over the blackness of an ever-present past.

I tell what I am told. Who is the speaker? If it is memory, then why does it sometimes whisper, sometimes shout, often chatter, and mostly remain in sullen silence? Ancient telephone numbers from my parents' apartment in Vienna are followed incoherently by the timid half-smile on a little girl's face, and I am eight. Busy ghosts with briefcases run through corridors that no longer lead anywhere. Blind mirrors reflect frightened faces; a bright-red satanic mill engorges bodies and excretes packages of phosphates; gold teeth are sorted, numbered, and melted down; all this to the accompaniment of the sweet and labyrinthine music of the fourth act of *Nozze di Figaro*. It is all in pieces, but the broken edges cut, and there is blood everywhere.

I am, therefore, condemned to writing as a fragmentist. This is a sentence that I do not appeal, for I have always been in love with small forms. A fragment excels through its very raggedness; the more torn the edges, the better. An aphorism, in contrast, is perfect like a tiny egg; it is a concentrate of the beginning and the end, with everything between, be it ever so essential, left out.

A Department and its Keeper

A FEW YEARS after I had joined Hans Clarke's Department of Biochemistry at Columbia University, a visitor told me that, on getting off the elevator on the fifth floor of the College of Physicians and Surgeons, the quaint eighteenth-century designation of the medical school, he thought he was in a madhouse. People ran past him, some screaming, others carrying weird vessels or apparatus; a door opened, and an elderly professor ejected, brachially and in a loud Germanic falsetto, a graduate student who, with faked dismay and in a great hurry, rushed to hide among his equals. Most doors were open, and a rich mixture of Brooklynese, Bostonese, but mostly Hamburg-American, filled the air.

Traffic density was high in the shabby corridors and laboratories, but some individuals stood out from the general disorderly and aimless fervor of Insanity Square. There was, for instance, one who seemed to rehearse a bizarre ballet: surrounded by a copious array of various motionless apparatus and empty vessels, he poured nothingness from one into the other. An empty beaker was raised and slowly and carefully emptied into an empty separatory funnel, the noncontents of which, after being shaken, divided into two layers of nonentity, separating nothing from nothing. Both nothings were then collected cautiously, each in its own vessel. A visitor, seeing all this, would, of course, have been baffled, but those who had observed the beautiful spectacle before knew that this was a "dry run" for an experiment to be performed on one of the subsequent nights. There were, in fact, more acts to this dumb show: many other operations — crystallization, distillation, sublimation — partook of the ghostly pantomime. That most of this activity did not lead to anything handed on to posterity was perhaps a pity. But does this count in the face of a human life? Does not the great *corpus mysticum* of the world contain all that was once felt or thought, suffered or overcome, created or forgotten, whether written or unwritten, made or destroyed? Are we not in this sense parts of a greater organism, kept alive through the ever more vividly circulating blood of an enormous past?

A large part of the population seemed to be marginal: they came and they went. A few did nothing, a few worked hard; others — owls of Minerva — flew only at night. The place was very crowded, the laboratories were in part quite irregular in shape, and some of the inmates were stacked away in the oddest corners. My wayward memory throws up many iridescent bubbles: a short man with a blue-black beard speaking, for unknown reasons, with a Maltese-British accent; a charming Chinese lady, not unconnected with one of the greatest historical undertakings of our time — Joseph Needham's awe-inspiring *Science and Civilisation in China;* a benign walrus presiding somewhere and intermittently over a sort of kymograph. The latter — tolerated in the department but not really belonging, and later separated from it — now reveals himself as the discoverer of a very important group of physiologically active substances, the prostaglandins. This was the good-hearted Raphael Kurzrok, an excellent and friendly obstetrician, dear to our family annals for having delivered our son Thomas in 1938. At that time I was taken to task for not handing out cigars: I was stingy, poor, and averse to any form of folklore.

A department at an American university is, or was when I began my life, something entirely different from a German "Institut." It reflected some of the most admirable qualities of the American character, which at that time had not yet been entirely submerged or denatured by the overpowering moral and physical noises that the drumfire of the mass media, including all that is called government or administration, set loose on a good-natured and helpless people. I know, in fact, no other nation that is as little represented by its representatives — public or private, business or art or science — as is the American people. In any event, the openness and informality, the absence of pomposity, the helpfulness and true collegiality, the resigned recognition that we were all in the same leaky boat, the good-humored lack of ambition: all this and much more must have impressed every newcomer from Europe. The last-mentioned attribute explains, in part, the relatively low quality of the science departments. This was actually not due to the low caliber of the individuals who constituted the departments, but to the feeling on their part that nothing they could do counted on the scientific stage, which was occupied by the loud-mouthed and conceited European heavyweights. They took it for granted that all beauty contests would be won by the decibelles from Germany and England. In other words, university departments in the United States, pleasant as they were in their well-ordered family lives, lacked all power of percussion.

I believe it is no exaggeration to say that, as concerns biochemistry, this was changed radically through Clarke's coming to Columbia University. It is time for me to say a few words about him.

Hans T. Clarke (1887–1972) was born in England of American parents and educated there and in Germany. He received his training in organic chemistry in London and worked subsequently in Emil Fischer's celebrated laboratory at the University of Berlin. At the outbreak of the First World War, he came to the United States and spent fourteen years as an organic chemist with the Eastman Kodak Company in Rochester, New York. During that time he was instrumental in developing the imposing line of organic chemicals sold by this firm, a huge repository of often difficultly accessible substances without which the great advance in organic chemistry in this country would have been impossible.* In 1928, when the medical school moved uptown to Washington Heights, to form part of the Columbia-Presbyterian Medical Center, Clarke came to the Department of Biochemistry as chairman. He remained there for twenty-eight years.

When I first saw Clarke in 1935, I met a rather tall, aristocratic-looking man with a human face and friendly eyes. His British upbringing, or perhaps his innate temperament, had endowed him with the special kind of shy aloofness that has baffled continentals in their dealings with the English upper class since times immemorial. In his case, it did not go all the way to stammering, the true attribute of the empire-builders who, while the rest of the world looked at them with bewilderment, managed to stutter away entire continents. For this reason, Clarke was not a good lecturer. But he was a very good organic chemist of the old observance; one of those who liked to putter around in the laboratory with test tubes and small beakers and watch glasses and who was happy when crystals appeared. He belonged to a vanishing species, when science was young and adventurous, when real experiments could still be performed, when the sense of smell still served to identify classes of compounds.

In contrast to the eager beavers among whom I have spent most of my life — all surface and polished professionalism — there was a very private side to Hans Clarke: he loved music and was an ardent clarinetist. I often heard him play chamber music with his first wife, who belonged to the Max Planck family.

He published very little and knew more than he showed. He

---

*Many years later, when I occupied the tabouret of biochemistry at Columbia, which in Clarke's time was still a real Chair, I wrote to the firm, suggesting that they help us in setting up a professorship in Clarke's honor. The answer I received will remain a monument to American corporate shabbiness.

belonged to the conscientious generation: every day of his long life he came in early each morning, and there he sat in his shabby office, door open to the corridor; you could see him and speak with him by sticking your head in. His dignity required no ceremony. When I think of my slick contemporaries in thick plush — receptionists and intercom and all the abstract art that foundation money can buy, cars with chauffeurs, private dining rooms — I can gauge the long, devilish way that we have traveled in forty short years.

Clarke would not have impressed one as very bright, nor was he a profound scientific thinker. He was, perhaps, the most unselfish scientist I have encountered, and I have often wondered whether in science a certain lack of passionate involvement is not the only way to true disinterestedness. But he had an uncanny sense of quality. After a short interview with an aspiring graduate student, in which he mostly asked the young man how he would make sulfuric acid or something of similar import, he arrived at a judgment which, at least nine times out of ten, was correct. He may have rejected a few who did not deserve to be, but he was almost never wrong in those he took. In my later years I have often envied him this gift, which I lack completely. The graduate students whom Clarke assembled in the department were, therefore, of high quality on the whole, and their subsequent careers have borne this out. He showed the same feeling for quality in selecting the members of the department with whom he surrounded himself, but of this more later.

Like many well-to-do people, Clarke was frugal and had little appreciation of the importance of money for those who had none. The salaries which he negotiated for his faculty members — one of the foremost functions of a department head in an American university — were largely below the average and mostly insufficient; he had no understanding of the material difficulties that beset some of his younger colleagues, and he did little to keep those who were pushed or pulled away.

He built the foremost department of biochemistry in the United States. The group that he had assembled and that he led benevolently through nonleading—faculty members, guests, and students—represented the first serious group in this science, which lifted biochemistry way above its previous status as an ancillary discipline in the education of physicians. Clarke's ideal was F.G. Hopkins, who had done something similar at the University of Cambridge. I had met Hopkins first in Cambridge in 1934 when he showed me his laboratories with absent-minded and paternal friendliness. I saw him again during the war, when he called on Clarke at Columbia, and I know how happy Clarke was about that visit. Hopkins was a wise and decent man, and so was Clarke. They both had what I would call the wisdom of the heart.

When, in 1956, the time had come for Hans Clarke to retire from his university chair, he asked to be let remain at Columbia in a small laboratory. The request was refused.

A Happy Family
and its Unhappy Members

IN THE BEGINNING of October, 1935, I entered Columbia, as almost everybody did, through one of its many back doors. In the first part of this brief memoir I recounted my return to the United States at the end of 1934. This was made possible by the hospitality of The Mount Sinai Hospital of New York and especially through Harry Sobotka, who was in charge of biochemistry there. I spent a few months in his laboratory, doing almost nothing except listening to his pleasant conversation and to his many jokes. He had been a student of the two great Richards of Munich, Willstätter and Kuhn, and later a collaborator of another great and unpleasant biochemist, P.A. Levene of The

Rockefeller Institute. Like many scientists who came to this country prematurely, i.e., of their own choice and before being propelled by the Great Migration, Sobotka never really fitted into what he had, and his quick intellect went to waste on petty matters.

It was through Sobotka that I made the acquaintance, at about that time, of the only genuine genius of my life, Bertolt Brecht. He had come to New York to supervise the unsatisfactory performance of his play *The Mother*, which he had adapted from Maxim Gorki's novel. I spent one unforgettable afternoon with Brecht, mostly fighting about our very divergent views of the blackest monster of these horrible times, Adolf Hitler. In retrospect, I must concede that I was wrong in that discussion: I had not realized that, in gauging the historical importance of a potentate, his weight must be increased by that of all the corpses he has created. This insight, acquired later, has helped me to do justice to the historical significance of some of our own congenitally insignificant statesmen.

The first few months of 1935 were spent on a search for a job. I already had thirty papers to my credit, but did not know anybody who could be of much use. After unprofitable visits to Boston, Philadelphia, Baltimore, and Chicago, it occurred to me to visit Hans Clarke and to present myself as a former collaborator of Rudolph Anderson at Yale, with whom Clarke was on good terms. I underwent the same baffling interview, at the likes of which I later assisted innumerable times, but nothing seemed to be on the horizon. My knowledge of sulfuric-acid manufacture must, however, have satisfied Clarke, for a few weeks later he telephoned me, asking that I come to see him again. He suggested that two surgeons at Columbia were looking for a biochemist and that I might be suitable for this position. This proved to be the case: Drs. Frederic W. Bancroft and Margaret Stanley-Brown of the Department of Surgery had received a small grant from the Carnegie Corporation to help them in research on blood coagulation. I was given the job, at

$300 a month.

This was, then, the back door through which I entered Columbia; and since nobody ever called me away, I stayed there throughout the rest of my professional life. I had been promised the title of assistant professor of biochemistry, which, in view of my having been on the way to a *Privatdozentur* in Berlin and of my advanced age, thirty years, was the least to be expected. But when I moved in with my spatula and my notebook, Clarke hemmed and hawed and disclosed to me that they had decided to start me at a lower rank, that of research associate. Always meek before the inevitable and caring, in fact, very little about such things, I acquiesced. It was an unpropitious beginning of a far-from-brilliant academic career: assistant professor at thirty-three, associate professor at forty-one, professor at forty-seven. I suppose that, at some time during this dazzling ascent, I received tenure; nobody told me and I did not ask. As so many other things, that grail of the American academic escaped me entirely.

I found myself in what would be called a happy place: a chief one could respect, colleagues one could admire. The title of this chapter requires, therefore, some justification. To begin with, such words as "happy" or "happiness"—done to death by the advertising jargon of our times—are not easily understood by someone brought up in a Latin, Germanic or, for that matter, Slavic language. I remember my surprise when, on learning English, I first read about "the pursuit of happiness." *Glückseligkeit, félicité*? Other languages do not possess a single word expressing the complete absence of malaise. In any event, looking around the happy department, I noticed that its members were far from a state of bliss. This was partly due to the human condition, partly to Clarke's disregard of the future of the people under him, which I mentioned before, but mostly to the fact, which took a long time dawning on me, that we were working in the middle of an American medical school. The education of health-care delivery boys is actually the function of a trade school, and that is what the medical schools were in the course of becoming. Sincere or excellent as some faculty members may have been—I remember with affection Palmer of Medicine and Whipple of Surgery—the ridiculous technicolor aureoles glued to the physicians' heads by their busy medical chamber of commerce or by a gullible and deadly afraid public have corrupted them all.

It is regrettable that most biological research has become concentrated in the medical schools; a development furthered by an insane funding policy on the part of government. Although I recognized this early, I remained. What else could I have done? I am, perhaps, the most impatient stoic there ever was, but I am a stoic. Since then, things have become much worse: the medical schools have been taken over by a particularly virulent type of scientific entrepreneur, those who are best described as wheeler-healers or, if you prefer, as healer-dealers. The inchoate mob which is called the public suffers them gladly; but when the water gates of what goes by the name of "biomedical research"—MD's getting the money, PhD's doing the work—once are opened, there will be quite a flood.

Ocean of Names and Faces

TURNING NOW to what I found in Clarke's department when I joined it, in 1935, I enter, happily and fearfully, the realm of the living. I am certain that my colleagues or, as one says in the United States, my friends, who still eat their shabby pensions, will be glad if I do not describe or characterize them. The old precept *de mortuis nil nisi bonum,* which undoubtedly was coined by a Neolithic undertaker, ought not to be converted to something like *de vivis nil nisi malum.* On the other hand, Cassandra should not be invited to address the Kiwanis. Even the most heartfelt panegyric sounds false when uttered in public. So let us assume that I am saying the best of everybody.

The supreme council of the department, as it were, was composed of three older, helpful, and friendly men: Clarke, Edgar G. Miller, and G.L. Foster. They were not old at all— forty-eight, forty-two, and forty-four, respectively—but to me they appeared old. They undertook most of the teaching load, which consisted mainly of rather poor lectures for the medical students. As the graduate students received practically no formal instruction, this left much time for us younger ones. Several already had reached distinction or were soon to do so, although the university showed little recognition of this fact: an old Columbia habit.

When one grows old, one is surrounded by an ocean of unremembered names and of young familiar faces. When you remember the names, they are forgotten; when you see the faces, they have grown old and sad. The only way to cross this Malebolge—and without a Vergil as your guide—is to tell yourself that what was is; that once young, always young; once beautiful, always beautiful; once bright, always bright; that what lived cannot die.

I lay, therefore, my hand in that of Mnemosyne, the goddess of remembrance, and let her guide me. There were several who had already established themselves as scientists of high rank: Michael Heidelberger, the founder of immunochemistry, a new branch of biochemistry—it was only the day before yesterday that I sat in the bus next to him, nearly ninety years old, on his way to work, and admired again the handsome face of a humanist scholar who should have been painted by Quentin Matsys or Holbein. Perhaps because Heidelberger also played the clarinet very well, Clarke had a low opinion of immuno-chemistry. For that reason, Heidelberger was, in my time, never really in the department. His laboratory was two floors higher up, in the department of medicine; and there I visited him often to speak about sugars or the world, more about the first. He gave rise to an entire school of excellent researchers in the field of immunology.

There was Oskar Wintersteiner, a fellow Austrian, who played the piano beautifully. He had already done very good work on progesterone and was to do more in many fields of the steroid hormones and other complex natural substances. At that time he collaborated with J.J. Pfiffner, who later went into the pharmaceutical industry. Wintersteiner was, like many Austrians, a quiet, sensitive, retiring, and slightly melancholy man. I was very fond of him, and so was Clarke; but instead of urging the promotion of one of the best organic chemists we had seen, he let him go. Wintersteiner went to Squibb, where he had a distinguished career.

The prize exhibit, when I came, was, however, Rudolf Schoenheimer. Not long before, he had come to Columbia from Germany, where he had been the chemical assistant in Aschoff's famous department of pathology at the University of Freiburg. From there he had brought with him a brilliant idea which he had the good luck and the energy to transform into reality in Clarke's department. The professor of physics in Freiburg, G. von Hevesy—later, I was to know him well—had been the first, before the 1914 war, to introduce isotopes* as markers in biological reactions. Those available until the early thirties were, however, of no great interest in biology. The elements of the greatest importance for biological studies are hydrogen, oxygen, carbon, nitrogen, phosphorus, and sulfur. When Schoenheimer came to New York, the heavy hydrogen isotope, deuterium, had become available, thanks to the work of Harold Urey at Columbia, and Schoenheimer began an ambitious program on the use of this isotopic marker in the study of intermediary

---

*The term "isotope" has now become a household word; it is, in fact, quite probable that one of them will eventually be the cause of the end of our world. It is, therefore, hardly necessary to explain that this designation stands for a sort of sibling of any of the elements making up the periodic table. Isotopes of a given atom occupy the same place in the table and have the same number of protons in their nucleus, but different numbers of neutrons.

metabolism. He was helped in the work by one of Urey's former students, David Rittenberg, who had joined Clarke's department a short time before I did. Their work — the first consistent use of stable isotopes in the investigation of biological reactions — is of lasting historical importance. Science has, however, moved so fast in my lifetime that the actual has become the historical almost before the print has dried, and even the youngest scientists are condemned to survive themselves. Many must go around pitifully, clowns of their own achievement, beating a drum that long ago had gone out of tune. This is why I have often compared the sciences of my time to soap sculpture.

Schoenheimer had an interesting, histrionic face. He was a marvelous lecturer, an ambitious, assertive, but at the same time a very nervous and easily wounded man. In 1941, at what would appear the height of his success, he took his own life; he was only forty-three years old. Universities being notoriously gossipy places, there were many rumors, none of any interest. Not given to boring into souls, neither my own nor those of others, I can only deplore the circumstances that drove this gifted man to so deep a despair. In my cool and witty way, I had never realized the misery in which he lived.

There were others when I came, and each explored, or began to explore, a field of great significance. Erwin Brand, an irascible, kind-hearted, protein chemist, a former pupil of the great Max Bergmann; Warren Sperry, who worked on lipids; Karl Meyer, who was just about to make his first important discovery in the chemistry of connective tissue. These people, together with three or four more, made up the department as I saw it before me. There were few areas of biochemistry, as it was then understood, to which the group of men chosen by Clarke was not making distinguished contributions.

In addition, there were the graduate students, not many, but of excellent caliber. I mention just a few of the early crop and more or less haphazardly: Joe Fruton and David Shemin, Ernest Borek and deWitt Stetten, Konrad Bloch and Bill Stein, Elvin

Kabat and Seymour Cohen, who was my first graduate student at Columbia.

When I came, the migration from Europe had barely got under way. Great numbers of scholars and scientists arrived during the next few years, and Clarke took several into the department. It would be a great mistake to believe that they were received with open arms in those days. It was not too difficult for the young ones, with little offended pride to swallow; but the more distinguished, the more famous a man was, the greater was the reluctance to welcome him. These poor luminaries had a hard time. Their manners were imperial, their accents ridiculous; their cant was entirely different from the one practiced in the country to which they had come.

A Bouquet of Mortelles

WHEN I ENTERED the biochemistry department of Columbia University, the population density of American science was extremely low. Clarke's group was one of the larger ones. In the spring of 1935 I attended my first "Federation meeting" in Detroit. The abstracts of the papers read there occupied a thin booklet of one-hundred pages that fitted into my breast pocket. The corresponding yearly publication of the "Federation of American Societies of Experimental Biology" now is the size of the New York telephone directory. The friendly, but lugubrious and slightly depressed, tone of the gathering showed to what extent American science then vegetated at the outskirts of society. This has changed radically, to the benefit of neither science nor society.

Few people have the strength, or the temerity, to decide early what they want to do in their life and then to attempt to follow it through. I am certainly not one of those. The gusts that pushed me in one direction or another are an important, perhaps the most important, part of my life. I never had a choice, or I never could afford to wait for an alternative to appear. Clarke's offer was the first I got, and so I accepted it without hesitation. Man's fate, I believed early, comes from his own heart; and this heart, as I learned later, is not programmed for him by his DNA. The conditions under which I was taken on demonstrated to me, however, the precarious position of a practitioner of pure scientific research—but is there such a thing?—in a medical school. There were, for instance, two kindly surgeons who had received a grant to study thrombosis and embolism, two important clinical complications of undoubted interest to surgery. Since biochemistry then was highly quoted on the medical stock market, a biochemist was hired to help them consume the meager gift. As I was that biochemist, I took the direction of studying the mechanism of blood coagulation: a biological system that has remained fascinating to this very day, and one from which the natural philosopher can learn as much as the natural scientist. With three joint publications the obolus was paid. From then on I was a free agent, and have remained one until very recently, when a much worse and more degrading form of servitude, namely to the public hand doling out the research money, made itself felt. But of this more will be said later.

In any event, between 1936 and 1948 I published a large number of papers on various aspects of the coagulation of blood, first unaided and later with the help of several gifted younger colleagues. The manner in which the animal organism manages and regulates the fluidity of its circulating blood presents a most interesting and instructive biological dilemma. I have tried to state it in the opening sentences of the lecture on the biochemistry of blood clotting that I gave to the Columbia medical students between 1942 and 1957. "Blood coagulation is an eminently protective mechanism, but there is a curious antinomy: blood must stay liquid in circulation; it must clot when shed. Otherwise, there are indications of pathological conditions." In all of my lectures, on many different topics, I have tried to stress the dialectical character of the life processes. One-half of a generation of physicians must have heard me; but I wonder how much of an impression I made.

Our work in this field gained quite a bit of recognition at that time; but it now seems to be forgotten. This is one of the many wilted flowers forming the bunch that lent its name to the title of this chapter. To be a pioneer in science has lost much of its attraction: significant scientific facts and, even more, fruitful scientific concepts pale into oblivion long before their potential value has been utilized. New facts, new concepts keep crowding in and are in turn, within a year or two, displaced by even newer ones. We worked on the activation of clotting by tissue lipids; we isolated and purified the tissue factor that triggers the physiological coagulation process, the so-called thromboplastic protein; we were among the first to introduce the anticoagulant heparin into clinical application, studied its mode of action, and discovered that circulating heparin can be inhibited by the injection of protamine. I shall mention here only one review article on blood coagulation that I wrote in 1944,[1] since I should like to quote the sentences with which it ends.

> It is quite possible that the clotting of blood represents only one example of coagulation processes of a much more general biological importance. In what manner the living organism controls these coagulation processes is completely unknown. One may assume that the various factors that constitute the clotting phenomenon, although continually formed and destroyed and continually acting on each other, are held in a delicate equilibrium. This is, in fact, what constitutes both the difficulty and the fascination of the problem: the difficulty, because it is a borderline problem, involving some of the most refractory and least explored substances and reactions; the fascination, because in the coagulation of blood there is brought into the open, as it were, one of the innumerable systems through which the organism maintains, by predetermined oscillations, the condition of life.

What I have taught about all this may be outdated and surpassed, but not what I have learned from it. This is, in fact, the great predicament of the scientist: that what he leaves behind is his experiment, not his experience.

The lipids—those intriguing and complicated fatlike cell constituents whose real biological function still is obscure—play an important role in blood clotting. In addition, other representatives of this class formed the object of my initial research work, as I mentioned in the first section of this account. It was natural for me to continue work in that direction, as well. There were quite a few panels to this polyptych. One had to do with the chemistry of various lipids, work that went on to the middle Sixties. Another line dealt with a group of important high-molecular cell components designated as lipoproteins. This is the form—a complex combination with certain proteins—in which some of the lipids occur in the body. I wrote one of the first reviews on the subject.[2] Clarke's esteem for me, never at fever heat, was increased considerably by that article; he told me that he found it written most amusingly—which shows that even lipids can be funny to the prepared mind.

Another series of investigations, which at that time had the charm of great novelty, concerned itself with the metabolism of the phospholipids. The radioactive phosphorus isotope ^{32}P was beginning to be available, although with difficulty. It was simultaneously used for such metabolic studies by a few other people, especially by Camillo Artom, a charming, lovable man, dried and concentrated by the sun of Sicily, but swept by the turbulent hurricanes of our century all the way to Winston-Salem, North Carolina. When I took up this work, one had to prepare one's own radioactive phosphorus, and I was helped in this home-industry alchemy by a young Columbia physicist, John Dunning, who was later to go on to a distinguished career. Although we were excited at that time, the results, as I look back on them, were uninspiring: it was to be expected that the different phosphorylated lipids of the body were not all formed at the same rate. Were I to expose the details of our findings to the uninitiated, they would perhaps say what a Shah of Persia is reputed to have answered when refusing an invitation from Emperor Franz Joseph to attend a horse race: "That one horse runs faster than another, I have always known. And I don't care to know which." It is, however, the very business of science to "know which." At any rate, I thought so when I was young, although much later I began to change my mind.

There was, however, a curious by-product of the work: I published the first synthesis of a radioactive organic compound. The few times I tried to preen myself on this feat, I encountered angry disbelief and ridicule. But there it is[3]: "Synthesis of a radioactive organic compound: alpha-glycerophosphoric acid."

A few more dusty specimens out of my mournful herbarium, and I shall have done. Blood clotting, lipids, lipoproteins, and radioactive tracers were not the only things on which I worked. I should like to mention three more areas of research. We did considerable work on the inositols, a group of sugarlike substances, of which one is nearly ubiquitous in living nature and is often listed among the vitamins. We worked on the biological fate of the hydroxy amino acids. We also studied the mechanisms of the inhibition of mitosis.

In everything I did I was impressed by the marvel of the cell, in which I saw nothing but order and beauty. I did not believe that we could ever unravel the plan of construction in which cohesion and crowding were only two of the many elements that we were forced to destroy in order to investigate them. Although I am now told that this plan has become clear to us, I cannot help feeling that it is not what I was dreaming of in those long-gone days. My laboratory was one of the first to prepare mitochondria and look at their chemistry, and also to use the high-speed centrifuge to isolate the organelles of the cytoplasm, such as the microsomes. It is not surprising that a little later, when I got a group of laboratories of my own, I called them the Cell Chemistry Laboratory.

This far from complete list of my activities covers the first twelve years of my stay at Columbia. The more than sixty regular papers published during that period dealt with a very wide field of biochemistry, as it was then understood; and a few of them may even have contributed a little to the advance of the science, which, at that time, was still slow, i.e., it had human proportions. The work was done with very little outside support: a small grant from the Markle Foundation and, during the war years, a little money from the Office of Scientific Research and Development. There was no publicity; I have never given a press interview. In fact, the "gentlemen of the press" have, on the whole, stayed away from me: a rare instance of the rabbit hypnotizing the snakes.

All was done with human hands: four graduate students, one or two post-docs, one technician. Almost the only use of electricity was for rather primitive centrifuges. Substances still were isolated, and even crystallized, in a visible form. The marvelous power of chemistry to demythologize and substantialize mysterious phenomena of nature was invoked. No claims were made that went beyond the evidence of reality. No questions were asked that only God can answer, nor were answers given on His behalf. No attempt was made to improve on nature.

Nevertheless, when I look back on what I did during those miraculous years, there come to mind the words ascribed to St. Thomas Aquinas: *Omnia quae scripsi paleae mihi videntur.* All he had written seemed to him as chaff. When I was young, I was required—and it was easy—to go back to the origins of our science. The bibliographies of chemical and biological papers often included references to work done forty or fifty years earlier. One felt oneself part of a gently growing tradition, growing at a rate that the human mind could encompass, vanishing at a rate that it could apprehend. Now, however, in our miserable scientific mass society, nearly all discoveries are born dead; papers are tokens in a power game, evanescent reflections on the screen of a spectator sport, news items that do not outlive the day on which they appeared. Our sciences have become forcing houses for a market that in reality does not exist, creating, with the concomitant complete break in tradition, a truly Babylonian confusion of mind and language. Nowadays, scientific tradition hardly reaches back for more than three or four years. The proscenium looks the same as before, but the scenery keeps on changing as in a fever dream; no sooner is one backdrop in place than it is replaced by an entirely different one.

The only thing that experience can now teach is that it has become worthless. One could ask whether a fund of knowledge, such as a scientific discipline, can exist without a living tradition. In any event, in many areas of science which I am able to survey, this tradition has disappeared. It is, hence, no exaggeration and no coquettish humility if I conclude that the work we did thirty or forty years ago—with all the engagement that honest effort could provide—is dead and gone.

"The Hereditary Code-Script"

EARLY IN 1944 somebody told me about a paper he had seen in the *Journal of Experimental Medicine*. This was the celebrated paper by Oswald T. Avery, Colin MacLeod, and Maclyn McCarty entitled "Studies on the Chemical Nature of the Substance Inducing Transformation of Pneumococcal Types."[4] The basic observations are not difficult to describe. There exist several types of pneumococci: avirulent and virulent, from their biological characteristics; "rough" and "smooth," from their surface properties. In 1928, the British pathologist Frederick Griffith made a very important discovery, namely, that when live nonvirulent organisms are injected into mice together with a killed preparation of virulent cells, lethal effects can be observed and virulent organisms are found in the animals. Similar observations on what came to be called "bacterial transformation" were later made in the test tube; it was clear that the virulent smooth cells contained some principle that could transform, permanently and inheritably, avirulent rough cultures into something resembling the smooth virulent donor organism. Avery and his collaborators set out to isolate, purify, and identify this principle. They suceeded; and these are the words with which they concluded their paper:

> The evidence presented supports the belief that a nucleic acid of the desoxyribose type is the fundamental unit of the transforming principle of Pneumococcus Type III.

It is difficult for me to describe the effect that this sentence, and the beautiful experimentation that had given rise to it, had on me. My reaction is, perhaps, best represented by some words I spoke much later in an address commemorating 100 years of nucleic-acid research.[5]

> As this tranformation represents a permanently inheritable alteration of a cell, the chemical nature of the substance responsible for this alteration had here been elucidated for the first time. Seldom has more been said in so few words. The man who had written them, Oswald Theodore Avery (1877–1955), was at that time already 67: the ever rarer instance of an old man making a great scientific discovery. It had not been his first. He was a quiet man; and it would have honored the world more, had it honored him more. What counts, however, in science is to be not so much the first as the last.
>
> This discovery, almost abruptly, appeared to foreshadow a chemistry of heredity and, moreover, made probable the nucleic acid character of the gene. It certainly made an impression on a few, not on many, but probably on nobody a more profound one than on me. For I saw before me in dark contours the beginning of a grammar of biology. Just as Cardinal Newman in the title of a celebrated book, *The Grammar of Assent,* spoke of the grammar of belief, I use this word as a description of the main elements and principles of a science. Avery gave us the first text of a new language, or rather he showed us where to look for it. I resolved to search for this text.
>
> Consequently, I decided to relinquish all that we had been working on or to bring it to a quick conclusion, although the

problems were not without interest and dealt with many facets of cellular chemistry. I have asked myself frequently whether I was not wrong in turning around the rudder so abruptly and whether it would not have been better not to succumb to the fascination of the moment; but these biographical bagatelles cannot be of interest to anybody. To the scientist nature is as a mirror that breaks every 30 years; and who cares about the broken glass of past times?

Before I go on I should, perhaps, say a few words about the group of substances that had so suddenly been thrust into the center of scientific attention, the nucleic acids. When the biochemist examines living tissue, regardless of whether he deals with animals, plants, or microorganisms, he will find certain features that they all have in common, and he will also find many differences. It will depend upon his plane of vision and also upon the goal of his search, whether he stresses the similarities or the divergences. It is sometimes difficult to see common characteristics among things that are ostensibly different; it is immensely more difficult to perceive differences among things which seem to be the same. What all living cells have in common are the four classes of compounds that make up their bulk: the proteins, the polysaccharides, the lipids, and the nucleic acids. The first three groups had been investigated successfully for a long time. Only with respect to the nucleic acids, seventy-five years had to elapse between their discovery and the beginning of an understanding of their functions and their structures.

The chemist distinguishes between two types of nucleic acid according to the sugar which they contain: deoxyribonucleic acid, generally nicknamed DNA, and ribonucleic acid, abbreviated as RNA. (Actually, these singulars are very much plurals, and the recognition of this fact is, perhaps, one of the fruits of my efforts.) At the time when Avery made his great discovery, it already was known that in animal and plant cells most of the DNA was found in the cell nucleus, which was also known as the seat of the—at that period—still mythical units of heredity, the genes. The new finding made it, therefore, extremely probable that the genes contained, or consisted of, DNA. I believe that few people now would deny that this is one of the most important discoveries in biology.

At the time the publication appeared, however, most people—including the Nobel Prize Committee, as it was then constituted—did not pay the slightest attention to it. Those who should have known were all too busy spinning their own tops through the corridors of power. Never having found the entrance to these useful burrows, I was not one of them. In fact, I immediately realized the importance of the observation and I even began to write an article, entitled "Professor Kekulé's Second Dream," in which many of the later developments were predicted fairly correctly. I regret that my only attempt to write science fiction, which was soon to become science truth, no longer exists.

I was not entirely unprepared. Two floors up from where I worked, Martin Dawson, who died young, had been doing excellent work on bacterial transformation, and in my own laboratory I had twice encountered nucleic acid: once, in the form of RNA, as a component of the thromboplastic protein mentioned before, and once, as DNA, when, during the war, we were doing research on the biochemistry of the rickettsia that causes typhus. But more importantly, I had at about that time been deeply impressed by a little book[6] written by the great Austrian physicist Erwin Schrödinger which carried the modest title *What Is Life?* Great scientists are particularly worth listening to when they speak about something of which they know little; in their own specialty they are usually great and dull. Speaking about the chromosomes—the rodlike nuclear bodies, constant in number for a given species, which can be discerned when the nucleus gets ready to divide—this is what Schrödinger had to say.

It is these chromosomes . . . that contain in some kind of code-script the entire pattern of the individual's future development and of its functioning in the mature state. . . . In calling the structure of the chromosome fibres a code-script we mean that the all-penetrating mind, once conceived by Laplace, to which every causal connection lay immediately open, could tell from their structure whether the egg would develop, under suitable conditions, into a black cock or into a speckled hen, into a fly or a maize plant, a rhododendron, a beetle, a mouse or a woman. . . . But the term code-script is, of course, too narrow. The chromosome structures are at the same time instrumental in bringing about the development they foreshadow. They are law-code and executive power — or, to use another simile, they are architect's plan and builder's craft — in one.

The hereditary code-script? The cryptographer hidden in every soul was intrigued. "Chromosomes!" I exclaimed. "DNA, builder's craft! Let's work on the nose of Cleopatra!"

The Exquisiteness of Minute Differences

WHAT WAS to be done was clear to me, but not at all how to do it. Avery's work had shown that the deoxyribonucleic acid of a *Pneumococcus* strain had biological properties lacking in the corresponding preparation isolated from calf thymus. It was, therefore, evident to me that these two substances must be different chemically; and from this to the assumption that all nucleic acids were species-specific seemed an easy and obvious step. When I first mentioned this to others, I was astonished to notice that it was not at all evident to them. They were not interested in the problem, nor were they willing to listen to my unassertive arguments. The initial incommunicability of truth, scientific or otherwise, shows that we think in grooves, and that it is painful for us to be torn away from the womblike security of accepted concepts.

If art represents the highest form of reality that man — or at least modern secular man — is capable of attaining, the many instances in which great creations were rejected initially, and often with incredible malice, show how reluctant we are to grasp reality. We accept only what has been predigested for us by the so-called tastemakers; but this is then a spurious reality, "a micro-idol of an Easter Island of the mind."[7] In another place[8] I have had an occasion to speak of the mysterious power of fashions.

When, in 1945, I began to think seriously about the nucleic acids, it grew, of course, out of my life-long fascination with the appearances of life, with its immense diversity, its majestic uniformity. So many colors, but they all fade; so many forces, but they all dissipate; being born to die; dying to be born. Even as a child, I felt that I was living in a gentle universe, ordered by a wisdom that I could never hope to comprehend. The great goddess Ananke appeared to me as a faithful friend. When later I learned chemistry and began to think about the chemistry of life, my trust in the superior wisdom of the living cell had by no means abandoned me. It remained clear to me that there must be one level on which all of life is chemical, just as there are many other levels of life whose understanding could only be distorted by exclusive reference to the laws of chemistry. My greatest defect as a scientist—and one of the explanations of my lack of success—is probably my reluctance to simplify. In contrast to many others, I am a "terrible complexifier."

Our understanding of the world is built up of innumerable layers. Each layer is worth exploring, as long as we do not forget that it is one of many. Knowing all there is to be known about one layer—a most unlikely event—would not teach us much about the rest. The integration of the enormous number of bits of information and the resulting vision of nature take place in our minds; but the human mind is easily deceived and confused, and the vision of nature changes every few generations. It is, in fact, the intensity of the vision that counts more heavily than its completeness or its correctness. I doubt that there is such a thing as a correct view of nature, unless the rules of the game are stated clearly. Undoubtedly, there will later be other games and other rules.

It was, hence, with the chemistry of the cell that I was concerned. Most of the efforts of the preceding generation had been spent on establishing the unity of nature. They were very successful in emphasizing how uniform living matter is in its general composition, its metabolic reactions, and in the economy of energy required to keep life going. But I was more attracted by the other face of Janus, by the enormous diversity of living nature.* From the point of view of the chemist, this diversity is expressed not only in shape, that is, morphology, but even more in the innumerable substances that are specific for one organism or for another. It was, however, clear to me that all these different pigments or odors or toxins could only be the symptoms, not the causes, of biological specificity. The agent specifying differences had to be looked for elsewhere.

The decisive influence on biological diversity and the agents maintaining the hereditary constancy of this diversity had to be searched for among the cellular constituents of high molecular weight that make up the bulk of all tissues: the proteins and the conjugated proteins, such as lipoproteins, mucoproteins, etc.; the polysaccharides; and the nucleic acids. As concerns the first two, the proteins and the polysaccharides, biological activity and great chemical divergences had been recognized for quite some time. It was, in fact, the great family of proteins that was generally considered to play the crucial role in specificity. The nucleic acids were only thought of as the coat-hangers for the all-important proteins. All this was changed abruptly by Avery's discovery, which established the deoxyribonucleic acids as the hub of the biological command structure. I considered this to be the real coming of age of chemistry as the central science of

*In one of my earliest papers, published when I worked in Berlin,[9] there already was some discussion of "structural specificity." To indicate their dubious nature, these speculations were, however, banished by the editor into small print.

the life processes.

Until 1944, DNA and RNA each was very much a singular. It was known that the nucleic acids were composed of four building blocks, the nucleotides. Each nucleotide consisted of three interlinked chemical substances: a nitrogen-containing base (the purines, adenine and guanine; the pyrimidines, cytosine and thymine or uracil), a sugar (deoxyribose or ribose), and phosphoric acid. The nucleic acids were formulated as small chains in which the four nucleotides were bound to each other by phosphate bridges. This structural model was referred to as a tetranucleotide, a term that served to relegate these unimportant and uninformative compounds to the role of a biological glue. It was my work and that of my colleagues that, starting in 1946, made out of a modest singular a huge plural.

As I have said before, it was under the influence of Avery's discovery that I concluded that DNA must carry species-specificity. This could, by my reasoning, have been due either to different building blocks or to differences in the arrangement of the same building blocks. The first alternative could be symbolized by the difference between the two words: ROSE and ROME. Three letters—that is, nucleotides—identical, one different. A simple example of the second type of divergence would be ROSE and EROS: the same components arranged differently. All these speculations were, however, worthless, since there existed no procedure to test them. Looking back at this comparatively recent past—not much more than thirty years ago—we may find it difficult to realize how little was then actually known. Only two preparations had been isolated in some quantity, although in a badly degraded state: the deoxyribonucleic acid of calf thymus and the ribonucleic acid of yeast. Even for the characterization of the basic components, enormous amounts were required; a quantitative analysis was out of the question. If my assumptions about the nucleic acids were to be proved correct, it was evident that extremely accurate quantitative methods had to be discovered. Moreover, those methods had to be applicable to minute quantities of nucleic acids, because several organs of many different species and also relatively inaccessible microorganisms were to be compared.

When, in 1946, I thought seriously of attacking the riddle of the nucleic acids, I was favored by a great deal of luck: 1) a new approach to the separation of minute quantities had been developed; 2) a new instrument, which was to prove crucial to our work, had become available commercially; 3) and most importantly, I acquired two excellent collaborators—Dr. Ernst Vischer and Mrs. Charlotte Green.

The method was the one described in 1944 by R. Consden, A. H. Gordon, and A. J. P. Martin for the separation of minute amounts of amino acids. This procedure, which came to be known as paper chromatography, consists in the application of a drop of a solution, containing the substances to be separated, to a sheet or a strip of filter paper, which then is irrigated with a solvent mixture. This results finally in the production of discrete spots, each containing one of the components. We succeeded in adapting the method to the analysis of the nucleic acid constituents, the purines and pyrimidines. That we could, for the first time, make the procedure strictly quantitative was due to the availability of the first commercial ultraviolet spectrophotometers, for the purines and pyrimidines exhibit strong and characteristic absorption spectra in the ultraviolet.

As for Ernst Vischer, his training and knowledge, acquired in his native Basel, were just as solid as the impressively robust Swiss shoes on which he first marched into my laboratory. That was in the autumn of 1946. One look at him, and I called him *der getreue Eckart*. His calm diligence, his imperturbable thoroughness, his intellectual honesty, proved invaluable, especially to me who, in those my younger years, certainly was one of the least tranquil of quietists.

We went to work, first the three of us, later joined by a few others: Stephen Zamenhof, Boris Magasanik, George Brawerman, David Elson, Ed Hodes, Ruth Doniger, and others. I made most of the nucleic acid preparations, Vischer and Green developed the quantitative analysis. We succeeded, and our first paper, a brief preliminary note, was published in May, 1947.[10] It was a modest beginning; the methods were still very rough; the solvent systems and the visualization of the separated spots were primitive; but we could separate and identify as little as five micrograms of each substance. I am not sure whether, before our work, even the millionfold quantity would have given equally reliable results.

When we began getting our first results on the composition of DNA from different types of cells, they were, of course, fragmentary, as our methods were crude. But they were sufficient to confirm me in my belief that different species contain different DNA, and I began to think about the ways in which differences in composition, even slight differences, could influence the content of "biological information." (It is probable, though, that I did not use this term at that time.) "Professor Kekulé's Second Dream" began to throw up various spectral schemes: I thought about variations in the nucleotide sequence which could carry species specificity, but even more about specific sterical arrangements. I was in love with topology, and all forms of twisted rings filled the office, rings splitting longitudinally and giving rise to intertwined structures. Thus, when I first discussed in public our initial observations, at a Cold Spring Harbor symposium and at the cytology congress in Stockholm in the summer of 1947, DNA was pictured as a Möbius strip. In a way, I am still sorry that these speculations remained a figment of the imagination.

One of the simplest surfaces studied in topology is the so-called Moebius strip. It consists of a long paper strip whose two ends are pasted together after one has received a definite number of twists. If, for instance, one end is twisted once completely round (i.e., through four right angles) before being joined to the other end and the strip then is cut along the center line, two interlaced rings are obtained each of which has inherited the particular twist. It can again be divided into two interlaced rings, and so on. An inquisitive child, by varying the arrangement, can make many fascinating discoveries about the inheritance of geometrical pecularities; and when it grows up and remembers them, they may help to take some of the terror from the seemingly automatic nature of the life processes.[11]

This is probably the first childish adumbration of strand separation in DNA. The terror, however, has not been removed; it has increased, for we have begun to define life by its very automatism. The majesty of the book *Genesis* has been replaced by a technology of biopoiesis which may well make the centuries to come into an undreamed-of nightmare.

It was very fortunate that in our first attempts to determine the structure of deoxyribonucleic acids we had chosen DNA specimens from yeast, from ox tissues, and from tubercle bacilli, for especially the first and last of those differ from each other dramatically in their composition. This gave me enough confidence to consider even small differences as significant if they were reproducible. Had I, on the other hand, decided to compare calf thymus DNA with pneumococcal DNA, I should probably have concluded that the two were indistinguishable chemically.

To finish this particular episode, it may be of interest to quote both from the preamble and the conclusions of the first comprehensive review of our work, which was published in 1950 in the Swiss journal *Experientia*.[12]

We started in our work from the assumption that the nucleic acids were complicated and intricate high-polymers, comparable in this respect to the proteins, and that the determination of their structures and their structural differences would require the development of methods suitable for the precise analysis of all constituents of nucleic acids prepared from a large number of different cell types. These methods had to permit the study of minute amounts, since it was clear that much of the material would not be readily available. The procedures developed in our laboratory make it indeed possible to perform a complete constituent analysis on 2–3 mg of nucleic acid, and this in six parallel determinations. . . .

We arrive at the following conclusions. The desoxypentose nucleic acids from animal and microbial cells contain varying proportions of the same four nitrogenous constituents, namely, adenine, guanine, cytosine, thymine. Their composition appears to be characteristic of the species, but not of the tissue, from which they are derived. The presumption, therefore, is that there exists an enormous number of structurally different nucleic acids; a number, certainly much larger than the analytical methods available to us at present can reveal. . . .

A decision as to the identity of natural high polymers often still is beyond the means at our disposal. This will be particularly true of substances that differ from each other only in the sequence, not in the proportion, of their constituents. The number of possible nucleic acids having the same analytical composition is truly enormous. . . . I think there will be no objection to the statement that, as far as chemical possibilities go, they could very well serve as one of the agents, or possibly as the agent, concerned with the transmission of inherited properties.

It must be admitted, compared to Ezechiel these prophecies read rather dry; but, on the other hand, they were swifter of fulfillment. The particular episode to which my sentences referred was, however, not quite at an end, for into the galley proofs of my article I had inserted two more sentences.

The Miracle of Complementarity

AFTER MUCH STRUGGLE I prevailed upon myself to add the following brief paragraph to page 206 of the proofs of the essay.[12]

The results serve to disprove the tetranucleotide hypothesis. It is, however, noteworthy — whether this is more than accidental, cannot yet be said — that in all desoxypentose nucleic acids examined thus far the molar ratios of total purines to total pyrimidines, and also of adenine to thymine and of guanine to cytosine, were not far from one.

For a long time I felt a great reluctance to accept such regularities, since it had been impressed on me that our search for harmony, for an easily perceived and pleasing harmony, could only serve to distort or gloss over the intricacies of nature. Many people had in the past attempted to find unifying formulations for the proteins and other natural high polymers, just as the nucleic acids had been considered as tetranucleotides, because they were built of four nucleotide constituents. All this I knew to be wrong, and I wanted, as I once said, "to avoid falling into a streamlined version of the old trap which in the past tripped so many excellent workers in the field of nucleic acid chemistry."[13]

Our first results on the base composition of DNA were marred by the fact that separate procedures were employed for the determination of the purines and of the pyrimidines. A higher percentage of the purines was always recovered than of the pyrimidines, as judged by reference to total phosphorus or nitrogen. But I could not help noticing that in DNA preparations from either ox or human tissues or from yeast there was always more adenine than guanine, more thymine than cytosine, whereas in the nucleic acid from tubercle bacilli these relationships were reversed. When I computed the molar ratios of adenine to guanine and of thymine to cytosine, I found them nearly equal for a given source and apparently characteristic of the species.

One late afternoon, while sitting at the desk in my narrow tube of an office on the fifth floor of the medical school, I asked myself: "What would happen if I assume that DNA contains equal quantities of purines and pyrimidines?" I took all the data we had on the molar proportions of adenine and guanine and of cytosine and thymine and corrected each set to give a total of 50 percent: there emerged—like Botticelli's Venus on the shell, though not quite as flawless—the regularities that I then used to call the complementarity relationships and that are now known as base-pairing.

This form of equipoise never having been encountered in nature, I was perhaps more confused than happy about the discovery. The ability to write a beautiful poem would have astounded me less. This happened either late in 1948 or early in 1949. When, in the summer of that year, I gave several lectures in Europe, I mentioned these observations, but again nobody seemed interested. Since I myself, being a scientific primitive, did not like laws of nature to be based on correction factors, I omitted complementarity when fashioning the review out of my lecture notes.[12] In the meantime, we had, however, improved our methods considerably: we now could determine all nitrogenous constituents in one analytical run; we had many more specimens to analyze, and recoveries became so good as not to require correction. I gained confidence and inserted the statement quoted before. A lecture I gave early in 1951 oozes assurance.[14] It stresses explicitly the species-dependent differences in DNA and the compositional regularities that all DNA specimens have in common; it points out the existence of "AT types" and "GC types" of DNA, according to whether adenine + thymine or guanine + cytosine predominate; and it ends with the following final remarks:

> It is fitting to conclude this all too sketchy survey with a confession of ignorance. What our studies have taught us more than anything else is how little we know as yet about the chemistry of nucleic acids. The chemical specificity of macromolecules and the interactions between them through which the organization of the cell is maintained can only partly be understood in terms of our present knowledge. In the approach to a scientific problem two principles are operative: generalization and simplification. Both are necessary and both dangerous. It is obvious that we can learn more geometry from the illustrations in a textbook on projective geometry than from the beautiful pictures in Sir D'Arcy Thompson's *On Growth and Form*. But it is difficult to say where the danger line lies beyond which oversimplification will produce a dogmatic ignorance. Should we stress the multiformity of Nature, which makes us forget the simplicity of its basic designs; or should the essential shape win over

the accidental form? In Wycherley's *The Country Wife* a quack is addressed as follows: "Doctor, thou wilt never make a good chemist, thou art so incredulous and impatient." If patience and credulity were all the chemist needed, the problem of the nucleic acids — still so baffling and elusive — would have been solved a long time ago.

The regularities of the composition of deoxyribonucleic acids — some friendly people later called them the "Chargaff rules" — are as follows: (a) the sum of the purines (adenine and guanine) equals that of the pyrimidines (cytosine and thymine); (b) the molar ratio of adenine to thymine equals 1; (c) the molar ratio of guanine to cytosine equals 1. And, as a direct consequence of these relationships, (d) the number of 6-amino groups (adenine and cytosine) is the same as that of 6-keto groups (guanine and thymine).

In some ways I was the wrong man to make these discoveries: imaginative rather than analytical; apocalyptic rather than dogmatic; brought up to despise publicity; uncomfortable in scientific gatherings; fleeing all contacts; always happier with my youngers than with my betters; more afraid of an absurd world than trying to understand it; but ever conscious, day and night, that there is more to see than I can see, more to say than I can say, and even more to be silent about.

I do not believe that my article, published in *Experientia* in 1950,[12] made much of an impression. Even the principal beneficiaries of my findings did not refer to it; but this may have been deliberate. All in all, I should think that the scientific climate was not yet ready to accept ideas on biological information, its conservation and transfer, and that an enormous publicity effort — or, to put it more gently, an enormous educational effort — was required to bring this about. Such an effort could not have come from me.

It is nearly impossible to reconstruct the moral, intellectual, and material atmosphere of a past period, quite in contrast to the relative ease with which the historical events that took place in it can often be listed.* This makes the history of ideas a precarious undertaking and renders the history of science almost impossible, unless we are satisfied with an anecdotal and crudely chronological account.

For this reason, I find it difficult to trace with historical accuracy the development of my ideas about nucleic acid, and when I want to know what I was thinking in the summer of 1948, I have to look it up in a collection of anecdotes.[15] Always more a polymaniac than a monomaniac, I was thinking of so many different things!

In any event, it cannot be denied — although many would still like to deny it — that the discovery of base complementarity in DNA has had a far-reaching effect on the development of biological thought. This effect has probably not yet run its course and the "last word" about any scientific problem will only be spoken when conscious life comes to an end on this planet; but the heavy golden seals attached to the bulls of molecular biology make it ever more difficult to reopen the documents for the addition of further codicils. When, twelve years after our original publication, I looked back, I was myself surprised:

> Few recent advances have, for better or for worse, had such an impact on biological thinking as the discovery of base-pairing in nucleic acids. These complementariness principles do not only underlie current ideas on the structure of the nucleic acids, but they form the foundation of all speculations, more or less well-founded, on their physical properties (denaturation, hypochromicity, etc.), on the transfer of biological information from deoxyribonucleic acid to ribonucleic acid, and on the role of the latter in directing the synthesis of specific proteins. They form the basis of present

---

*What Napoleon did on the 18th of Brumaire can be ascertained, but not what he thought, which is not the same as what he said he thought. When it comes to the reception of an event by individual minds, we are even more at a loss. Reading recently the letters exchanged by Goethe and Schiller, I was struck by the fact that the entire voluminous correspondence, reaching from 1794 to 1805, and comprising more than a thousand letters, contained only one mention of Bonaparte.

explanations of the manner in which the amino acids are activated before being assembled to make a protein; they are being invoked incessantly in attempts to unravel the nucleotide code which is thought to be responsible for specifying the amino acid sequence of proteins.[7]

When I began to realize how unique were the regularities we had discovered, I tried, of course, to understand what it all meant, but I did not get very far. My inclination has always been more to marvel at a mystery than to explain it to the onlookers. This, most people would say, is a highly unscientific bend of mind, and I am afraid I would agree with them. Nevertheless, I attempted to build molecular models of the nucleotides, since I remembered from our work on the inositols how crucial the inspection of correct models can be. Unfortunately, the atomic models I had at that time were few and very large and clumsy; no sooner was a nucleotide constructed than it broke apart at one or more of its many links. After making a trinucleotide, I ran out of atoms and even more of patience. I did notice, in playing with models of adenine and thymine, some sort of a special fit—the guanine-cytosine pair I do not remember—but I never had enough of two nucleotide chains to try anything reasonable. Soon I dismissed the whole traumatic experience, since the "terrible complexifier" that I was—always two steps ahead of reality—dreamed of something much more grandiose than a plain code-bearing tape. What I did not want to acknowledge is that nature is blind and reads Braille. In fact, even now I am not entirely reconciled to it. Thus, I missed the opportunity of being enshrined in the various halls of fame of the science museums.

In the meantime, we continued publishing many papers on nucleic acid structure, and these began to attract some attention. The first important scientist to be interested in my work was the Swedish biologist John Runnström. He invited me to his laboratory in Stockholm, where I prepared DNA from many varieties of sea-urchin sperm, and he also visited me in New York.

I was very fond of this benign and un-Swedishly lively man who was still a remnant of those great naturalists of the past who combined daring with deep respect for nature. Through him I met Georg von Hevesy and Einar Hammarsten. Although Hammarsten had demonstrated, more convincingly than anybody else, the high-molecular nature of DNA, he seemed unimpressed by what I told him. This was not the case with Hevesy or with Erik Jorpes, a man whose contributions to biochemistry have, perhaps, not received the credit they deserve.

Two outstanding British X-ray crystallographers, J. D. Bernal and W. T. Astbury, were aware of the great interest offered by the nucleic acids. Astbury came to see me in New York in September, 1950, soon after the publication of my *Experientia* paper, and subsequently I sent him some of my DNA preparations. One year later another British biophysicist, M. H. F. Wilkins, visited us and received several DNA specimens that I had prepared. This was at the time of a Gordon Conference in New Hampton, New Hampshire, in which I took part together with many excellent protein and nucleic-acid chemists, among whom the wonderful Linderstrøm-Lang stands out in my memory. I had first met Lang at the International Cytology Congress in 1947, when he undertook to convey us to some address in Upsala. His car described a complicated topological flourish; but when the same small church offered itself to my view for the fifth or sixth time, I told him that we seemed to be going in a circle. "It was not a *circle,*" he replied, and left the circuit. Although I do not remember where we were going, possibly to see Arne Tiselius, it is obvious that we must have arrived; otherwise I could not be writing this now.

The DNA preparations that I gave to the X-ray people were, as I warned them at that time, probably not particularly suitable for physical investigations. They had been made with special attention to chemical purity and homogeneity, and were completely dehydrated in a vacuum in the frozen state. The snow-white felt that resulted from the evaporation was excellent for chemical studies, but there must have been severe depolymerization. Actually, this was not of great consequence. What I did not then realize was that we were on the threshold of a new kind of science: a normative biology in which reality only serves to corroborate predictions; and if it fails to do so, it is replaced by another reality. And as to dogmas, they are in no need of experiments. What is currently considered as the structure of deoxyribonucleic acid was established by people who required no recourse to actual DNA preparations, whether polymerized or degraded.

Gullible's Troubles

WHEN I FIRST MET F. H. C. Crick and J. D. Watson in Cambridge, in the last days of May, 1952, they seemed to me an ill-matched pair. This intrinsically unmemorable event has so often been painted—"Caesar Falling into the Rubicon"—repainted, touched up, or varnished in the several auto- and allo-hagiographies[15, 16] that even I, with my good memory for comic incidents and great admiration for the Marx Brothers films, find it difficult to scrape off the entire legendary overlay. I hope that the resulting portraits will be in sharper focus than the famous picture of Parmigianino in the Vienna museum.

This is the way it all came about. The summer of 1952 promised to be an unusually busy time for me: the biochemistry congress in Paris; lectures at the Weizmann Institute and in several European cities; trying unsuccessfully, as twice before, for a professorship in Switzerland. My first talk was scheduled in Glasgow, and on the way there I spent May 24 to 27 in Cambridge, where John Kendrew put me up in Peterhouse. He asked me to speak with two people in the Cavendish Laboratory who were trying to do something with the nucleic acids. What they were trying to do was not clear to him; he did not sound very promising.

The first impression was indeed far from favorable; and it was not improved by the many farcical elements that enlivened the ensuing conversation, if that is the correct description of what was in parts a staccato harangue. Lest I be accused of *crimen laesarum maiestatum,* I have to point out that mythological or historical couples—Castor and Pollux, Harmodios and Aristogeiton, Romeo and Juliet—must have appeared quite differently before the deed than after. In any event, I seem to have missed the shiver of recognition of a historical moment: a change in the rhythm of the heartbeats of biology. Moreover, the statistical likelihood of two geniuses getting together before my eyes here at Cavendish seemed so small that I did not even consider it. My diagnosis was certainly rapid and possibly wrong.

The impression: one, thirty-five years old; the looks of a fading racing tout, something out of Hogarth ("The Rake's Progress"); Cruikshank, Daumier; an incessant falsetto, with occasional nuggets glittering in the turbid stream of prattle. The other, quite undeveloped at twenty-three, a grin, more sly than sheepish; saying little, nothing of consequence; a "gawky young figure, so reminiscent of one of the apprentice cobblers out of Nestroy's *Lumpazivagabundus.*"[17] I recognized a variety act, with the two partners at that time showing excellent teamwork, although in later years helical duplicity diminished considerably. The repertory was, however, unexpected.

So far as I could make out, they wanted, unencumbered by any knowledge of the chemistry involved, to fit DNA into a helix. The main reason seemed to be Pauling's alpha-helix model of a protein. I do not remember whether I was actually shown their scale model of a polynucleotide chain, but I do not believe so, since they still were unfamiliar with the chemical structures of the nucleotides. They were, however, extremely worried about the correct "pitch" of their helix. I do not recall how much of the X-ray evidence of King's College (Rosalind Franklin, Wilkins) was mentioned. Because — at that time, at any rate — I set little trust in the biological relevance of X-ray photographs of stretched and pickled high-polymer preparations, I may not have paid sufficient attention.

It was clear to me that I was faced with a novelty: enormous ambition and aggressiveness, coupled with an almost complete ignorance of, and a contempt for, chemistry, that most real of exact sciences — a contempt that was later to have a nefarious influence on the development of "molecular biology." Thinking of the many sweaty years of making preparations of nucleic acids and of the innumerable hours spent on analyzing them, I could not help being baffled. I am sure that, had I had more contact with, for instance, theoretical physicists, my astonishment would have been less great. In any event, there they were, speculating, pondering, angling for information. So it appeared at least to me, a man of notoriously restricted vision.

I told them all I knew. If they had heard before about the pairing rules, they concealed it. But as they did not seem to know much about anything, I was not unduly surprised. I mentioned our early attempts* to explain the complementarity relationships by the assumption that, in the nucleic acid chain, adenylic was always next to thymidylic acid and cytidylic next to guanylic acid. This had come to nought when we found that gradual enzymic digestion produced a completely aperiodic pattern; for if the nucleic acid chain had been composed of an arrangement of A-T and G-C dinucleotides, the regularities should have persisted.

I believe that the double-stranded model of DNA came about as a consequence of our conversation; but such things are only susceptible of a later judgment:

> Quando Iudex est venturus
> Cuncta stricte discussurus!

When, in 1953, Watson and Crick published their first note on the double helix,[18] they did not acknowledge my help and cited only a short paper of ours which had appeared in 1952 shortly before theirs, but not, as would have been natural, my 1950 or 1951 reviews.[12, 14]

Later, when molecular prestidigitation ran wild, I was often asked by more or less well-meaning people why I had not discovered the celebrated model. My answer has always been that I was too dumb, but that, if Rosalind Franklin and I could have collaborated, we might have come up with something of the sort in one or two years. I doubt, however, that we could ever have elevated the double helix into "the mighty symbol that has replaced the cross as the signature of the biological analphabet."[19]

Matches for Herostratos

WHEN the Artemision—one of the world wonders of antiquity—went up in flames in 356 B.C., a man was apprehended who confessed that he had done it in order to make his name immortal. The judges, in condemning him, decreed that his name must remain unknown. But soon after, the historian Theopompos claimed that the name was Herostratos. Whether this really was the name or whether Theopompos merely wanted to annoy, say, his father-in-law, cannot be ascertained. Recently, when I mentioned Herostratos in an article, the editor called up to say that nobody in the editorial office had ever heard of him, thus giving belated satisfaction to the judges of Ephesos.

If Herostratos has earned immortality for having burned down the temple of Artemis in Ephesos, maybe the man from whom he got the matches ought not to be entirely forgotten. I am that man.

I am afraid I shall be misunderstood if I say that all great scientific discoveries—or, as some would say, all great scientific advances—carry a Herostratic element, an irreversible loss of something that mankind cannot afford to lose. This may have been less noticeable as long as the sciences were small and powerless, and the greatest of all scientific minds—the discoverer of fire, the inventor of the wheel, the brains that first formulated such concepts as time or force—remain hidden, as benefactors of humanity, in ancient mist. Whether Prometheus deserved to be tortured by the eagles cannot be decided; the creators of the myth obviously believed that the gods had a case.

In early historical times there was, it would seem, a strict separation between scientific inquiry and technology. The latter could, with a few exceptions, hardly be considered as an application of scientific research, but rather as an empirically growing learning process. With the onset of the modern phase of the natural sciences at the beginning of the seventeenth century, the distinction becomes much more difficult; and, with regard to the last 150 years or so, it may be argued in each particular case whether science acted on technology or vice versa. I shall not try to weigh the gain or loss.

The philosophical and moral impact of the sciences varied with the historical and social conditions. Newtonian physics had a very different effect on Newton than it had on Voltaire. Descartes, Malebranche, and Diderot may have read the same books, but their conclusions were different. There is no evidence that Pascal forgot his mathematics when he began to work on the *Apologie*. Science shook the shakable and confirmed the firm. Its use as an ideological weapon came later.

Among the sciences, biology occupies a special place. Although late in growing out of its purely descriptive and classificatory phase, its impact was immediate. Only astronomy, in the times of Copernicus, Tycho, Kepler, Galilei, can be compared with it. But the great upheaval in our view of nature that modern biology has brought about has given rise to neither threnody nor paean; neither John Donne's *The Sun is lost, and th'earth* . . . nor Goethe's *Die Sonne tönt nach alter Weise* . . . .

The great names in the biology of the last hundred years are Darwin, Mendel, and Avery. Darwin's influence on thought and action was almost instant. He is, in many respects, the Richard Wagner of science; and it is not an accident that a susceptible mind such as Nietzsche's fell victim to both. Mendel's fame took a long time to establish itself; but once genetics was recognized as a distinct, though popularly misunderstood, science, it became as rapidly and as shamelessly vulgarized as did Darwinism. It would be foolish to charge one or the other scientist with the misdeeds perpetrated in their names—the slaughterers no doubt would easily have found other tutelary saints—but the stench emanating from such slogans as "the improvement of the master-race," with all the concomitant unheard-of atrocities, will never again be dissipated. Mendel is entirely innocent in all this, not so Darwin; but the blame must mostly go to the sloganeers.

Avery's influence was of an entirely different order. It was exerted only within the biological sciences; his name still is widely unknown. Whereas Mendel's successors were able to demonstrate that the heredity rules discovered by him were due to distinct units of inheritance which had physical reality, being localized in the chromosomes, Avery's findings pointed to the chemical nature of those units, the genes. The observations of my laboratory completed the quest by showing that the deoxyribonucleic acids could indeed represent texts carrying specific information and, furthermore, that these texts had one entirely novel feature in common, namely, a most peculiar and unexpected pairing of the DNA constituents. These findings all were the result of inductive reasoning based on numerous experimental observations, as were also subsequent important discoveries, such as the mechanisms by which the nucleic acids are replicated and the establishment of the genetic code.

The double helix model of DNA, which has had an enormous

influence on the biological sciences, is something quite different. It is, as formulated, essentially a packaging job, an extremely neat and witty one; and it lent itself easily to the vigorous promotion campaign that was put in motion without delay. Looking back on the hubbub twelve years later, this is what I had to say[20]:

> This is not the place to write the *histoire intime* of a discovery; but you know that the outstanding charismatic symbol of our time—the spiral staircase leading, I hope, into heaven—has been advertised with a truly remarkable intensity. It has been used as an emblem, it has been put on neckties, it embellishes letterheads, it stands outside of buildings as what might be called commercial sculpture. It has even invaded the higher forms of mannerist art. The semirigid flexible nature of the DNA structure may have reminded Salvador Dali of his watches; and the Arcimboldi of our times has repeatedly painted the portrait of a somewhat flabby, perhaps partially denatured, double helix.* If you consider that no echo of Copernicus is found in Titian and none of Kepler or Galilei in Rubens or Poussin, this may teach you something about our art; but I am afraid, it may also teach you something about our science.
>
> All these merry noises, the exuberant carnival spirit of what I like to call Pop Biochemistry, have had one unfortunate effect: most students no longer study nature; they test models.

Quite a few years have gone since this was written. It has become quieter, because science is being suffocated slowly, partly by overproduction, partly by underfinancing. The ill effects alluded to in the last sentence of my quotation persist. The Texas spirit of doing the impossible in a little while longer has produced many short-lived triumphs; but the new science which grew out of the fusion of chemistry, physics, and genetics, i.e., molecular biology, has remained normative and dogmatic. One of the obnoxious dogmas to which it has given rise—the so-

---

*In a Dali exhibition in New York in 1963, the title of one of the paintings was *Galacidalacidesoxiribunucleicacid;* and in a lengthy explanation in the catalogue the names of the proponents of the double helix were linked with those of Isaiah and Christ.

called Central Dogma: DNA makes RNA; RNA makes proteins—is no longer valid. (I had never accepted it, as shown in lectures I gave in 1957 in Moscow and in 1958 in Vienna.[21, 22]) But the fact that dogmas could be handed down from the mountains shows that science had changed disastrously.

This was the time when I began to feel awfully alone. Neither country nor profession, neither language nor society, and not even the tranquil and reverential inspection of nature, seemed to offer a refuge. We all die in an armor of ice, I used to say. But I was not yet 55 years old. The orderly, loving, and careful study of life had been replaced by a frantic and noisy search for stunts and "break-throughs." An entirely novel kind of scientist filled the laboratories and congresses. I asked myself whether I, too, if only in a small part, had helped to bring this about; and I had to give the same answer as did Emperor Franz Joseph in 1914. After Austria, through its ultimatum to Serbia, had unleashed the war, the Emperor was made to publish a very beautifully written manifesto. *Ich habe es nicht gewollt*, said the helpless old man.

In the Light of Darkness

In 1969 I was invited to give a lecture in Basel. The lecture was to serve a double purpose: to commemorate the centenary of Friedrich Miescher's discovery of DNA and the twenty-fifth anniversary of the Swiss scientific journal *Experientia*. Being no stranger to DNA nor to the journal in which had appeared my ancient review article on nucleic acids, announcing the observation of the complementarity relationships in DNA,[12] I was glad to accept the invitation. The lecture took place on a pleasant May day in the elegant, large auditorium of the University. The room was full of young people, my favorite audience. It was an unusual, questioning crowd, for this was the time of great ferment among students all over the world, an exaltation into new and undefinable horizons; but soon it was to dissipate itself, unfortunately, without leaving much of a trace, unlike the romantic movement 150 years earlier, of which it reminded me in many respects. The students had certainly not come only to hear me; the eminent Nikolaas Tinbergen was due to speak on ethology. The audience was, of course, not composed solely of students; there were many scientists of great distinction. One of them, the noted organic chemist Leopold Ruzicka, his eighty-two years notwithstanding, followed my words with lively attention, and afterwards he got up and said some much too flattering things about me.

Before choosing my subject, I had given much thought to the attractive figure of Friedrich Miescher, who appeared to me as one of the rare scientists whom I was wont to call "the quiet in the land." I was also thinking about the way in which, in calmer times, a new scientific idea arose and flowered. For a scientific concept to be formulated successfully, a concerted interaction of many requisites must occur. First of all, the right man must ask himself the right question. This may well be a random event that occurs much more often than we are aware; not to speak of the many "Raphaels born without hands" to whom Lessing alludes in *Emilia Galotti*. Less fortuitously, this man must find an audience, i.e., he must be able to publish and to find readers; and this may not have been so easy even in the bucolic days of the last century. But, most importantly, the times must be ripe for both question and answer. In many instances, what a time takes to its heart dies with the time. Scientific best-sellers are, on the whole, not more durable than are other best-sellers; and one could have said that it augured well for the permanent value of Miescher's work that it found so little echo during his lifetime.

My lecture, which was a very informal review of a hundred years of nucleic acid research, was eventually rewritten in the form of an essay entitled, in its original version, *Vorwort zu einer Grammatik der Biologie*. In the belief that it ought to reach a wider audience, I offered it to the German monthly *Der Neue Merkur,* but the editor turned it down and it appeared finally in *Experientia.*[23] There it was read by the late Sam Granick of The Rockefeller University, a fine and decent biochemist, who was so much impressed by it that he suggested to the editor of *Science* that an English translation be published. Although I had always defined one's mother tongue as the language out of which one cannot translate, it fell to me to prepare the English version,[5] and in this form it became, perhaps, the most widely read of my articles.

Recently, when getting ready a book of which this essay was scheduled to form a part, my eyes fell on the final paragraph. I should like to quote it here, for it tries to bring out something that has been at the center of my appraisal of our present-day sciences. Halting and incomplete though this statement may be, I believe it is valid.

> It would seem to me that man cannot live without mysteries. One could say, the great biologists worked in the very light of darkness. We have been deprived of this fertile night. The moon, to which as a child I used to look up on a clear night, really is no more; never again will it fill grove and glen with its soft and misty gleam. What will have to go next? I am afraid I shall be misunderstood when I say that through each of these great scientific-technological exploits the points of contact between humanity and reality are diminished irreversibly.

Somebody who had read these words said to me: "You seem to appreciate the natural sciences only as long as they are not successful. Darkness illuminated becomes light." I could only answer: "What is success in science? Illuminated darkness is not light. We find ourselves in the cavern of limitless possibilities. Take a flashlight with you, and you may find you are only in a lumber room. If I know what I shall find, I do not want to find it. Uncertainty is the salt of life." And he said: "When you say darkness, you mean obscurity." This I denied; but I do not think we achieved conciliation.

This brought me back to ancient times. I was twelve years old and invented devices or mottoes for my future life. These were properly heraldic and, therefore, in Latin, as befits the escutcheon of an *Untergymnasiast* (high-school boy). There was *oculis apertis* or *larvatus prodeo;* but most often there was an armorial mole, and it said *fodio in tenebris.* "I dig in darkness," said the mole, and was hopelessly subterranean. The sun may have shone on the ground; but deep down there was the stylized animal performing its blind excavations. Do we really change during our lives? "As you began, so will you remain," Hölderlin wrote in his poem *Der Rhein.* We look at shriveled, toothless Helena, not realizing that, if she once was, she still is: the most beautiful of women. I, too, have attempted to remain faithful to my beginnings.

What I remember of my beginnings is the truly lyrical shudder with which I contemplated nature. I am not sure that I even knew what I meant by nature. It was the blood and the bones of the universe, its dawn and dusk, flowering and decay, firmament and graveyard. The alternations of the spiritual and the material tides, the oscillations between future and past, the mysterious fates of everlasting stone and short-lived fly: they filled me with admiration and reverence. Nature, it seemed to me, was almost the entire non-I, the entire non-small-boy. If anybody had asked me then whether I did not wish to go out and do away with some of the riddles of nature, I do not believe I should have understood him. Was I not born and sustained by the darkness that enveloped equally my past and my future? A small boy begins by being unable to explain the explainable, but when he grows old he often looks away from what cannot be explained. I am grateful that fate has preserved me from this form of blindness. Surrounded by a surfeit of solved riddles, I am still struck by how little we understand. I would not go so far as to claim that knowledge and wisdom are mutually exclusive; but they are far from being communicating vessels, and the level of one has no bearing on that of the other. More people have gained wisdom from unknowledge, which is not the same as ignorance, than from knowledge.

I could, therefore, say that sitting as a child in a large forest I was satisfied with admiring its immensity without inquiring about the names of the trees. That came later, and there even came times when I wanted to dig; but my motto remained unchanged: I dig in darkness. When I was fifteen I began to read Pascal's *Pensées*, probably before I knew how great a scientist Pascal was. We take from others only what we already have in ourselves. What I took from Pascal was, perhaps, the depth and the intensity of observation, but not the razor-sharpness of the "spirit of geometry" or the sparing elegance of his prose. Convinced by him that I, too, was a "thinking reed," it was more the noun than the adjective of which I was conscious. I was hurt by his claim that witty people were bad characters, for I prided myself on being a wit. Nevertheless, I thought that Pascal could teach me the compatibility of a life of deep religious thought and a life of scientific investigation, although it is possible that he had to renounce the second before entering on the first.

With this temperament of mine, should I not have thought of becoming a painter or a poet? But I was entirely ungifted for the first and not courageous enough for the second. My trouble was that I could do many things well and nothing superbly. I loved music, but I was a clumsy piano player; I loved writing, but my own attempts filled me with disgust. Even as a child, I was a disillusioned observer of myself; I had a strong sense of the ridiculous, especially as it concerned my own little person. There was no profession, no vocation that I could see myself choosing freely. Most of all, I loved to read, and I was a disgustingly erudite child; but I should never have thought of making use of what I knew. I was a monad searching for a destiny that did not exist. Even as a child I seem to have had a strong feeling for what Unamuno has called "the tragic sentiment of life."

What I had at that time—and it has never left me—was a dream of a reality that we could only touch tangentially, an awe of the numinous of nature whose power rested in its very unattainability. It was a feeling for the necessity of darkness in the life of man. In the Sistine Chapel, where Michelangelo depicts the creation of man, God's finger and that of Adam are separated by a short space. That distance I called eternity; and there, I felt, I was sent to travel.

That this may be a voyage without a destination was no concern of mine: How often have I said that only the road counted, not the goal? It could, however, be argued that Jakob Böhme did not have to be accurate to two decimals and that mystics should not have to equip themselves with electronic pocket calculators. But we live in peculiar times. Besides, when I floated into science, a naive young man could still imagine that he was devoting himself to the study of nature. This may, in fact, have been due to my simple-mindedness, but I became aware of the dissociation between nature and the natural sciences only late in my life. In any event, for me nature has still remained a synonym for the highest form of reality.

An earlier chapter has described how I, a "weakly motivated" young man, got into science. What one really wants to do when one is young is to overcome the horrible black beast called "future." In any event, I chose—and even that for frivolous reasons—what appeared to me the least problematic of sciences: chemistry. Vienna was far from the stench emanating from the Leuna Works; and even if I had smelled it, I doubt that it would have made me aware of the many insoluble problems that the chemical industry was to pose to our survival on earth. Like all good things in life, we seem to have noticed the environment only when it began to deteriorate. Altogether I have the impression that my life must have been out of phase, and that for me the Biedermeier period ended in 1933.

When I received my doctor's degree from the University, the diploma stated that I had studied chemistry. This seemed to confer on me the right, and at that time also the ability, to practice the science in all its subdivisions. Specialization had not yet overwhelmed the sciences, as all other branches of knowledge, to the bizarre extent that it has done since. Of course, one decided to be an inorganic or analytical chemist, a physical or an organic chemist, a technological or a biological chemist; but the barriers were weak and easy to displace. The direction one chose was left to contingency or fate, and very rarely to predilection. This ostensible freedom of choice created a sense of freedom that is now, I fear, completely lacking in the sciences. The shrinking of latitude has been accompanied by, or has been the cause of, an outright change in the types of individuals entering the various disciplines. Science has become a hard and pitiless and, what is even worse, a thoroughly humorless master.

I had a diploma. Did this make me a scientist? Of course not. How does one become a scientist? I wish I could describe the stages; they are obscure. Furthermore, the steps are not the same in the different branches of the natural sciences. The confined reserves of physics or chemistry are one thing, the giant and seemingly shoreless ocean of biology an entirely different one. The geologist knows what is meant by the earth that he carries in his very name; but does the biologist know what life is? It was the lure of a mystery that pulled men into numberless concentric cycles of darkness. This was, in fact, the principal reason why I wanted to apply my chemistry to questions of biology. The profound Lichtenberg had taught me that for people to find something they must first know that it exists. This was an assurance that I have never lacked during my entire life. What became weaker as I grew older was the conviction that the way of searching which we had chosen was the right one.

The feeling that there is always more than he can find, that he is only pulling shreds out of an unfathomable continuum, forms part of my definition of a scientist. This definition will fit few of my contemporaries, and certainly not the "successful" ones. But what is success in science? Prizes, titles and other honors, lots of money? Some would say glory and a lasting name. But how long does "lasting" last? The winds of fashion, those inscrutable winds, blow dust also on the most glittering achievements. There is a great danger that Professor Ozymandias will look funny long before he is dead. The library catalogues will list him as "Mandias, Oscar ('Ozzy')"; and soon there will not even be libraries.

Most people entering the sciences nowadays are being driven by the winds of fashion — something from which I was preserved completely in my youth — and they will try to attach themselves to a man who follows the trend of the moment or, even better, who is himself one of the trend-setters. A few of these young people may, in the course of their apprenticeship, become scientists, but most never will. They will turn into specialists. What form of individuation the production of a true scientist may comprise, I cannot say; but among the thousands of practitioners of science I have met in my life, there were perhaps twenty or thirty to whom I should have granted the name of scientist. I have often doubted whether I would have included myself among this number.

It is the sense of mystery that, in my opinion, drives the true scientist; the same force, blindly seeing, deafly hearing, unconsciously remembering, that drives the larva into the butterfly. If he has not experienced, at least a few times in his life, this cold shudder down his spine, this confrontation with an immense, invisible face whose breath moves him to tears, he is not a scientist. The blacker the night, the brighter the light. Who knew this better than San Juan de la Cruz when in the dark night he sent his soul on its eternal search?

> . . . *sin otra luz y guia*
> *sino la que en el corazón ardia.*

(. . . with no other light and guide/except the light that was burning in the heart.)

Are we not forever burning, tied to the stakes of Giordano Bruno or Servetus? Are we not forever rotting in Galilei's dungeons? Is not each of us dying of thirst in his own cloud of unknowing? So many questions; no answers.

But when I step out on the brightly lit stage of our present-day sciences, how different is the spectacle. Break-through chases break-through; and there is always room for more, as long as the funds are forthcoming. One thing leads to the next, and at the end we shall know everything. "Money is the seed of the sciences," a modern Tertullian could have concluded; although, thinking of our last World War, he might have substituted, tautologically, "blood" for "money." And what arrogance, what overbearing! I cannot imagine an eminent cheese merchant getting up and claiming that he was an unregenerate cheese merchant, for he would know that there was more even to Edam or Emmenthaler than his brain could encompass. But have I not recently seen and heard one of our foremost scientific establishment figures get up and cry out in open assembly that he was an "unregenerate reductionist"? Just give him and his like a little more time and much more money, and while they fly between EMBO and NATO, between NIH and CNRS and MRC, their postdocs will keep busy, and soon there will be no mysteries any more and the eternal day of total knowledge will dawn.*

And how many of our great did I hear announce that what we needed was more science, that is, more of themselves? This is quite in contrast, presumably, to the ancient Egyptian priest-hood whose members may not have realized that it required a

---

*Whether at that time a totally devastated earth will still carry *homo non nimis sapiens,* I do not know. But, in the meantime, space probes will have made the universe familiar not only with the genetic code and the picture of a chimpanzee, but also with Mr. Jimmy Carter's voice on tape or disk—assuming, of course, the universe to have provided itself with suitable hi-fi equipment, presumably made in Japan. It was reassuring to learn that full instructions and a replacement stylus were included in the capsule.

critical mass of mumblers before the Nile could be made to return.

It is, hence, no wonder that I have been feeling so alone throughout my life as a scientist and that I have been painfully aware of the difference that separated me from almost all other scientists I have met. We all started in the same way, but then our paths diverged and I had to go a lonely way. I did not choose it; it chose me. In our thoughtless times, which put quotation marks around every thought and punish outsiders by pasting silly sobriquets on them, I have been called a "maverick" or a "gadfly." But I do not believe that bovine appellations will settle the case, nor have I, in contrast to the nasty insects, ever had a particular taste for ox blood.

In science, there is always one more Gordian knot than there are Alexanders. One could almost say that science, as it is practiced today, is an arrangement through which each Gordian knot, once cut, gives rise to two new knots, and so on. Out of one problem considered as solved, a hundred new ones arise; and this has created the myth of the limitlessness of the natural sciences. Actually, many sciences now look as feeble and emaciated as do mothers who have undergone too many deliveries.*

For me, there has always been something exhilarating in the observation that there are as many philosophies as there are philosophers, for this showed me that philosophy was a truly human undertaking. The same freedom of choice could certainly not be claimed for, say, physicists or chemists. The iron corset of axioms, laws, and theories, and, equally effectively, of the methodologies currently acceptable in the respective sciences, prevents aberrations and flights of fancy. Most sciences are predictive and most of their results are predictable. I should say, however, that for me the real interest begins when these attributes no longer apply, i.e., when darkness reigns as a threat and a lure. The hospitable illumination of the sciences to which

---

*I have attempted to discuss the limits of science in a recent essay.[24]

we have become accustomed has attracted much too many scientific gnats.

Is there anything that can be done? Attempts to remedy an intolerable situation are usually classified as Utopian. The construction of a Utopia signifies, in fact, despair with the world as it is. This feeling of despair must have begun with the end of the *aurea aetas* or, if you prefer, shortly after the expulsion from Paradise. It was an entirely justified feeling. Considering the role of science in our time, generally agreed to be flourishing as never before, I have not been able to decide whether its enormous ascendancy was the cause of, or was caused by, the disappearance of the religious sentiment. There can, however, be little doubt that the whole complex of the natural sciences has become a substitute religion, fulfilling the double roles of mysterious incomprehensibility to the lay public and a means of livelihood for its practitioners. The first function could easily be taken over by another creed or pseudo creed, but not the second. The institutionalization of science as a mass occupation, which began during my lifetime, has brought with it the necessity of its continual growth — similar in that respect to such mythical entities as the "gross national product" — not because there is so much more to discover, but because there are so many who want to be paid to do it. Any attempt at reform is, therefore, met by insincere cries about the "freedom of scientific inquiry"; and this will be followed by the immediate constitution of all sorts of pressure groups, marching under the banner of Galilei. Entrepreneurs disguised as freedom-fighters may look ludicrous, but they are usually effective, for there is little as irresistible as the momentum of the pocketbook.

At the beginning of this memoir I described the effect that the atom bombs of Hiroshima and Nagasaki had on me and on my attitude to science. Since that time, when I thought about the direction in which science was going, I had the feeling that this cannot go on much longer; but at the same time, with the passing of so many years, I could not help noticing that it did go on. I should, therefore, have concluded that apocalyptic inclinations are not of much use in forecasting the future. What I did conclude, instead, is that the future always is a little farther away than it appears to the prophetic eye. On the whole, professional pessimists prove right at the end if one does not hold them too tightly to a time scale. Most people shun Cassandra, for they know that they will hear only the most unpleasant of possibilities. In spite of the aroma of decline and fall that I exude, I have often been asked for my ideas about the future of science. This is, more or less, my answer.

A scientist attempting a dialectical meditation on science is faced immediately with a dilemma: on the one side, the harmonious beauty of science, its orderliness, its openness, its attraction for the acute and searching mind; on the other side, the dehumanizing and cruel uses to which it has been put, the brutality of thinking and imagination to which it has given rise, the increasing arrogance of its practitioners. No other mental activity offers such contrasting aspects. Art, poetry, music wield no power; they cannot be exploited or misused. If oratorios could kill, the Pentagon would long ago have supported musical research.*

The forecaster can act as a realist or he can act as a Utopian. If he does the first he will pay equal attention to the two horns of the dilemma stated before. As a Utopian he will, in deference to his predecessor Tommaso Campanella, walk only on the sunny side, disregarding any black shadows the present may throw. Inclining to the first choice, I shall assume that the natural sciences will, at least for some time, continue on the

---

*Scientific findings, however, can be misapplied even if they are erroneous. Long before nerve action began to be understood, nerve gases were manufactured. Many nasty things have, in fact, been made on the basis of wrong hypotheses; but this did not diminish their nastiness. In our incomplete understanding, death is not a very specific event. Whereas there is only one way of being born (so far!), there are many ways to die, helped along by numerous chemical and physical events.

path they entered around 1940: an ever-greater fragmentation of our vision of nature; a rapidly increasing specialization, driving the scientific disciplines farther and farther from each other; an enormous rise in the costs required to maintain and expand the scientific establishment, with a concomitantly increasing gap between claims and achievement.

I see only two safety valves against the dangerously augmenting pressure in the cauldron. In view of the troubles that lie ahead, the countries may, one after the other, run out of money; and secondly, though not unconnected with the first, the sciences may run out of a sufficient number of young adepts. But, as has been observed so often, safety valves usually open too late and in the wrong direction. (This could be called the Seveso syndrome.*)

Eventually, of course, this too will come to an end, perhaps because at that time the brains will be so full of lead or mercury that the ancient programs of the computers will no longer be understood. Also, humanity will doubtless have so many other worries that our way of doing science may well lapse by default, as did so many seemingly indispensable institutions of the past. Immense historical changes are usually not recognized while they happen; and it is entirely possible that the demise of our kind of science already has been under way for some time without its being noticed.

This is, however, not the note on which I should like to end this chapter, but rather with an arcadian pastel. Before doing so, one argument ought to be disposed of. It is usually held against the critics of science that they interfere with its progress. But what does the expression "progress of science" mean? Can science be measured in quantitative terms, can it be subject to a five-year plan? Are six laws of thermodynamics better than

---

*Seveso is a town in northern Italy where, in 1976, an explosion in a pharmaceutical factory sprayed the region with the poison dioxine, necessitating evacuation of the residents.

three, are the highest melting-points the best? Is there an optimum speed to scientific growth, does "faster" mean "better"? And, for that matter, does everything have to grow? In no other field of intellectual endeavor has the Victorian distortion of the idea of progress done as much harm as in scientific research. The people of Prague who, at its premiere, applauded Mozart's *Don Giovanni* with all their hearts may, for all I care, still have believed in the existence of phlogiston; they lived in a better world. I do not know whether there can be too much of a good thing, but I am convinced that there must be moderation in the growth of science, as of almost everything else. I believe that our world is pushing science too fast, just as it disregards reason for the sake of intelligence. Misdirected curiosity killed more than the cat.*

If it is the real purpose of science to teach us true things about nature, to reveal to us the reality of the world, the consequence of such teaching ought to be increased wisdom, a greater love of nature, and, in a few, a heightened admiration of divine power. By confronting us directly with something incommensurably greater than ourselves, science should serve to push back the confines of the misery of human existence. These are the effects it may have had on men like Kepler or Pascal. But science, owing to the operation of forces that nobody, I believe, can disentangle, has not persisted in this direction. From an undertaking designed to understand nature, it has changed into one attempting to explain, and then to improve on, nature. This has brought about an overemphasis of the mechanical side: how the postulated wheels and gears operate to produce presupposed effects and to reach posited goals. Generations of scientists have given many final and conclusive explanations, but these explanations changed with

---

*If instead of the IQ, the intelligence quotient, somebody succeeded in working out the HQ, the humanity quotient, I believe the latter would yield surprising test results.

the times. I am not sure whether the analogy is correct, but I cannot help thinking of the deplorable fact that when the child has found out how its mechanical toy operates, there is no mechanical toy left. Although in scientific research the investigation does not usually consume the object with similar irreversibility, it seems to influence the direction, and often to limit the extent, of reasoning. The stress on mechanisms has given rise to one of the curses of our time: the expert. It has made body mechanics out of physicians and cell mechanics out of biologists; and if the philosopher cannot yet be called a brain mechanic, this is only a sign of his backwardness.

I see only one salvation: the return to what I should call "little science." In contrast to the great undoubting Thomases — Morus, Campanella — I have seen the Neverlands that I describe. That is where I came from, the science of the Thirties of this century, that is where my contemporaries began. The times were surely as beastly as now, although in a different way; but the institutions were small, and so was the number of scientists working in them. The slow pace of discoveries made it relatively easy for the public to adapt to them. There was much less noise, for it is indeed the enormous number of voices now crying in the wilderness that has produced the wilderness.

The wish for a return to another kind of science is based on esthetic and ethical considerations — two branches of philosophy that the philosphy of science seems to have slighted. Just as the great scientists were moved by a vision of the harmony of the universe, everything that is beautiful in the world is beautiful by virtue of its shape. In his *Enneads* Plotinus writes:

> We maintain that the things in this world are beautiful by participating in Form; for every shapeless thing which is naturally capable of receiving shape and form is ugly and outside the divine *logos* as long as it has no share in *logos* and form. This is absolute ugliness.[25]

I should claim that precisely this has happened to our scientific endeavor: it has gotten out of shape.

I do not, of course, advocate a return to the sort of science that would have pleased Plotinus, not to speak of his master Plato. They would most likely not even have recognized what we are doing as being worthy of human efforts. It is much rather Aristotle who would have felt at home in our laboratories, although he, too, would have raised weighty objections to our unreflective ways of going about our ill-defined jobs. "What is the purpose of your actions?" he might have asked. "What do you want to achieve? Greater riches? Cheaper chicken? A happier life, a longer life? Is it power over your neighbors that you are after? Are you only running away from your death? Or are you seeking greater wisdom, deeper piety?"

The ghosts I meet are always very loquacious, and I could certainly not have answered this one; the less so, since I am of the opinion that the sense and the goal of the natural sciences have become obscured, or even effaced, by the vastness of the spaces into which they have expanded, by the masses of devotees trampling them down. *Thyrsigeri multi, paucos afflavit Iacchus.** This may once have been true; but now poor Bacchus, instead of arranging bacchanals, must worry about how to get the money to pay all those hungry thyrsus-bearers.

What I should like to see established are conditions in which one man, perhaps together with two or three younger ones, can pursue his search in a quiet and dignified manner. I should like to see the noises and the crowds of the market place or the sports arena kept away. Presumably, this can happen only after the disappearance of mammoth grants and of the sloganeering concomitant upon them: "scientific break-throughs" and "centers of excellence," "interdisciplinary team research" and "peer

---

*Roughly translated: "There may be many candidates to the party, but only a few get into the politbureau." Incidentally, I was surprised to find the famous analogous passage in Matthew 20:16, about the many called and the few chosen, omitted from the text of my Greek New Testament; it was relegated to a footnote, whereas in the Vulgate and in the various translations it forms part of the main text.

review" will be memories of an ugly past. Gently and reverently, the scientist of the future, this pale dream of mine, will try to bring into the clear what is inside nature, and the way in which he does it will determine the quality of what he finds. He will attempt to avoid the gray strips of eroded nature that his measuring machines tend to leave behind and he will stay away, as much as he can, from METHOD, that bulldozer of reality. He will be slow, for he will be one of few. He will be aware of the eternal predicament that between him and the world there always is the barrier of the human brain. But above all, he will be conscious of the perpetual darkness that must surround him as he probes nature.

THE SUN AND
THE DEATH

Le soleil ni la mort ne se peuvent regarder fixement.

LA ROCHEFOUCAULD

A Medal Made of Sterling Silver

It is early October, 1974, and I am sitting in my old office at the Medical School. It is a small room at the end of a flight of laboratories, full of books and papers and heaps of recent journals whose tall and irregular piles, all accumulated within a few months, seem to raise desolate arms to heaven, offering a sacrifice, as it were, to dust and to the vanity of earthly knowledge. The room has the sort of untidiness out of which anything required can be extracted promptly, though only by the illuminate. The principle of Poe's purloined letter is observed, whatever should not be read by the uninitiated being exposed to full inspection.

It was a nice room when I moved in, with a beautiful view over the Hudson River toward the green shores of New Jersey. That was early in 1951, and The Rockefeller Foundation and the U.S. Public Health Service had contributed generously to make it possible for me to build and equip a very adequate group of laboratories which we called the Cell Chemistry Laboratory. Many young people had passed through these rooms, students and recent doctors; some were brilliant, most were decent; marriages were celebrated, children were born; no one died. The laboratory was truly a microcosm, perhaps more micro than cosmos. The departmental gossip and jealousies, the petty pastime of academia—only the Russian language concentrates in one noun so much vacuous and vapid shabbiness: the word is *poshlost'*—all this penetrated to us only slowly and incompletely, for we were separated by six floors from the locale of the Department of Biochemistry.

But now, twenty-four years later, as I sit in my room, the beautiful view has gone, water and sky have disappeared behind a multitude of tall buildings, the shadows have lengthened. A bitter malaise has come over science. Nothing seems to work any more. What is the cause, what is the symptom? Science partakes of both: guilty when blessed, guilty when damned.

Other shadows, destined for me only, have also become darker and more menacing. Dust has settled, not only on my books, but also on my hair, and that will not go away. I am an old man, and as I sit here in my office reading and writing, I am reminded of the old German rhyme: *Auf dem Dache sitzt ein Greis, der sich nicht zu helfen weiss.** I am not really the helpless type, but I have never been very fond of the sort of aggressive scholarship that is now encountered everywhere, trying to sell to humanity brand-new laws of nature as if they were used cars. A feeling of tentativeness; an appreciation of the provisional and fragmentary character of all human insight into nature; a consideration of how much arrogance and rashness must attend even the deepest understanding before generalizing statements can be made about life: all this will be part of the inheritance with which the many years have burdened the scientist as he grows older. If he is any good, he will become more modest.

The contemporary world always rejects the best and the worst and takes to mediocrity as to a mother's breast. For the solitary worker or thinker, speculating on all the obstacles that he finds

---

* Even this poor verse from a pre-1848 students' song is not really translatable. "On the roof there sits an oldster who doesn't know how to help himself." In this far from profound statement, all overtones of sound and association are lost in translation; nor will a freer version help: "On the roof the old dope / is at the end of his rope." For the German *Greis* — so expressive in its diphthongal despair — is neither "oldster" nor certainly "old dope," and the French *vieillard* or the Russian *starik* do not translate it either. How can another tongue mirror the avernal descent from *alter Mann* to *Greis* and then perhaps to *Urgreis*, *Mummelgreis*, and further decompositional subspecialties? And who can render the following metathetic concentrate of Viennese *fin-de-siècle* despondency? *Wie ist dem Greis mies vor dem Maisgriess!* That the old man detests the corn mush remains comprehensible, but the lyrical depth of revulsion is lost. (I dedicate this footnote to the memory of a great artisan of words, Vladimir Nabokov, *d.* July 2, 1977, who — a multilingual Sisyphus — spent many years on the attempt to translate Pushkin's *Eugene Onegin* into meager prose and luxuriant commentary.)

in his way, on the malevolence he encounters, the whispering rumors, the didactic stupidities of the established world, there arises a great danger of megalomania. He will remember what greater men said about the way they were received, for instance, Goethe in his conversations with Kanzler Müller (November 23, 1823):

> This is an old experience; as soon as there arises something considerable, there will appear as a contrast meanness and opposition. Let them have their way, they will for all that not suppress what is good.

Or Jonathan Swift in his *Thoughts on Various Subjects*:

> When a true Genius appears in the World, you may know him by this infallible Sign; that the Dunces are all in Confederacy against him.

But the victim would be wrong in letting the nitwits — Duns Scotus has deserved better than to be enshrined as the proverbial dumbbell — go to his head. The "dunces" simply are against all nondunces, and they do one more thing not foreseen by Swift: they elect their own geniuses from their midst and foist them on posterity, which, being inhabited by a new set of dunces, is likely to ratify the selections of their predecessors. Genius — who would dare assign this qualification? — is extremely rare, especially in science. I have not encountered, personally, a single one in my life; with the possible exception, in a very different field, of Bertolt Brecht.

On this clear blue October morning I am still sitting at my desk when, without knocking, there marches into my laboratory a small detachment, led by the recently appointed dean of the Medical School. He wished to show the Cell Chemistry Laboratory to a young man they wanted to hire for a clinical group. Not sufficiently gratified, as I should have been, by this Swiftian accolade, I realized suddenly that this was the elegant way chosen by Columbia to show me — after I had been here forty years—that I had to go away. This was three months after my official retirement.

Even earlier, within two weeks after I had reached the statutory retirement age, I had been notified by the vice-president's office that the University would no longer sponsor grant applications submitted in my name. It was suggested that I arrange to have someone else sign my application. This I refused, of course, thus terminating an ancient relationship. I feared that I had grown so corpulent that, were I to hide behind a middleman, I should be sticking out on all sides.

Shabbiness is so much built into the very fabric of our institutions that nobody who has lived in them for a long time could complain about their being as they are. It all came as I knew it would. And, secondly, the University did give a dinner to the retiring chairmen; there were brief, but moving, speeches, and we were given a sort of commemorative medal which, as the dean told me in a whisper, was made of sterling silver.

Pay as You Grow

THE MODERN American university has become a monstrosity. I am speaking of the spiritual department store, as I have come to know it. This may not always have been so, for I suppose that the small colleges that existed on this continent in the last century—provincial papier-mâché replicas of Oxford and Cambridge—were on the whole quite lovable institutions of what was euphemistically called higher learning. There may not have been much that was high or learned about them; but, especially before the Civil War, they fullfilled the function of helping young people grow into a society that still knew, or thought it knew, what it wanted. That what it wanted carried in it the seed of coming disaster nobody seems to have foreseen, although Henry Adams or, somewhat later, Santayana may have had a pretty good idea.

The rapid processes of dehumanization — a form of progressive disindividuation of which I have spoken in another place — that overcame the country and turned it into the nightmare it has become, produced, paradoxically, a tumescence of emptiness; a loss of direction, even where there could be no doubt about the direction; a hollow despair. The disappearance of the core, of what for want of a better word I should call individual character, became, perhaps, first apparent in the decay of language. (Compare an American text written, say, 150 years ago with an equivalent one of our days, and you will see what I mean.) This went along with a malignant growth of all institutions and their concomitant bureaucracies; with the substitution for reality of its "image," that is, an alleged reflection in the clouded mirror of a brutally promoted, but actually nonexistent, public opinion; with a distortion of the ancient values that had guided previous generations; with the discovery that human aspirations and achievements could best be expressed in cash. "In Hell everything has its price," I used to say when I was young.*

That the schools, and especially the higher schools, were among the first to be affected by these malformations is only natural. They literally forgot what they were here for; they were engulfed by the mad whirlpools of a consumers' society in which what went in at the top and what came out at the bottom could no longer be distinguished. The decision whether a given mush was food or excrement was left to so-called educationists, and

* A society that consists only of slaves must invent a master. This master might be called "will of the people," "public opinion," or something like it, but he does not, of course, exist. Since figments tend to go to sleep easily, the master must be kept awake, and this is done by an arrangement insuring incessant manipulation and propaganda, a *bourrage de crâne,* which is the task of the so-called mass media. More lies are told the people in one day than Beelzebub could think up in all the time he has been in business. And all this without a formal ministry of propaganda; no Goebbels is needed. The system functions almost automatically; so Beelzebub may have had a hand in it after all, as in all automats. The ways of the devil are so obvious that we do not see them.

they often changed their mind. After some time, when things got worse, it also made little difference.

When I first went to Yale University in 1928, the conviction that wisdom was cheaper wholesale had not yet penetrated to the surface. Although the class character of the great universities was quite unmistakable, their function of educating the young men of the upper classes for careers in business and finance was still exercised with a measure of decency and restraint. Yale University was, at that time, much more of a college than a graduate school; and the undergraduates — handsome young men with baby faces — were all over town. They were then, I suppose, digesting their last goldfish, for the period of whoopee, speakeasies, and raccoon coats was coming to an end, to be replaced by a grimmer America which was never to recover the joy of upper-class life.

The University proper — Mr. von Humboldt's Spiritual De Luxe Motel — was much less in evidence. Shallow celebrities, such as William Lyon Phelps, owed their evanescent fame to the skill with which they kept their students in a state of elevated somnolence. The graduate school, and the far from numerous students working on dissertations, remained barely noticeable. The American universities still were colonies of a Europe that itself had almost ceased to exist. This was not the only instance that reminded me of dying Rome. But the excellent Yale library reconciled me to much that was disagreeable. A few years before, when I borrowed books from the venerable National Library in Vienna, I was surprised to be given works by Pico della Mirandola or Swedenborg in the original editions of the sixteenth or eighteenth centuries. This was, however, nothing when compared to Yale. I had free access to the book stacks, and I could not get over my astonishment about the treasures that I was permitted to handle. In this respect, at any rate, I can claim to have been educated also at Yale.

On returning to the United States a few years later, to immure myself in Columbia University, I found a similar, though shabbier and livelier, school. The great economic depression of the early Thirties had not yet run its course. Depressions and recessions have, in fact, punctuated almost my entire life. If it was not the country that was depressed, it was I or my family. Only my first five years were free from this.

That Columbia was a livelier place than Yale had much to do with the fact that it was in New York City, which offers a great deal of intellectual, artistic, and other diversions. The economic misery itself contributed to the animation of the University. Its graduate school, more important than that of Yale University, was populated to a large degree by students who came from families of first-generation immigrants. The Promised Land, even if keeping few of its other promises, opened to their children access to the free, tough, and excellent education of City College. The Irish, Italian, or Jewish boys who came to Columbia made, on the whole, very good and intelligent graduate students, and they found many outstanding professors with whom to work. I do not wish to set myself up as Fra Angelico, painting a Paradise, but at that time Columbia was a good university; that is, it permitted many young people to find themselves. What Columbia has become now makes another and sadder story; but this is also the story of the entire country and even of the entire Western world. The face of the twenty-first century looks in through all the windows.

What made Columbia, during all my time, such a singularly disagreeable institution is difficult to explain. Its being located in the middle of a huge and rough city, many leagues away from the nearest ivy, may have something to do with it. Getting out of the subway and into the University, one hardly experienced a change in atmosphere. But all this cannot account for the peculiar *genius loci* of Columbia, which I would characterize as the complete absence of tradition. We are all brought up to consider tradition as something risible. When John Kendrew once informed me in Cambridge that only fellows of Peterhouse and their guests were permitted to step on the college lawns, that may have sounded ridiculous to an inhabitant of Central Park. When I was once shown in Padua the courtyard of the university with the escutcheons on the wall of the students who had been there in the seventeenth century; when I was taken to venerate Galilei's cathedra or the first anatomical amphitheater: I may have compared the past with the present. When once, before an audience with the Pope, the chamberlains entered, crying *Papa, Papa!* it may have reminded me of the last act of *Rosenkavalier*; but it did more. For tradition may constrain you as an iron corset; but when your back hurts badly, it also helps you. Sham and shame though tradition may often be, its absence was evident in Columbia.

I shall limit myself to a few examples. Avery, of whom I have spoken before, one of the most incisive forces in modern biology, received his degree from the College of Physicians and Surgeons of Columbia University in 1904. I have tried repeatedly to get the school to recognize this memorable fact, but to no avail. Whole buildings, individual amphitheaters, or lecture rooms and laboratories carry the names of assorted moneybags, with or without an MD degree, but there was no room for Avery. Schoenheimer, who revolutionized modern biochemistry, was so forgotten in his own department that a few years ago, when I was asked by a historian of science to provide some memorabilia, not one scrap of paper could be found and only by the greatest efforts a photograph. The oral history collection of Columbia is well known, but I wonder how many of the distinguished members of the University ever were interviewed.

The lack of collegiality, the impersonal character of all relationships with one's colleagues, and many other defects were, however, partly redeemed by one very agreeable feature: the University was pleasantly underadministered. One was left very much in peace; and a professor could easily have died in his office and his salary checks continued to be booked to his account for months, before ominous signs alerted the cleaning personnel to pay one of their infrequent visits to his room. This, as many other things, was changed by the "revolution" of 1968, from which the University never recovered. In order to guard themselves against both justified and groundless attacks, the universities have grown a heavy administrative carapace. At the same time, they have been invaded by a particularly malignant form of bureaucratic cancer: the numerous newly created administrative positions show no form of contact inhibition and keep on sprouting additional jobs, most of which produce no revenue. For this reason, the so-called "overhead" charged by the institutions to their outside supporters has climbed to fantastic proportions, in some cases 100 percent or more of the grant. The universities have taken on the appearance of transient motels in which one rents a laboratory or office through the overhead of a research grant, and when one loses the grant one is fired.

The function of the American high school in the last century and that of the American college and university in the present one was, it would seem to me, to impose a minimum of civilization. Reading one of Henry James's earlier novels, for instance, *Roderick Hudson, The Portrait of A Lady,* or *The Bostonians,* I get the impression that this function was exercised successfully. This is no longer the case; and I am not even sure that the universities still fulfill the task that I ascribed to the University of Vienna in my time, namely, to act as bureaus for the issuance of licenses. There is a general nausea abroad—and I believe it encompasses the entire world—a revulsion from art and knowledge, from search and thought; a leaden tiredness; an immersion in a two-inch nirvana. Baudelaire's artificial paradises have been changed into synthetic hells.

Coping under Hot and Gray

AT ONE TIME I bought at an auction the first edition of one of Max Beerbohm's collections of caricatures. The book is entitled *Observations*; it was published in 1925. Having been made in the good old days of English book production, it has withstood the assaults of time, climate, and pollution almost as well as my books from the sixteenth and seventeenth centuries. There is one section in it that I have always cherished particularly. It is called "The Old and the Young Self," and each of the drawings depicts the confrontation—sometimes silent, sometimes loquacious—of the very young and the very old varieties of the same famous man. There is, for instance, corpulent old Lloyd George dropping his cigar as he inspects with dismay the equally obese figure of the unpleasant and cocky Victorian schoolboy that he was. There is Joseph Conrad being addressed by his young self in what may be a sort of pidgin Polish and answering him in French. Or Baldwin, surprising the primordial urchin by the announcement that he now was the Prime Minister.

How often have I, Narcissus over a turbid pool, tried to bring about this confrontation of my young and old selves, seventeen versus seventy-one; and I have always found it surprisingly easy. Not only have these fifty-four years passed quickly, as a short breath; but the farther away the time is, the nearer it is to me. I have not changed my beliefs, although I may find it more difficult now to express them than in my youth, when I still had a mother tongue. I have had the good fortune of not being forced to make concessions; the absolute observer has not become a relativist. I have, thank God, not become much wiser, even if mellow savagery has turned into savage mellowness. These intimations of identity—the very opposite of the much written-about identity crisis—may all be mental illusions, but I do not believe so.

I have been moderately interested in my profession, although the belief that it was a noble one, if I ever had it, was certainly shattered in 1945, as I described at the outset of this account. That in the middle of slaughter and destruction, surrounded by general collapse and barbarism; that in a world of despair and oblivion, never far from one brink or another; that under these circumstances, I say, I have been able to survive together with my family, slowly writing one sentence or another, putting word upon word or thought upon thought—and sometimes only sitting in the sun—could be described, vulgarly, as happiness. I do not think that I was a particularly brilliant young man, especially when I remember one or two with whom I came into contact during my years as a university teacher. I have certainly not become more brilliant when getting older. It so happens that I have never been very fond of brilliancy. I have been looking for entirely different qualities and I have often found them in people who were not outstandingly clever.

When I think of myself in a historical context, I look upon myself as a latter-day Ausonius or Claudianus, one of those late Roman writers, desperate fighters against barbarism, but barbarized themselves, building, painfully and in a despoiled language, epigonic hexameters upon imitative pentameters, achieving nothing that has not been said better before. Is there anything sadder than this splendor of decay, this continual fight between "must" and "cannot"? This is an instance when the pendulum of life becomes a wrecking ball.

As to my own life during the later years, it became much quieter: the amplitudes of the pendulum diminished perceptibly. I had got into nucleic acid research as into a vise. The vested interest in a scientific subject compresses as it intensifies; it restricts as it deepens. Although I continued having excellent collaborators and a few very good students, people came to me not, as they had done before, to learn about the chemistry of life, but to learn about the nucleic acids. The latter objective will strike the naive observer as definitely exhaustible, but it is not, for it is inherent in, it is the very essence of, the natural sciences that they keep on creating their own problems. Once you embark, you will never land. You will, in fact, after a short time, forget that there is such a thing as land; ever-changing, unattainable horizons will lure you into the unknown that few people, it is true, really want to know. But you are paid to know.

I gain the impression that, in the last fifteen years, the world of science, or at any rate that part of science that I can overlook, has undergone a deformation whose dimensions I find it difficult to fathom. The swelling process may have begun to be noticeable at the end of the Second World War, but it was only ten or fifteen years later—some time after the Russian Sputnik—that it acquired the malignant qualities with which it has been operating since. Whereas before, every practitioner of a science, i.e., everybody doing original scientific research, was never very far from the core of his particular discipline, from what one could call its specific character and code of conduct, at present one is confined to the outskirts, which are ever more distant from the center. This is principally due to the truly explosive multiplication of efforts and publications. The best illustration of the complete break in tradition may be found in the bibliographies of scientific papers. In order to be fair, I shall compare two of my own papers, one published in 1946, the other in 1976. The bibliography of the ancient publication comprised thirty-nine references. Of these, sixteen cited papers older than thirty years, and only four had been published in the previous five years. The 1976 publication has sixteen references, of which one-half are to papers published in the last five years, with only two papers slightly older than ten years.

Modern science lives only in the day and for the day; it resembles much more a stock-market speculation than a search for the truth about nature: a search in which I thought, perhaps mistakenly, of engaging when I entered science nearly fifty years ago. In the meantime, science has swollen to such an extent that nobody can know enough about his subject. This is the way I put it some time ago: "The sciences, like other professions, cannot endure if their practitioners are unable to know more than an ever-smaller portion of what they must know in order to function properly." [1]

I continued as best I could: collaborators, young and not so young; papers, reviews, lectures, symposia, congresses; and committees, committees. We now have professors who do nothing but sit in committees, but I was never one of those. There was the ever-present dissatisfaction with myself: the feeling, which I do not believe has anything to do with ambition, that I was not spending my time as I ought to; that I was wasting whatever gifts nature had bestowed on me; that whenever *liber scriptus proferetur* my name would figure in scarlet. There were rare moments, getting rarer all the time, as if a cool, clear, blue sky were to open itself over Manhattan, though mostly the days are hot and gray or cold and dark.

One possibly useful thing I did was to edit, together with the late J. N. Davidson of the University of Glasgow, the large treatise *The Nucleic Acids*.[2] The first two volumes of this work appeared in 1955, the third in 1960. The chapter on the chemistry of the deoxyribonucleic acids, which I wrote myself, represented the first modern treatment of the subject. It is, in my opinion, one of the best articles I ever wrote; I have often regretted that I did not have an opportunity to disengage its general portions, of which there are many, from those containing no more than a heavy and laborious compilation of ephemeral facts. As happens always in science, it is the facts that pull the thoughts to the bottom of the sea of oblivion.

I can think of few people who would agree with me when I say that in the last fifteen or twenty years the sciences have grown in a direction that makes their eventual extinction very probable: they have, one could say, painted themselves into a corner. When I look back at my own life since about 1960, I must confess that my heart had gone out of what I was doing. The phenomenal growth of biology and biochemistry, the glory of their recent achievements, in which I myself perhaps played a small role, disheartened and frightened me. I saw an avalanche of triumphs with which those who ostensibly had brought them about were no longer commensurable. There was something wrong with ever-smaller people making ever-greater discoveries. There is no such a thing as an unearned creation of the mind, whether a lyrical poem, a musical work, or a painting; but I have witnessed many entirely unearned so-called "scientific breakthroughs." In his great novel, *The Man Without Qualities,* Robert Musil derives his forebodings of imminent enormous disaster and collapse from having read in a newspaper of a race horse with genius. I began to suspect that it was this species that had the most conspicuous successes in science, although the very notion of success is, in its reference to science, as spurious as is the notion of genius in regard to race horses, Olympic champions, or Nobel laureates. Science had become a spectator sport, even if one that had no real spectators. It had, it seemed to me, become one of the most effective tools for mass cretinization.

It was, however, much too late to break out, nor should I have known where to go. Freedom, that most elusive of ideals, has never been among the gifts bestowed upon me: I was no freer than a log floating on a mighty river. This I continued to do or, rather, to suffer.

One summer, in August, 1961, sitting in front of the tiny cottage in Maine that we used to rent, I decided to become worthy of the sobriquet that I sometimes applied to myself, that of *vieillard misérable,* by writing something entirely extracurricular. The dialogue *Amphisbaena,* taking place between an insufferably omniscient old chemist and an insufferably stupid young molecular biologist, was my first attempt at a critique of science in a free form, i.e., in a satirically distorted jargon and without the stately periwig of references and quotations. The definition of molecular biology, given there, as "the practice of biochemistry without a license" has become well known and much quoted.

This piece, together with other unpublished or previously published articles, appeared in 1963 in a book entitled *Essays on Nucleic Acids.*[3] I have always been grateful to the publishers, Elsevier of Amsterdam, for undertaking so unconventional a venture, and one requiring some courage. The dogma of the infallibility of science has become so strong and generally accepted that measures of excommunication, customary in weaker churches, do not even have to be contemplated. It is presumably for this reason that I have been spared the fate of earlier heretics. The refusal of research grants is, in any event, a more effective form of interdict; a retribution from which, in the last few years, I have been far from being exempt.

Since that time in 1961, when I wrote the dialogue, I have written several more, published together under the title *Voices in the Labyrinth*.[4] In that work, as well as in many general essays and lectures, I continued my critical evaluation of our kind of natural science. Some people have been reading these articles only for the few nuggets of information they may contain. This is understandable, for scientific papers have long ago given up any pretension to being more than quick purveyors of provisional knowledge. But what I attempted to do in those dialogues and essays was to lift the critical consideration of scientific questions to the level of literature. I shall speak of this later, but I may say that it was this form of not uncomfortable schizophrenia that preserved my sanity. In some respects, my position was similar to that of a prelate of the modern church in which almost everything is permitted as long as it is done with taste and circumspection.

Increase of Knowledge From Running To and Fro

EVERY SO OFTEN the telephone would ring in my pleasant office at the Columbia Medical Center, and my secretary—at that time the unforgotten Emmy Bloch—would tell me that there were two gentlemen from the Federal Bureau of Investigation or from the Central Intelligence Agency who wanted to see me. After some time, I was no longer surprised by this ominous news, for I knew what would happen. Two happily bovine men (F.B.I.) or two furtively vulpine ones (C.I.A.) would introduce themselves with much swinging of badges and ask me with a sheepish or insidious grin to tell them all I knew about a man usually called Abdul Mur Rahman or something like it. At the same time, they would extract a photograph of a bearded gentleman whom, in an instant flash of apperception, I would recognize as my paternal grandfather, known to me only from portraits, since he had died two years before I was born. Soon I learned to distrust these hasty recognitions, as it was clear that to me all bearded and most other faces looked alike. In any event, I had never met Mr. Rahman or whatever, and I informed the respective catchpoles accordingly. Always helpful, I used to ask them whether they did not mix me up with Dr. Chaikoff, who worked in California, and they, conceding that this was possible, would depart.

This happened mostly at the time when, under the leadership of Senator Joseph R. McCarthy, every American was supposed to behave as a true democrat, denouncing his fellow citizens, and when I—one of the sad exceptions—used to refer to the Bill of Rights as the Bill of Goods. Not all inquiries concerned people suspected of endangering the Free World. Often the detectives were merely engaged in a so-called security check: delving into the past of persons considered for the position of dishwasher in a federal laboratory, and the like. Once, however, the visit had a different purpose.

In the beginning of 1957, I was invited to attend a symposium on the origin of life—truly a subject for the scientist who has everything. The meeting, organized by the U.S.S.R. Academy of Sciences, was to take place in Moscow. Only a few days after I received the letter from Russia inviting me, two men from the C.I.A. came to see me. They were clearly of a higher type than the normal brand, not exactly aquiline, but let us say vulturous. They had obviously read the letter before I did, and they asked me whether I planned to go to the meeting. When I replied that I did not yet know, the financial question still having to be resolved, they said that they hoped very much that I should go and keep my eyes open. Not since the Good Soldier Schweik was offered the chairmanship of the Joint Chiefs of Staff could an apter choice have been made. "Have pun, will travel" — was that not one of my early mottoes? I showed my surprise; they offered to pay for my trip. I refused; they left.

This was, of course, not the end. The "intelligence community" threw another bubble, this time a lady, but not at all *la femme fatale*. After all arrangements for my trip had been made, there came a maternal type — we shall call her Mrs. Grizzly — looking very much like an underpaid mother with several difficult children. At this occasion, no money was offered; everything was strictly scientific, although the poor woman was clearly out of her depth. Mrs. Grizzly asked for help with difficult questions which she had trouble spelling correctly. It was not clear why she had come. She was pleasantly confused, exuded distrait warmth, wished me in parting a pleasant trip, and added, unfortunately, "See you again."

The symposium in Moscow and the subsequent visit to Leningrad, although interesting and even exciting, were somehow spoiled for me by the heavy-footed and heavy-haunched visitors I had left behind. "Keep your eyes open," hissed the vultures; "See you again," murmured Mrs. Grizzly. Of course I would keep my eyes open, for I was a well-meaning observer of the Russian scene. My wife and I had begun to learn Russian a few years earlier, and we were not lost when left to ourselves and eager to use our knowledge. But all my life I had been a very private person, fleeing boisterous contacts, feeling a revulsion for slime, even if it was patriotic slime. The only consequence of the silly attempt to enlist me was to make me see less than I should have seen otherwise, speak with fewer people, go more often to museums. My thorough knowledge of the beautiful Hermitage in Leningrad — including my failure to convey the difference between Manet and Monet to the guard, whose Russian ears could not distinguish between the two vowels — was largely due to Mrs. Grizzly.

I renewed my acquaintance with a few of the great Russian biochemists, Vladimir Engelhardt, Alexander Oparin. I met many colleagues, especially from Eastern Europe, whom I had not seen for years. I became quite friendly with Andrei Belozersky, one of the most likable gardeners in our common orchard. In addition to having much else in common, we discovered that we were of exactly the same age.

After we returned from a long summer abroad, there was Mrs. Grizzly among the first visitors. She was even vaguer than before and went away after some mumbling. Instead of diabolical guile, I began to suspect some mild derangement. But she came back; and this time one could not be clearer: her people wanted to know whether the Russians had succeeded in creating a homunculus, little men with whom to populate their spaceships. (At that time the Sputniks formed the center of an artificially whipped-up commotion.) At last, I could tell her the truth. That was the end of Mrs. Grizzly.

Of the many other trips, only those stand out that appeared to take me into regions offering some alternatives to the society in which I had to spend my life: Japan, Brazil, Vatican City. In general, there are few things as lugubrious as the professional travels of scientists. This has to do with the professionalization of our lives and with the unstated, unacknowledged, and possibly even subconscious, cultural imperialism of America. Wherever one goes, the same form of pidgin is spoken, the same cocktails, the same indigestible food, the same centrifuges, gradient makers, the same graphs, all superimposable. After some time, all lectures form one confluent blob; all lecturers stumble through the same ten minutes of automatic recitation; all problems are chattered to pieces, and then they coalesce again to the same meaningless phrase, something like "structure and function." The brutal clatter of a nonsensical machine engaged in the so-called dissemination of scientific information overwhelms all thought and imaginativeness. Diogenes with his lantern, looking for a human being, would be out of place in these assemblies.

This had not always been so. For centuries, travel was considered one of the foremost modes of education: it formed the man. What would Goethe or Stendhal have been without Italy? But, then, they did not have to fly from Hilton to Hilton. As journeys were very costly, few scientists traveled, except as governors of young noblemen making their grand tour. Georg Christoph Lichtenberg, the great German satirical writer and professor of physics in Göttingen, went twice to England; certainly he spent more time in the London theaters than in the Oxford observatory, and he learned more from Hogarth and Garrick than from Dr. Priestley; but the acute observer of fallible humanity got most of all from watching the life in a London street. The collectors of natural curiosities or of curious facts of nature were amateurs or dilettantes in the original sense of these words: they loved nature and were curious about it.

Belonging to a generation that will soon be past, I still traveled in the old style, although not unmarked by the depravation of the current one. I have, therefore, never attended a NATO workshop on one of the Cyclades or on Mount Erice, but I did go to many congresses and gave lectures in many places. The profit I derived from these trips had, however, less to do with science than with a form of enrichment that is difficult to describe. The wonderful and mysterious temples and gardens of Kyoto are reflected more vividly in my mind than is the Protein Institute in Osaka, which looked like all other laboratories in the world. The curves of the old bridges; the red pillars in the sea; the complex patterns of pebble and bush; the numbering of the admitted views of Mount Fuji; the domesticated volcanoes; the mannered recitations before the painted backdrop of a single hieratic tree; the praises of the stone-old vessel at the start of the tea ceremony: all this, degraded to lures for a touristified world, surrounded by the brutality of a Japanese working day, spoke to me with the voice of ages, and I listened in speechless deference. It showed me an alternative to the ailing Western world in which I lived; an alternative as inaccessible to me as were the temples of Paestum.

Brazil: the eternally crumbling monument of Latin colonialism; a giant groaning in his hot sleep; the horror of São Paulo, a greater Chicago without proper sanitation, but kept tender by its boneless Portuguese; the forever-fading, melancholy beauty of a Rio de Janeiro that never was; and most of all the north — torpid and torrid Belem, dozing in the tropical clatter of intermittent ventilation; the insane Baroque of Recife amidst the desperate, heavy-eyed stolidity of the surrounding Indian villages, a Symphony in Maize Major.

Or the Proustian visits to the Popes. I have seen two of them from nearby, caught in the congealed folds of an impossible office: to be both the keepers of the faith and the bookkeepers of God on earth, managers of a theocratical investment bank with a view of eternity. I saw the first in Castel Gandolfo, addressing an assembly full of hematological infidels whose cameras outclicked the sonorous cadences: Pius XII, in white robes a monument to Mannerism, gesturing, imperially fatigued, with beautiful long-fingered hands, the most elegant saint the world has seen, as if Zurbaran had suddenly produced a masterpiece of *bondieuserie*. This must have been in 1958. How different, three years later, everybody's but the prelates' favorite Pope: John XXIII. The occasion was a small symposium on biological macromolecules, organized by the Pontifical Academy of Sciences, with one of whose meetings it was to coincide. It was a small gathering, one of the most pleasant I have attended, the specifically Italian way of treating science showing itself from its best side, as if held under the auspices of Spallanzani or Malpighi, of Volta or Galvani: devotion and gentleness without the grimness of our days; a light, ironical sadness glancing through the graceful pillars of a Renaissance pavilion. The

"Casino di Pio IV," Ligorio's eclectic masterpiece, in which the meeting took place, ennobled even the crudest contribution; but standing in the beautiful oval courtyard in front of the portico, in the pale sunlight of a late autumn day, was even better.

One particularly crude sentence graced the beginning of one of the lectures (the italics are mine): "The essence of the dogma, *so acceptable to our time*, can be briefly summarized by the following familiar diagram: DNA → RNA → Protein." (It had not been acceptable to me; but, then, I am not of "our time.") I remember how funny I found this ovation from one orthodoxy to the other, in the midst of the Vatican gardens; and I said to someone: "A couple of *filioque's* more or less will make no difference." Actually, this particular dogma, on which free-thinkers and believers could agree so joyfully, has worn unusually poorly. Only a few years later the same peddlers flourished by hawking the reverse dogma.

At the end of the conference, John XXIII was scheduled to receive the guests, but he became ill and the reception was called off. Three days later he had recovered, and sent word that he would meet those still in Rome. Most of the vigorous beavers had, however, already departed in a hurry to their eager dams and lodges; and so the gathering that assembled in the Vatican palace was quite small: a few academicians and a few of the lesser breed. A small hall holding, perhaps, six or eight rows of seats; the members of the Academy in full dress: Otto Hahn, already eighty-two and very frail, Leopold Ruzicka, kneeling and kissing the papal ring, and a few others. I sat in the third row—there exists a photograph in the published transactions of the conference—and had a good occasion for a study at close hand. The old, heavy-set man, with an unusually good-hearted face and humorous peasant eyes, did not seem to act a part. Unselfconsciously adjusting his white zucchetto, which kept sliding off, he spoke in fluent Italianate French. He told us that he would not read a prepared speech, but that he preferred to reminisce about his early days at the *liceo*, when he had studied the natural sciences, and he praised particularly what he called "the noble periodic system of elements." Some people grin at old men's tales; others like to listen to them, as they dip again into the ancient rivers of their youth, smoothing, for a fleeting moment, the wrinkles of time and decay. I belong to the second group, and the old Pope's voice, telling us of the times when he was a child and a boy, has not yet faded.

Science as a Profession

A CLIOMETRICIAN — what a profession! — who has made himself a name through having estimated, by computer simulation, the number of fleas on the back of the dog that had once belonged to an American president of the second rank, will expect me to know his name, and oh shame, I shall; but he has never heard mine. And why should he have? Science is a hidden, private, hermetic occupation. It is not easily understood by onlookers, nor could even most of its practitioners say what it is.

The profession of science? When I was young, science as a profession barely existed. Among the pure sciences, only chemistry offered some reasonable hope of employment, as I mentioned earlier in this memoir; but even this took place mostly in the sectors devoted to applied chemistry, in industry or in government. Of my contemporaries at the University, I can think of only three or four others who could have been said to have entered upon a scientific career. The medical graduates, of whom there were many, may have considered themselves as scientists, but no one else did. Apart from chemistry, the demand for academically trained scientists was small: very few were needed to replenish the meager ranks of university teachers in such fields as zoology, botany, geology, physics, astronomy. The number of advanced students in these fields was naturally small, and many of those expected to find occupation in secondary education, as did also most of the students of the humanities.

The first convulsion in this fairly homeostatic and rather modest arrangement was brought about by the First World War and its ensuing economic and political upheavals. This was much more noticeable among the vanquished nations than among the victorious allies. There were many reasons, some quite obvious; but one factor has, I believe, not received sufficient stress: it had been Germany that had, even before 1914, gone further than any other country in making the natural sciences into mass occupations. Science as a profession, the concept of scientific research performed by large numbers and often in large teams, originated, I think, in imperial Germany, which had been late in joining the imperialist ranks. There were no Indies to be had any more; all lucrative colonies had been grabbed by more ancient greed; it was left to the Reich to direct its colonialist fervor against nature. The Kaiser Wilhelm Institutes would do what Kaiser Wilhelm could not.

In the second half of the nineteenth and the beginning of the twentieth century, the other great scientific countries—England, in particular, but also France—had produced several outstanding scientists, but basic research was very much left to the individual. Especially England was distinguished by a series of scientific amateurs, unsupported and unfettered, who made important and influential discoveries not only in physics and geology, but also in chemistry and biology. In many respects, these great men lacked all flavor of professionalism. The very designation of "expert" would have surprised them. Compared with these figures, even Liebig and Wöhler represent early examples of grim professionalism, as may be gathered from their very interesting correspondence.[5] And coming to later times, how could a Perkin be compared with an Emil Fischer?

When, in 1918, the central powers collapsed, Germany and the remnants of Austria were left with an apparatus for the production of academics, and especially of scientists, that was much too large for their requirements. I have mentioned this before. The consequence, less in Austria than in Germany, was the mass production of an academic proletariat, pretending to a social status that had vanished, condemned to brooding and malevolent unemployment. This group of malcontent mercenaries was of great importance for the eventual fascist bestialization of Germany. It is not impossible that the beginnings of a similar development can at present be discerned in the United States. A saving feature may, however, be seen in the fact that here the social standing of academically trained persons is much lower than it was in Central Europe.

To the extent that science as a profession requires the exercise of one's brain, that it is an intellectual occupation, it has always carried certain anomalous features: there is something absurd about receiving a fixed salary for thinking and searching. This does not, of course, apply to the scientist as a teacher, for all societies have, until recently, been agreed upon considering teaching as a socially necessary and useful activity. But natural science, as a feat of the mind, is probably the only salaried occupation of this sort in the noncommunist countries. I shall be told that this is not true and that all practitioners of *die Wissenschaften* — mathematicians, philosophers, historians, and so on — find themselves in the same situation. I believe, however, that in this instance, as in so many others, quantity has produced a new quality. Besides, in the case of the scientist in the United States, the proportion of "teaching" and "research" is distorted in favor of the latter to such a degree that his occupation must be compared with that of a painter, a writer, or a composer, rather than with that of a teacher. If, to draw the evident ultimate conclusion, scientists were forced to live from the sale of their products, as do artists, our sciences would return to a much happier equipoise. But would anybody buy the fruits of their minds?

Of course, no one would; but my absurd proposal brings out

one of the peculiarities of the scientific profession: those who do not partake of it often dislike it, though they may feel that it is needed. If they are asked what the sciences are needed for, the answers will show a deplorable, but prevalent, inability to distinguish between science and technology; for I shall be told that the sciences are required for the education of physicians or engineers. If science were only necessary for the formation of these eminently needed specialties, the world could get along on a small portion of the enormous number of scientists produced in the last thirty years.

I should say that the paradox became noticeable only when the United States decided—actually I do not believe there ever was a conscious decision—to enter the arena of scientific research in its well-known big way. When the national tendency to grandiloquence, when the elephantiasis of claim and expectation, are backed by what looked for a time to be unlimited resources, disaster is bound to ensue. As long as scientists formed a tiny minority of the educated population, questions of purpose and goal were no more asked than of, say, a linguist or a logician. In a developed, wide-meshed society there were enough interstices in which to disappear; no questions were asked, and it was easy to hide one's failure or achievement. But now the gentle shield of a tepid and comfortable invisibility has ceased to protect.

I have often wondered how scientific professions are chosen nowadays. I have tried to describe in the first part of this account the hare-brained way in which I chose mine. I may have been an ass, but certainly not of the Buridan variety, for I never had a choice. If there were two bundles of hay, there were twenty applicants. Nor, do I believe, did any of my contemporaries receive clearer indications that their God-given gifts lay along the line of coffee import, glass manufacture, or stock-market speculations. If man's character is said to be his fate, in my generation it was rather the lack of character. The aleatory manner in which I circumnavigated fearful decisions had the consequence that I never became a real professional, but only a strange guest at many strange symposia where wines of different colors were drunk, all tasting alike.

When I inspect the present scene I notice, however, that it has changed portentously. Everybody is supposed to be obsessed with his ridiculously narrow specialty. If you are an orthodontist, you must live orthodontics; if you are a sociobiologist, you must live and die as a sociobiologist. Day and night, forty or fifty long years, waking and sleeping, all you do, all you read, all you think, all you talk about will be devoted, for instance, to population genetics or to autoimmunity. It is decreed that thus will you live, thus will you die; and if there still are gravestones, they will duly note your expertise. Surely, there will be a funny crowd in the valley of Jehoshaphat (Joel 3:2).

I have probably lived through the creation of more scientific specialties than existed altogether at the time when I entered science. The priesthood of ancient Egypt was presumably also highly compartmentalized; but I do not know whether only certain priests were entrusted with the spells designed to quiet the pain from a given molar. In our time, it would certainly be so. One man or two may decide to study a certain beetle. Whether they do this because the animal is a pest or a biological delight is immaterial. If they find something of scientific interest, there will soon be ten others and more who will do the same. Once there are a hundred men studying the beetle, they will form a society and publish a journal. A society creates a profession, and a profession cannot be permitted to die. It is up to the nation to support it. If the nation can be persuaded, there will soon be a thousand members of the society for the study of the beetle. It is obvious that at this stage the beetle can no longer become extinct, for what would all these experts do who may well outnumber the beetle? Then a foundation will arise whose lay members—influential bankers, society ladies—will neither know nor care whether their function is to help with the eradication or the preservation of the beetles. They know one thing: they must support those who study the beetle. There may even be a Beetle Ball. But what if the beetle disappears after all? The National Infantile Paralysis Foundation has avoided the worst by finally omitting its objective from its name. The American Cancer Foundation may find this more difficult.

Thinking of the peculiar ways in which scientific interests become vested nowadays, I have often wondered whether the real impulse does not come from the simple and age-old desire of man for a carefree and pleasant way of life. After all, even in ancient times there must have been a few who, for a small remuneration, were eager to interpret the sun for their fellow Neanderthalers working in the sweat of their brows.

I have often spoken of these things, mostly with younger people, and of course not with my colleagues, for lepers cannot, any more than leopards, change their spots. Some of those lectures were converted to essays, gaining in polish what they lost in immediacy. A single specimen of an unrefined and unconverted lecture may, I believe, be of some interest. The following chapter reproduces, in the raw, the transcript of a lecture given in Madison before the graduate students of the University of Wisconsin on April 14, 1975.

The Great Dilemma of the Life Sciences

I AM NOT SURE whether the word "dilemma" is the correct description of the predicament in which the biological sciences find themselves. This predicament is, I believe, worldwide, although it has been exacerbated by the unfortunate fact that for all practical purposes science has become preponderantly American science. Let me say in a few words what I have in mind. For those of you who have decided to spend your lives in science, to devote your time to scientific research, it is important to ascertain what you are getting into and whether the profession you are choosing is really what you think you are choosing.

The name "life sciences," in the way it is mostly used, is just a fancy name for biology; but it also comprises the ancillary sciences, such as biochemistry, biophysics, and so on. There are even some confused people who believe that what is now called "molecular biology" makes up all the science of life. But that is not true, except in the superficial sense that all that we can see in this world of ours is composed of molecules. Yet, is this all? Can we describe music by saying that all instruments are made of wood, brass, and so on, leaving out the sounds? You will all agree that there is more to music, for in the brain of the composer, and even of most musicians, there exists a music without all the brass and wood. Someone will then, correctly, reply that our brain consists of molecules. And I shall answer in my dreamy way: "But is this all that our brain consists of?" and then we shall have the silly battle between the reductionists and the nonreductionists. The battle has been going on for nearly 2,500 years, and there is no end to it. It seems to be the human condition that there can be no consensus except on trivial matters. Maybe cats are all of one opinion with regard to mice, though I doubt it.

The dilemma of my title, that is, the choice between alternatives that are bound to be unpalatable to one or the other, is that biology will have to decide whether it can again become small, whether it can return to human proportions of research and funding, or whether it will continue on its present path to becoming an enormous technology, ever more costly and lumbering, ever more alienated from the people who must pay for it, and forever living on huge and necessarily unrealizable promises.

*   *

I used, just before, the term "human proportions." This presupposes that there is a proper size to everything in the world, that there is a measure to everything which must not be exceeded. Nobody knew this better than the Greeks with their famous μηδεν 'αγαν — of nothing too much. We have lost entirely this sense of measure, of reticence, of knowing one's own boundaries. Man is only strong when he is conscious of his own weakness. Otherwise, the eagles of heaven will eat his liver, as Prometheus found out. No eagles of heaven any more, no Prometheus: now we get cancer instead — the prime disease of advanced civilizations.

Professional scientists have, by necessity, limited vision. They should not be allowed to drive freely across humanity, because, with their eyes fixed on the highest, they are bound to produce collisions with the nearest. This does not mean that the professional nonscientists who run this country are any better; they are only different. I have always tried not to be a *professional* scientist, since I dislike professional professionals, but that is of no importance in the present context. In any event, for nearly fifty years I have been going to a laboratory in the morning and have come home at night. Or, to put it in the wonderful way that the people of Paris use to describe their life: *Métro, boulot, métro, dodo* (subway, job, subway, sleep). And even in such a limited, in such a truncated life as that of a scientist and teacher one cannot help observing changes, vast changes, in all our lives and in our daily surroundings.

What I used to call "human beings" are becoming rarer as I look around. There was a time — well, it is long gone — when St. Augustine could say: "The heart speaks to the heart." But now computer talks to computer. Most people I meet in my or other universities seem to be rejects from IBM. In fact, you can talk with them only in triplicate. Slaves or prisoners of NIH or NSF, of Xerox and Beckman — they are really the narrowest, the dullest kinds of experts or specialists; they are essentially molecular podiatrists: people who know all about the fifteenth foot of the centipede.

Incidentally, I now have a simple method by which I can recognize future Columbia vice-presidents and deans, especially at the medical school: they misuse the adverb "hopefully"; they "address a problem"; they speak of "input" as if they were dealing with a computer; they submit proposals as "a package," but if "a package" is offered to them, they "don't buy it"; they like to engage in a "dialogue" — with several hundred people at the same time — but if you answer, they tell you that this is "only semantics." I could go on, but I won't. That this is a profession which once was represented by Kepler or Faraday, by Mendel or Avery, is really hard to believe.

That we live in rotten times requires no argument. What made them so I have no license to explain. Even the great doctors of our time appear, when viewed through my glasses, as quacks. It is quite possible that the world has indeed become too complicated for human beings and that there is nobody left who can understand it any longer, let alone reform it. Maybe we all got too much lead into our brains.

In any event, it is no wonder that science, which is the most brittle, the most vulnerable of occupations, is affected and damaged by our century. In what follows, I shall touch principally upon three topics: (1) What is science? (2) How is science done in our days? (3) What are some of the special problems facing the life sciences?

*   *

What is science? Truly a big question about which large books have been written that I have great difficulty in reading. I shall give a simple answer. Science is the attempt to learn the truth about those parts of nature that are explorable. Science, therefore, is not a mechanism to explore the unexplorable; and it is not its task to decide on the existence or nonexistence of God or to measure the weight of a soul. It is very unfortunate that science has become extremely arrogant — this started at the time of Darwin, but is getting worse—and that scientists arrogate to themselves a special right to speak out loudly, and often stupidly, on almost any topic. For instance, the National Academy of Sciences, which is, after all, only a sort of chamber of scientific commerce into which some very funny characters have entered through various backdoors, is widely regarded as the true receptacle of wisdom. But when you spend your life watching a bubble chamber or running cesium chloride gradients you may become an expert bubbler or gradient runner, but there is little likelihood of your thus acquiring much wisdom. There is, in fact, a good chance that such people will turn into very dull fellows indeed, wasting their lives by trying to outrun ten other dull fellows with whom they are in competition.

I said that science is the effort of learning the truth about a part of nature; and the hope is, of course, that with truth there will come understanding. Now, nature is much too enormous for the human mind to encompass and understand as a whole. So it has to be subdivided into many discrete disciplines, each of which has unfortunately developed its own code of honor, as it were. If the different sciences talk with each other at all, it is only through a form of Esperanto, namely, mathematics; and mathematics is a beautiful, but very dry, language. In all other respects, the sciences have grown very much apart, and when I hear their several practitioners talking with each other, it is about automobiles and the price of gasoline. Sometimes also about Chinese restaurants.

If you asked a layman what science is, he would perhaps say that it consists in the rational and critical accumulation of verifiable or disprovable facts. If you asked him what a fact is, he would answer that this is what scientists collect. But if you then told him that grown-up people should avoid tautologies and that there is no point in trying to square a vicious circle, he would look at you with the empty expression that has become so familiar to us from the photographs of our leading statesmen, but the discussion would come to an end. For never before has science become so alienated from the common man, and he, in turn, so suspicious of science.

If we were willing to survey all the sciences from astronomy to zoology, we should notice that some can communicate with each other via mathematics and others cannot. And we should also notice that some sciences collect their facts in very different ways from others. For instance, chemistry derives from, and depends upon, an experimental approach in which experiments can always be repeated, if the conditions are kept constant. An organic substance whose synthesis has been described must always be capable of being synthesized if the same procedures are followed. It will have the same melting or boiling point, the same spectrum, and so on. We have here an ideal representative of an exact science. The same holds for physics, though not for all parts of it. But consider, on the other hand, astronomy. To a large extent it is certainly an exact science, but it is not an experimental science in the sense that physics and chemistry are. If Kepler wanted to verify his calculations, he could, of course, repeat his measurements and even improve on them. But he had no second sun and second set of planets to play with. The same, or even more far-reaching, restrictions apply to, say, geology or paleontology. But the success of the exact sciences, and therefore the pull they exert, has been so great in our times that many other sciences that are not suitable for this approach have begun to imitate them, not at all to their profit. For weighing and measuring may be the bread of life for one science, but it may make others look ridiculous.

When we come to biology, we meet a peculiar situation. For biology is the science of life, and life is something with which the exact sciences feel very uncomfortable. Even the other "nonexact" sciences do not quite know how to handle it. For this reason, the term "biology" comprises an entire landscape full of variations. On one side, there are disciplines that try to look as if they were exact, such as biochemistry and biophysics. On the other side, there are sciences that are mainly descriptive or even historical. Obviously, a man trying to work out a metabolic cycle or one putting reporter molecules on the active center of an enzyme has little in common with others studying the feeding or breeding habits of sea gulls or reconstructing a skull from an ancient jaw bone.

I hope to return to these questions at the end of my talk and shall now take up the second of my three topics.

*   *

How is science done in our days? Here I must immediately make a distinction between science as a profession and science as the expression of some of the faculties of the human mind. The two are not necessarily connected. When someone tells me "I am a professional scientist," it does not automatically mean that he is a scientist. The distinction I am suggesting here has nothing to do directly with the question of talent. There have always been more or less gifted scientists, and there were even a few, very few, scientific geniuses. But what I want to bring out is that as a profession science is one of the most recent ones. It barely existed when I began my studies. Perhaps the exception is chemistry, where, when you called yourself a professional chemist, people would assume that you worked in the chemical industry. This was about the only mass outlet for academically trained scientists. It was not an accident that, when the science departments of the universities began to swell and to expand, it was always the chemistry department that led the way; just as the first modern teaching and research laboratory at a university was Liebig's chemistry laboratory in Giessen.

Otherwise, one entered a career in science, just as in history or philosophy, by trying to become a teacher at a college or even a high school. There were very few jobs, and almost none that paid enough to live on, except for the position of the professor himself. And there was usually only one professor for a discipline. Hence the old students' saying that there were only two ways to make a university career: *per anum* or *per vaginam*. You tried to become the professor's darling or you married his daughter. Obviously, this limited the choice: some professors were very nasty, some daughters were very ugly. Girl students were altogether out of luck, but there were only a few of them.

You may conclude—and you are right—that this was a most unpleasant system. But it had one advantage: it acted as a sieve, letting through the few who could not do otherwise. By requiring what amounted to a pledge of poverty, it kept out all those who, to use a nasty term, were not "highly motivated." It produced a slightly smaller number, but probably a much higher density, of good scientists than does the present system.

I should by no means wish to give the impression that I am in favor of the old system. It was abominable. Nor am I, on the other hand, in agreement with the way things are done now; for I am convinced that with our methods of organizing and supporting it we are effectively killing science. We are destroying the whole concept of science, as it has developed over the centuries.

This may sound to you awfully apocalyptic, and I ought to clarify it a little. I shall try to do this under four headings: What has science done to the universities? What have the universities done to science? What has science done to the country? What has the country done to science?

All these interactions have to do with science as a profession. But you will remember that I have made a distinction between this aspect and that of science as a product of the human mind. In this respect—namely, as the search for truth about nature—science began as a branch of philosophy, and for me this connection has never broken off. Science is an admirable product of human reasoning, as admirable and astonishing as are music or poetry or the arts. Previous generations understood this very well. For instance, I am a member of the American Academy of Arts and Sciences and, until recently, before Columbia sent me down for recycling, I belonged to their Graduate Faculty of Arts and Sciences.

As a mental occupation, as a product of the human mind, science does not operate on a time scale. Just as nobody could have told Mozart how many operas he ought to write, there can be no five-year plan for science. It comes as it comes, it goes as it goes. Should all melting points be raised by 10 percent; are six laws of thermodynamics better than three? But when America decided to go into science in a big way—and this really took place only within the last thirty or forty years—it went into it in a crazy fashion. This country has always had the tendency to blow up every balloon until it bursts, and it has done it also with science.

What science has done to the universities is that it has inflated and disfigured them; it has left them more bankrupt than they were before. The large private universities have been turned into huge corporations whose only business is to lose money. There are exceptions, but, in general, power-hungry, empty-headed money grabbers have taken over. The true and only function of a university, namely, to help young people find themselves by bringing to them the accumulated memory of mankind, has been swept aside. By misunderstanding, through overemphasis, of the old adage of the unity of research and learning, research has been made into a teaching tool, into a most expensive and stultifying one, forcing every student to become a researcher and trivializing the purpose of scientific research. Thousands of meaningless and costly experiments are performed to persuade the young that water boils at 100°. We are now paying the price for the excessive veneration of the value of inductive reasoning.

Now to my second question: What have the universities done to science? They have bled it for overhead; they have cheapened and vulgarized it to the point of nonrecognition; they have made it into a public-relations "gimmick." If the products of this kind of education often still are so good, it testifies only to the resilience of young minds. But many are damaged irreversibly.

What has science done to the country? Obviously, a lot of good and a lot of evil. If the republic envisioned by Plato had come to pass, that is, a dictatorship of wise philosophers, maybe no evil would have come to the state from science. But how many wise men will you meet in your future long lives? When I look at our leading statesmen, there are brought back to me the immortal words that the Duke of Wellington once spoke of his generals. "They may not frighten the enemy, but, by God, they frighten me!" The thoughtless, almost automatic use of science as the seed of technology has landed us in a fearful mess. The cry that what we need is more and ever more science has lost all persuasion, as far as I am concerned. The republic will not be saved by geese, not even by geese with a PhD.

What has the country done to science? In a way, I have already answered that question. When you have been a scientist all your life, going to the laboratory every day and spending all your days among other scientists, it becomes hard to imagine that there still are people in this country other than scientists, although an optimistic forecast made a few years ago promised me that in less than hundred years there would be more scientists than people in the United States. In any event, as I have already mentioned, the country at large views science with great diffidence and often with dislike; and the rain of suspicion falls alike on the guilty and on the just. I don't want to go into the tedious arguments about pollution and DDT and all the rest. I shall also not discuss whether ten million blackbirds ought to have been killed, by Tergitol or otherwise; nor shall I have anything to say about Napalm, that innocent pastime of a Harvard professor.

Our kind of science has become so dependent on public support that nobody seems to be able to do any research without a handout. If their applications are turned down, even the youngest and most vigorous assistant professors stop all work and spend the rest of their miserable days writing more applications. This continual turning off and on of the financial faucets produces Pavlovian effects and a general neurasthenia that are bound to damage science irreversibly. It would have been much better if it had never got so rich before getting so poor, for in the meantime many young people have been lured into a career that may never materialize.

*　　*

What are some of the special problems facing the life sciences? In speaking of biology, I leave out of consideration the applied sciences, such as agronomy or medicine. For this reason, I shall not mention, for instance, the ethics of organ transplantation and similar problems, although a lot could be said.

The special problems I do have in mind are both of a general nature—you might call them philosophical—and of a specific nature. To begin with, no other science is as limitless, as wide open, as is biology. No other science deals in its very name with a subject that it cannot define. In no other science is the span so wide between what it ought to understand and what it can understand. The concept of "method" in itself and of the application of "methods" has entirely different consequences in, say, chemistry and in biology. There can very well be a method, a procedure, to determine the iron content of a mineral, but there is no method to study life. There are, however, many tricks or shortcuts claimed to accomplish this. But their very number and variety have produced such a fragmentation that a unified vision of living nature has become impossible, although ancient Aristotle may have believed that he was not far from it. The tremendous mass of information that has come down on us with unexpected suddenness has produced more confusion than enlightenment.

This is directly related to the loss of human proportions in science which I mentioned before. Science—at any rate in my way of considering it—is a mental activity, something that you do much more with your head than with your hands. The human brain has a vast capacity for storing and retrieving bits of information; but its capacity is presumably not limitless. To put it crudely and metaphorically, the more telephone numbers I am called upon to memorize, the less chance for me also to commit to memory the whole of *Paradise Lost*. Now, you might reply that there is no need for me to memorize the entire Milton, for there is a book on my shelf whose spine says "Milton," and I can look him up when I want to. Correct; but that is not the way in which creative science operates. Here, we require a minimum of ever-ready information without which fruitful analogies and even completely original ideas are impossible. This minimum has been increasing at a truly frightening speed. At the same time, more and more telephone numbers and other similarly trivial information are being thrown at us, and our poor brain cannot distinguish any longer between what it may need and what is useless. Thus we arrive at a stage that in another context I used to describe as follows: "The more I know the less I know."

It is, moreover, no consolation when I am told that there will always be a computer to help me. Quite apart from the probability that there will not always be a computer, for we are going into uncertain and dark times, a computer would be entirely useless to me: the idiot's best friend is an idiot himself. What the scientist needs is a selective and nonautomatic memory and, even more, he needs plenty of empty spaces, as it were, between the reminiscences, for he works as in a dream of reason. Great scientific concepts often have an entirely noninductive, dreamlike quality. So what a scientist requires more than anything is the ability to maintain empty spaces, both around and within himself. But our entire teaching establishment is directed against this need. Having ourselves lost the umbilical connection with the center of science, we always cram the newest into our students: lost souls teaching the young how to lose theirs.

I realize I have begun to sound like a minor apocryphal

prophet, and I might as well continue along that line a little while longer before coming back to earth. What I wanted to say has to do with the "usefulness" of such human activities as scientific research. This is a very delicate subject, especially when discussing it with such dyed-in-the-nylon pragmatists as Americans are supposed to be.

There is, of course, a limited number — not a very large one — of basic human actions that may be considered necessary for survival, such as growing and building and making. The production of food, housing, and clothing belongs to them. Most people, not all, would probably include teaching among these vital and, therefore, useful activities. There are other activities that are really useless, but can claim usefulness because of the particular social and economic conditions of the people among whom they are practiced: for instance, law, banking, advertising, or journalism. I am undecided where to put medicine. A very limited amount is probably useful or even necessary, most of it is a nuisance. When I hear that we are being exhorted to produce more and more physicians, I shudder, for I ask myself: Will the nation be able to produce enough sick people to guarantee to all these doctors the level of comfort to which they consider themselves, for unknown reasons, to be entitled? But never fear: doctors make patients. That is an old rule that still holds.

But now I have to make a confession: I am not at all worried by this talk about usefulness and uselessness. These are not categories with which I wish to be concerned. Some of the nicest occupations in the world are entirely useless by strict criteria of cost-accounting, and yet they have been with us from times immemorial. I am thinking of all the arts, in all their forms. What should we be without them?

Some of you may already have seen what I am driving at. From where I sit, stand, or lie, the sciences are not essentially different from the arts. I only wish they could have remained equally "useless." Let me quote from a recent article of mine:

> Scientific induction is actually the resultant of a parallelogram of
> rational and irrational forces. That is why in many respects Science
> is not a science, it is an art.

I should say that unpredictable associations and the free play of
imagination are no less important in science, that is, in real
science, than they are in writing.

But there are two important differences. One is that the arts
create their own truth, whereas the sciences are said to reveal
the truth that is hidden in nature. Therefore, if you fake in
science, you may first be allowed an extra page for your paper
in the Proceedings of the National Academy. But then you are
found out and must consult one of the useless professions, a
psychoanalyst. In the arts, what could be called faking is of a
completely different nature, but for this I have no time. The
other difference is the way in which the several occupations are
supported or, if you wish, financed—and this brings me back to
earth with a loud thump.

For I should say that our era is extremely ambivalent when it
comes to the problem of how scientific research ought to be
supported. "Ambivalent" is perhaps a misnomer—I should have
said "nullivalent," for the people are entirely lost in front of
science. They do not know whether to support it, how to
support it, nor what to support. This has landed us in the mess
in which we find ourselves now. The less the people are willing,
the more promises must be made. Instant longevity, freedom
from all diseases, a cure for cancer—soon, perhaps, the abolish-
ment of death—and what else? Whereas no singer did ever have
to promise to make a better man of me if I listened to her trills.

Maybe someone would reply that this is so because there is
very little pleasure to be had out of science except for those who
do the work. Maybe he would be correct. And this brings me
back to the "dilemma" of my title. You will either have to work
in huge laboratory factories producing the snake oil for the
impresario who has hired you, leaving it for him to sell the
snake oil to other impresarios, or science will have to become

166 *The Sun and the Death*

small again: an activity of a few selected and devoted individuals. The sign over the door of the laboratory reads: "There is no hurry; there never is any hurry."

Science as an Obsession

SCIENCE HAS TAUGHT US that man is an animal; a view often expressed by people wishing to excuse the bestialities they perpetrate. Somehow I have never become reconciled to this view. When as a child I was taken to the zoo, the "Menagerie" in Schloss Schönbrunn, my nearest relative, the ape, was of course shown to me; but I looked at him with dismay and even with horror. He reminded me threateningly of frightful figures seen in my dreams: archetypal images going back all the way to the expulsion from Paradise. This should not be taken to mean that I am anti-animal; quite the contrary: some of my best friends were animals. I can only think with a feeling of sadness of my dear Minka, the cat of my *Gymnasium* years, who died such a horrible death. And if I ever met a knight, rash and courageous, mild and quick, it was the friend of my later years, Terry the Irish terrier, who left a permanent hole in my heart as in my carpet. In any event, the animals of my acquaintance did not require persuasion that their animality was worth the effort; they were as they were. In that respect, as in a few others, they were quite different from those other friends of my later years, the graduate students.

It is really in their futile attempts to explore the mind, human or animal, that the sciences have revealed their nakedness. For all I know, Terry the dog was capable of unbounded imagination and deep thought; but he showed no sign of it. These qualities — unbounded imagination, deep thought — are, in fact, the attributes that liberate man from the bondage of matter, from the chains of the flesh. They render him human, they lift him eternally out of the pale sea of nothingness. These were certainly the gifts that attended the onset of humanity, and it was through them that man was impelled and enabled to think about nature into which he found himself thrown. But there must soon have developed a curious antinomy: as profound thought about nature progresses, it is in danger of encroaching upon imagination. Actually, it took a long time before this danger became evident, for there is an enormous distance between thinking itself and the decision to test its validity and to use its fruits. The first decision may have been made early, but thousands of years had to elapse until the second came about.

Logic, the branch of philosophy concerned with the criteria of correct reasoning, has, since the time of Aristotle and the Stoa, naturally undergone many changes in the course of history, but from early days it has accompanied, as a watchman, the thought processes of man. In the evaluation of scientific reasoning, logic is, however, not sufficient, for when the explorations apply to matter or, in general, to measurable or weighable phenomena, other criteria testing the validity of scientific statements must be called upon. The dominant themes, at any rate in those sciences with which I have been in contact, may be listed as (a) experiment, (b) method, (c) model. Each of these processes has contributed to the polytomy, the fearful fragmentation, of our vision of nature with which the scientist is daily confronted. Each has widened the gap between human imagination and scientific thought, upholding the ever-increasing separation of the scientist from the rest of mankind. At the same time, experimentation and methodology have made possible the impressive increase in our knowledge of nature, although one may ask whether this is really the kind of knowledge that mankind requires.

Only in the last 350 years or so has the predominance of the experiment brought forth the several experimental sciences; a development with which the overrated philosopher Francis Bacon usually is credited, in my opinion undeservedly. Whereas in ancient Latin the word *experimentum* stands for tribulation, and Goethe referred to the "torment of nature," the word experiment itself, more or less in its present connotation, appeared in the European languages around 1300, although experiments must, of course, have been performed occasionally during antiquity. But if questions were asked of nature, I do not believe that the answers received served for the construction of systems of knowledge, except, perhaps, in astronomy and geography; nor were they really, in most cases, the sort of question that would now be called an experiment. The more limited and circumscribed the question, the more likely a definite and comprehensible answer, i.e., one that adds to, and fits into, a previously conceived system or model. In limited sciences, such as physics or chemistry, which are surrounded by boundaries, as it were, the multiplicity of frequently overlapping answers, collected in the course of centuries, has produced a broad area of understanding, though even here much is still obscure.

But biology is limitless, and our experiments are only drops out of an ocean that changes its shape with every rolling wave. Because our questions must skirt our fundamental ignorance of the nature of life, the answers we receive can be no more than a travesty of truth; a truth, moreover, that may be so much of a plural that we can never comprehend it. The manner in which questions are asked, i.e., experiments designed, is either completely random or conditioned by our ideas of a preestablished harmony, a harmony that we seldom recognize as a contract with God that He has never signed.

I am not sure whether one can say that man—just as he possesses an almost instinctive sense of symmetry—is governed by an equally elemental desire for simplicity. But Ludwig Wittgenstein writes in his diary of September 19, 1916: "Men have always searched for a science in which *simplex* is *sigillum veri.*" This longing for simplification has, in fact, been one of the intellectual driving forces during the growth of modern science. The attempt to find symmetry and simplicity in the living fabric of the world has, however, often given rise to false conclusions or to anthropomorphic short-cuts. The world is built in many ways: simple for the simple-hearted, deep for the profound. Our time is rather feeble-minded, but science is growing ever more complex, some people knowing more and more about less and less. The ideal state which we approach asymptotically is to know all about nothing.

The edifice of the animated world rests, one could say, on two pillars: one is the unity of nature, the other its diversity. To pay attention only to the unity, as is usually done, completely distorts our vision and condemns us to the kind of analogy research that fills our journals. Who could understand music only from an analysis of the composition of the instruments of an orchestra? The news that all trombones are made of brass is trivial when measured against the immensity of the musical universe. Saint Cecilia may have blown sweetly on a trumpet of glass.

The insufficiency of all biological experimentation, when confronted with the vastness of life, is often considered to be redeemed by recourse to a firm methodology. But definite procedures presuppose highly limited objects; and the supremacy of "method" has led to what could be called by an excellent neo-German term the *Kleinkariertheit* (piddling pedantry) of much present-day biological research. The availability of a large number of established methods serves, in fact, in modern science often as a surrogate of thought. Many researchers now apply methods whose rationale they do not understand.

For the experimentalist, a tested method is like an extremely sharp tool serving to cut tiny and regular shreds out of the flesh of nature. What he learns holds for the particular fragment, but not for the contiguous areas. Those may be similarly investigated by other methods. The hope is that all this shattered universe of knowledge will eventually coalesce into a total vision; but it has never done so, nor is it likely to happen in the future, for the more we divide, the less we can integrate. (Even a child learns at the end that a whole doll, together with the illusion that it is a real baby, is worth more than a lot of splinters.)

A few years ago I tried to describe some of the consequences[6]:

> The fashion of our times favors dogmas. Since a dogma is something that everybody is expected to accept, this has led to the incredible monotony of our journals. Very often it is sufficient for me to read the title of a paper in order to reconstruct its summary and even some of the graphs. Most of these papers are very competent; they use the same techniques and arrive at the same results. This is then called the confirmation of a scientific fact. Every few years the techniques change; and then everybody will use the new techniques and confirm a new set of facts. This is called the progress of science. Whatever originality there may be must be hidden in the crevices of an all-embracing conventional makeshift: a huge kitchen midden in which the successive layers of scientific habitation will be dated easily through the various apparatuses and devices and tricks, and even more through the several concepts and terms and slogans, that were fashionable at a given moment.

The role of fashions in science is a very interesting subject which I have treated in more detail in an essay first published in 1976.[7] This influence makes itself felt in all sciences, but particularly in biological research, where the direction in which nature—or what is considered as nature in biology—is being probed is as much under the sway of fashion as is the choice of methods and of models. Models may have had their part in many forms of deductive reasoning; but they were usually under firmer control than in my time. Especially, the onset of molecular biology was accompanied by an orgy of model-building, much of it of a transparent stupidity. The journals were full of models no sooner published than discarded. Even then I counseled moderation, thus contributing to my reputation as a "controversial figure." I said in a Harvey Lecture in 1956: "I should advise to wait and see. Models—in contrast to those who sat for Renoir—improve with age."[8]

One of the most insidious and nefarious properties of scientific models is their tendency to take over, and sometimes supplant, reality. They often act as blinkers, limiting attention to an excessively narrow region. No application of logic can prove a model to be true, though its lack of plausibility can often be demonstrated easily. The extravagant reliance on models has contributed much to the contrived and artificial character of large portions of current research.

However, the helplessness of science before life has, in my opinion, profounder reasons. It is probably not accidental that, of all sciences, biology is the only one that is unable to define its object: we have no scientific definition of life. The most exact studies are, in fact, performed on dead cells and tissues. I say it with all due diffidence, but it is not impossible that we are encountering here a form of an exclusion principle: our inability to comprehend life in its reality is due to the very fact that we are alive. If this were so, only the dead could understand life; but they publish in other journals.

The appearance and the growth of the natural sciences in their present form is nearly contemporary with the emergence and the ascent of the bourgeoisie; and it is not accidental that, if one historical event could be said to mark the onset of modern science, it is the French Revolution. The *tiers état*, which has not enjoyed a good reputation among the creative minds that suffered from it — I do not believe there ever existed a bourgeois genius — has always been able to point to the flowering of science and technology as its greatest triumph. Since we are now witnessing the beginning of the end of this progress-drunk epoch, it is to be expected that a new historical era will give rise to an entirely different kind of science; a science that we, looking out from the jail of our notions, could hardly recognize as such.

In the meantime, however, the great successes — many would perhaps call them the triumphs — of the experimental sciences, especially physics and chemistry, have had a curious effect on the scholarly disciplines that are usually designated as the humanities; an effect that has been rendered more conspicuous since the entrance of those well-known pragmatics, the Americans, on the scientific scene. In an attempt to emulate their successful brethren — with all their logarithm tables, slide rules, calculators, and computers, with their graph paper and their statistical camouflage techniques; in other words, with all their triumphant decimalization of nature — the humanities have also begun to go scientific. This spread of scientism to history and economics, psychology and linguistics, sociology, philosophy, and philology, is about to deform them into many grotesque shapes. But the very ease with which matters of the mind can become trivial by catching mathematics has also shown that what is good for Judith may not be good for Holofernes. For there are certain phenomena that gain in comprehensibility by being weighed and measured and others that do not. I do not need statistical word analysis to show me that former President Ford cannot be the author of *King Lear;* the number of belly laughs per week the merry slave had on a plantation does not interest me; nor do I require a personality profile with "in-depth analysis" of Cleopatra or Jan Hus. The incredible twaddle let loose by all these computerized humanists is probably not worse than that of the scientists; but since the former have only begun to develop a coterie jargon or an animal language of their own, they are still forced to use more or less intelligible words, and these give them away.

The Trembling of the Balance

A READER of this book may get the impression — erroneous, but not entirely unjustified — that it was written by a man who was was slightly to the right of Ivan the Terrible or Genghis Khan. One should have thought that it was the experience of a long life, and the reflections flowing from it, that brought me to this undesirable position. The truth is, however, that as long as I can think back I was never far from it. I remember distinctly that when I was very young, sixteen or seventeen years old, I described myself once as a red reactionary. This was youthful exaggeration, and if a sobriquet then had to be applied it would have been that of a radical conservative, although I have grown so tired of slogans that I should hesitate to characterize a cockroach in two words. In contrast to the imperial malefactors mentioned just now, I have always been very much opposed to violence, and the lyrical universe in which my mind grew up drew its reason from its rhyme.

But we live in a world in which rhymes have become impossible, and reason is a convert to despair. (Is it really an accident that it was in our time, and almost simultaneously, when rhyme and verse disappeared from poetry, melody from music, and the recognizable object from painting and sculpture?) Ours is indeed a twilight world in which soulless puppets throw blood-red shadows on a screen of instant oblivion. They come and they go at a speed that contracts centuries into days, their names sooner forgotten than spelled out on the transparencies proclaiming their eternal fame. What has taken away their souls I do not know. The very word "soul" has, in fact, become as absurd in our day as would be Shakespeare's or Pope's rhymes. Man seems to have been turned into a "biodegradable" plastic.

Even as a child, a most unchildish child, I must have been conscious of being born in a rent between the times, for I grew up in a cloud of sadness. Although our ghastly century was in its beginnings, the intimation of abominable things to come was inescapable, as was my feeling that I could do nothing about it, except to bear witness to my revulsion. As a safety valve to this oppression of helplessness there came times of savage wit: an escape into the immutable and ever-changing landscape of language and imagination. The inexhaustible fountains of poetry and later of music refreshed me when I was despondent and they strengthened my belief in powers that transcend our misery. Even now, reading a page of Goethe, Hölderlin, or Stifter can throw a little light into the mirthless prison of my years. The conviction that "I shall not all die," *non omnis moriar*, so often repeated to me in the stillness of the night, had less to do with the cry of glory-drunk Horace and his stainless-steel monument than with the incandescent loveliness of Mozart's music.

Three historians, none a card-carrying member of the guild, have been of influence: Machiavelli, Gibbon, and especially Jacob Burckhardt, as disabused a mind as La Rochefoucauld. He taught me that only a pessimist can make a good prophet; an ambition, however, that I have never had, knowing that even in the times of Isaiah the servants of God were despised.

Living in cramming and shamming times, when the prevailing winds all blow from the side of hypocrisy, shabby make-believe, insincere eye-rolling; living in a country where one does not die but passes away, where bitter chocolate must be called semisweet, and a man may be *worth* a million dollars; living in a city that envies Detroit for having recently celebrated its first murderless day since 1928—in other words, living in the sewer into which the juices of a rotting epoch drain, I find it difficult to explain that the human gift that I prize most highly next to sincerity is intensity. That quality, especially of the creative mind, has become very rare; it must not be confused with aggressiveness or impetuosity, properties so frequent among salesmen or scientists. For me the word connotes the ability to concentrate one's powers of imagination and execution so as to convey an overwhelming impression of blinding reality. Perhaps a few examples of what I mean by intensity will help: Shakespeare and Donne have it, Milton or Shelley do not; Bach and Pope have it, Telemann or Wordsworth only rarely; Dante in every line, Leopardi not at all; Yes for Tolstoy, Dostoevsky, or Joseph Conrad, No for Thomas Mann or Heine; great applause for Schubert, but very little for Wagner; and the loudest cheers for Mozart and Haydn. Because of my ignorance, or for other reasons, I know of no American artist or writer, if I exclude Henry James, who would qualify, since in speaking of intensity I am not thinking of the noise-making potential.

Two great religious writers have accompanied me during my entire life: Pascal and Kierkegaard. Especially Pascal's *Pensées*, gaining so much in profundity from the disorder in which they were recovered at his death, I have never given up reading. Pascal was particularly memorable for me, as here was a great physicist who had succeeded in escaping from the labyrinth of science under the guidance of his own heartbeats, as it were; "a Moses," I once called him,[9] "who must curse the Promised Land." The third great writer who influenced me in a very special way, Karl Kraus, I have also mentioned before.

In countries trying to live up to Anglo-Saxon standards of gentility, one is always asked for one's hobby; a question that would surprise an Italian stone-cutter or a French peasant. The answer must be original: collecting Parthian coins or raising borzois. Were I given to replying to silly questions, I should probably have said that my hobby was biochemistry, but that what I really did was nobody's business. One thing I have been doing most of my life is learning languages. In the course of the years I have, at one time or another, occupied myself with something like fifteen languages, at least to the extent of being able to read them. I do not read for instruction—my marvelous library can supply that—but for the delectation of the mind. I have long ago stopped reading translations; but there seldom passes a day without my reading a few pages in three or four languages. Even the shortest text of any value is untranslatable: one of the most striking examples of the wonderful diversity of living nature.

Not long ago, reading Lichtenberg's delightful letters, truly representative of my favorite century, I was dismayed to discover that he did not share my opinion regarding the importance of studying languages. In a long letter which he wrote to one of his older brothers on August 13, 1773, he says, speaking of a nephew:

> Etwas habe ich an ihm bemerkt, . . . nämlich eine grosse Neigung zu Sprachen, und auch eine Überzeugung, dass es sehr nützlich sei, viele Sprachen zu lernen. Dieses muss er ja nicht tun, wenigstens werde ich ihm nie dazu raten. Es ist der gradeste Weg zu dem *ex omnibus aliquid,* der nur genommen werden kann. . . . Etwas zur Erquickung von den Haupt-Sprachen zu erlernen, und was man, wenn der Verstand erst seine Form hat, leicht zu einem Grad von Vollkommenheit erweitert, die der Sprachgeck nie erreicht, ist allerdings nützlich. . . . Wenn man seine Muttersprache, Latein und Französisch versteht, so lernen sich, wenn zumal ein etwas philosophischer Geist dazu kommt, die andern gewöhnlichen Sprachen unglaublich bald, ohne über den *verbis irregularibus* und deren Konjugation die beste Zeit zu verlieren.*

Lichtenberg had one of the sharpest and wittiest minds of a century unusually rich in acute intellects. He was a great writer, arguably the greatest aphorist known to man, and a distinguished physicist. It will be noticed that his minimum demands — mother tongue, Latin, French — are far above what our schools can now supply. The barbarization of our time is nowhere as noticeable as in its obtuse indolence about language, one's own or others. There are many causes, and I have often discussed them, from apocalypsis to zoology, but the natural sciences and those other disciplines trying to ape them carry a heavy share of the guilt. Recently I spoke with an eminent linguist who assured me that he got along on English and

---

* There is something I have noticed in him, namely, a great love for languages and a conviction that it is very useful to learn many languages. This he must not do, at least I shall never advise it. It is the shortest way to "a little of everything" that can be taken. What is, however, useful is to learn, for one's delectation, something of the principal languages; once the mind is fully formed, one may expand this to a degree of perfection never attained by a linguistic snob. If you understand your mother tongue, Latin, and French, the other common languages can be learned with incredible speed, especially if you are a little gifted for philosophy; and you will not waste your best time with irregular verbs and their conjugation.

Yiddish. But, then, he had a Cartesian mind, and he could truly have said: *Scribo, ergo cogito.*

A time and a country babbling of machine translation cannot understand what I am talking about. Nausikaa coming down to the seashore — the Greek language arising from the morning mist of Mycenaean shudders, or the French returning to them: *La fille de Minos et de Pasiphaé,* a verse that has condemned centuries of French poetry to euphony.

The murder of my mother and of my mother tongue are of one piece: they fell into the same ashes. But language can rise again, and it will undoubtedly do so when the metaphysical blood, staining and paralyzing all growing fibers of the language, has bleached. The regeneration can only come through great writers. For the time being, however, the most considerable German writers of my day — all, peculiarly, Austrians — remain Kraus, Kafka, Trakl. Drunk as I was even as a child on the sound and the senses of words, in which the phantasies of the boy and the imagination of the man could meet as in a lovers' tryst, I attempted naturally with all my force to keep the connection. I continued to write, and very rarely also to publish, in German; but I was a light-weight Antaeus. Easily lifted and dislodged, I became no prophet in many fatherlands. It was not without emotion that I found this cry of anguish in one of Franz Kafka's letters to his friend Max Brod (June 1921). In speaking of the desperate situation of German-Jewish writers living in Prague, writing in a language not quite their own and hearing another, even stranger one, spoken around them, he was thinking of himself; and this from one of the purest masters of German prose:

Zunächst konnte das, worin sich ihre Verzweiflung entlud, nicht deutsche Literatur sein, die es äusserlich zu sein schien. Sie lebten zwischen drei Unmöglichkeiten . . . : der Unmöglichkeit, nicht zu schreiben, der Unmöglichkeit, deutsch zu schreiben, der Unmöglichkeit, anders zu schreiben, fast könnte man eine vierte Unmöglichkeit hinzufügen, die Unmöglichkeit zu schreiben . . . also war es eine von allen Seiten unmögliche Literatur, eine Zigeunerliteratur, die das deutsche Kind aus der Wiege gestohlen und in grosser Eile irgendwie zugerichtet hatte, weil doch irgend jemand auf dem Seil tanzen muss.*

A balance that does not tremble cannot weigh. A man who does not tremble cannot live. One thinks, one dreams, and then one thinks again; but the two functions must be kept apart. Goya wrote on his 43rd Capricho: *El sueño de la razon produce monstruos* (The dream of reason brings forth monsters).

The caricatures of the past become the portraits of the present. The devils that the old masters painted on the walls have detached themselves and walk among us. Satan, dispenser of delights to Faust and of horrors to Ivan Karamazov, now hopes to achieve tenure. He, like all of us, has come down in the world, for we live in shabby times. But we must not repeat the mistake of Ivan, who found the devil stupid. Discovery and Invention, the dearest idols of our grandparents, may have lost much of their healing power, and certainly a great deal of their ambrosian aroma, but am I not surrounded by people who tell me that the only way to remedy the harm done by science is more science?†

---

* To begin with, that into which their despair broke forth could not be German literature as which it appeared outwardly. They lived among three impossibilities: the impossibility not to write; the impossibility to write in German; the impossibility to write in another language; one could almost add a fourth, the impossibility to write. It was therefore a literature impossible from all sides, a gypsy literature that had snatched the German child from the cradle and fixed her up somehow in a great hurry, as there must be somebody to dance on the rope.

† I should like to erect here a modest stele to the memory of Sir Arthur Helps (1813–1875), a secretary and confidant of Queen Victoria. It was probably he who invented the marvelously useful verb *to disinvent*. The only illustration of this word in the *Oxford English Dictionary* (Vol. III) is a quotation from Helps dated 1868: "I would disinvent telegraphic communication." The word is not listed in Vol. I of the Supplement (1972), but a recent use will be found s.v. *fantasy* in the same volume. If I were younger, I would found the *Coverers' and Disinventors' Club*.

Breathing in and breathing out, I became suddenly an old man, trying to comfort the quadragenarians when they complain of getting old. It was only yesterday when I came with my parents and my sister to war-disrupted Vienna — the Vienna of 1914 — where people had to sleep in bathtubs because the rooms were crowded with refugees. I must thank God that if the scales went up and down, the beam held firm. The oscillation between manual science and matters of thought and language, the eternal systole and diastole of heart and mind, permitted me to keep a measure of sanity in an atrocious world.

Mrs. Partington's Mop, or the Third Face of the Coin

THE REVEREND Sydney Smith was a very witty man; I should have liked to meet him, just as I should have liked to meet Lichtenberg, Chamfort, Rivarol, Peacock, or, for other reasons, that most likable of German writers, Theodor Fontane. On October 12, 1831, the *Taunton Courier* reported a political speech Smith had given. Here is a passage:

> I do not mean to be disrespectful, but the attempt of the lords to stop the progress of reform, reminds me very forcibly of the great storm of Sidmouth, and of the conduct of the excellent Mrs. Partington on that occasion. In the winter of 1824, there set in a great flood upon that town — the tide rose to an incredible height — the waves rushed in upon the houses, and every thing was threatened with destruction. In the midst of this sublime and terrible storm, Dame Partington, who lived upon the beach, was seen at the door of her house with mop and patterns, trundling her mop, squeezing out the sea-water, and vigorously pushing away the Atlantic Ocean. The Atlantic was roused. Mrs. Partington's spirit was up; but I need not tell you that the contest was unequal. The Atlantic Ocean beat Mrs. Partington. She was excellent at a slop, or a puddle, but she should not have meddled with a tempest. Gentlemen, be at your ease — be quiet and steady. You will beat Mrs. Partington.

Having once wanted to found the Bureau of Lost Causes, I must have realized early that there were not enough Mrs. Partingtons around. Most people are wise and applaud the inevitable; but I, inexplicably, love to be on the losing side. I should certainly have enlisted under Julian the Apostate; I am the born Albigensian; I admire Thomas Müntzer. In other words, I am an inveterate Catonist: *Victrix causa deis placuit, sed victa Catoni* (The winning cause was liked by the gods, but the lost one by Cato—Lucan's *Pharsalia*). Cato, I am sure, had his good reasons, and so have I. If there were two faces to the coin, one preferred by austere Cato, the other by the frivolous gods, and if the coin were thrown in a world of pure chance, then the gods and Cato would be satisfied evenly. There is, however, more than one "but": (1) winning and losing are not the same as good and bad; (2) the gods may not really like the winning cause, but the cause wins because the gods like it; (3) ours is not a world of pure chance*; and (4) we are often dealing with, so to speak, a three-faced coin, of which only two sides, both evil, are visible to us and only one can be on top. I could almost summarize my life in saying that I have been searching for the third face of the coin. We seem often to be resonating between two devils, with the one angel remaining discreetly invisible. I am also convinced that in this imperfect world the good side can never win, for if it wins it does not remain good for long. What I would call the Actonian corruption principle will set in, and absolute power will corrupt absolutely. Whereupon the Brahman would assure the Manichaean that he was not surprised. "Tear," he would say, "the veil of Maya ever so little, and you will see nothing but grinning skulls."

This reminder of the vanity of vanities encourages me to say something shamefully naive. In my opinion, nothing that has been done or thought is ever lost. If it existed once, it keeps on

---

* How happy I was to read recently in a work by one of the most admirable representatives of an admirable century, in David Hume's *Dialogues concerning Natural Religion* (part IX): "Chance is a word without a meaning."

existing. The lost tragedies of Aeschylus or Sophocles; *Dafne,* the only opera that Schütz wrote, or Monteverdi's *Arianna;* Kleist's *Die Geschichte meiner Seele,* the manuscript of which he gave to a friend before killing himself; Giorgione's frescoes in Venice or the missing books of Livy; the innumerable buildings, paintings, sculptures, writings, or music that perished irretrievably—they may be lost to us, but in a higher sense they are not lost: they have entered the *corpus mysticum* in which all is contained, every breath that was breathed, every deed that was done. In this sense, no cause is ever lost, no battle ever won.

In any event, I have fought losing battles, for, like Mrs. Partington, I have been prone to meddle with tempests. One strictly scientific battle, the biological importance of the nucleic acids, I could have been said to have won, but it was a funny victory: the victorious army decided to move to another battlefield. This happened, I am told, because I had called my discovery "base-complementarity," and the others preferred to call it "base-pairing." It is true, I was singularly uneager, and unfit, to found a new scientific religion.

More important struggles were not really lost—winners are declared only by posterity—but they led to nothing. The principal one was my quixotic attempt to maintain a science with a human face. This means small science, one for which an individual can stand up, in which a human voice can still be heard. This also means a science that is governed by human conscience, and not merely by scientific conscience. The latter advises me to stick to the truth about my discoveries, for otherwise I may be found out and, among other unpleasant consequences, lose my reputation, which, in lieu of worldlier goods, is the only thing the scientist can accumulate.

Small science was, in fact, the sort of science in which I grew up, as I have mentioned before. It changed its character rather abruptly during the Second World War. We came out of it with a bloated establishment which carried the seeds for further uncontrollable malignant growth. At the end of the war, hundreds, yes, thousands of "pure scientists" had become used to working in scientific concentration camps, such as the "Manhattan Project." The results produced by these phalansteries, skillful applications of the most recondite laboratory observations, will live forever, if "live" is the correct word for the manufacture of the atom bomb. The image, however, of the absent-minded professor—never true in the experimental sciences, in which abstraction would soon lead to self-combustion—has outlasted the happy hour when the same scholar was busy perfecting the hydrogen bomb.

My life has been marked by two immense and fateful scientific discoveries: the splitting of the atom, the recognition of the chemistry of heredity and its subsequent manipulation. It is the mistreatment of a nucleus that, in both instances, lies at the basis: the nucleus of the atom, the nucleus of the cell. In both instances do I have the feeling that science has transgressed a barrier that should have remained inviolate. As happens often in science, the first discoveries were made by thoroughly admirable men, but the crowd that came right after had a more mephitic smell. "God cannot have wanted that!" Otto Hahn is reported to have exclaimed. Did he ask Him beforehand, did He remain silent? I have the impression that God prefers to be left out of these discussions.

The impact that the discovery, the bloodstained discovery, of nuclear energy had on me I have tried to describe in the first pages of this account. From that time the Devil's carnival was on, for me at any rate. As the dances became more frenetic, the air turned thinner and harder to breathe. That science, the profession to which I had devoted my life—and a life is the heaviest investment a man can make—that science should engage in such misdeeds was more than I could bear. I had to speak out, for I was bound to ask myself: Is this still the same kind of science that I thought of getting into more than fifty years ago? And I had to reply: it is not.

Several essays of mine dealing with this question are about to be published as a book,[10] but I believe I ought to explain myself briefly. When I began, the natural sciences were constituted — although, as all best constitutions, theirs was unwritten — as an international community of scholars intent on learning the ways of nature. (A few centuries earlier one would have said "the ways of God in nature.") It was, and I have mentioned this before, a very small community; even the beginner did not find it difficult to start on his way. Most of the principles were established; axioms, theories, and hypotheses abounded; but as the number of researchers was small, the pace was slow. There seemed to stretch before our eyes an unending sunny plain, and even at night one could walk securely at one's own speed. The purpose did not appear questionable: it was a good thing to understand more about the world in which we lived. There were no immediate goals of a practical or conceptional nature; the Grail was out of reach, Montsalvat would never be climbed by us. Matter was built of molecules, most of them still to be investigated; molecules consisted of atoms, all of them known and in good order; atoms could not be split. Had anybody asked me, the chemical apprentice, I should have added: atoms must not be split, for I was a foolish young man growing up in great reverence for nature.

The degree of my foolishness may be gathered from the fact that I had studied radioactivity at the University of Vienna, which housed one of the early important radium institutes. I could also have remembered the paranoiac suspicion and almost hatred — but the paranoia of a genius is often prophetic — with which August Strindberg regarded the Curie couple. I had been an admiring reader of Strindberg's remarkable diaries, the *Blue Books*, and I knew well that the nightmares of a genius have a way of generating the horsemen of the Apocalypse. But although I knew about radium and its decay, the great revolution in the physics of the atomic nucleus had somehow passed me as a not very attentive bystander. Only when the work of the Joliot-Curies and of the Fermi group broke upon me as I was beginning to employ the radioactive isotope of phosphorus ^{32}P, and when this was followed by the ominous discovery of nuclear energy, did I begin to realize with horror the dimensions of this most revolting of all scientific revolutions. The incessantly tortured atomic nucleus seemed to be taking its revenge on mankind. I had to think of a saying of Goethe that I had always found particularly moving: *Die Natur verstummt auf der Folter; ihre treue Antwort auf redliche Frage ist: Ja! ja! Nein! nein! Alles Übrige ist vom Übel.** If tormented nature fell silent, the cries of the victims of these astounding *in mortuo* experiments grew that much louder. Would Goethe still have celebrated the lack of "basalts and of ruined castles" that endeared America to him? †

The public, if there is such a thing, had no opportunity beforehand to discuss, or deliberate on, the development and the use of the atom bomb. It was all a very well-kept war secret. But would an open discussion have made any difference, would it have halted the truly inexorable progression? There would have been a great deal of gabble and of drab and dull posturing, but the movement, a movement without movers, a fall without gravity, would have continued. Ask the lava where it flows. It would answer with what I have called the Devil's doctrine: *What can be done must be done.*[1] And a lot can be done!

In the case of the splitting of the atom and its sequels we were faced, one could say, with an accomplished atrocity. The second instance I have mentioned before, the exploitation of the discovery that the inheritable properties of the cell are encoded in its deoxyribonucleic acid, is perhaps more instructive, for here we can discern the misdeed in the course of being accomplished.

The direction of the drift is clear, but the steps are impercep-

* (Nature falls silent on the rack; its candid answer to a sincere question is: Yes! yes! No! no! Everything else is of harm. Goethe, *Maximen und Reflexionen*, Nr. 115.)

† (*Amerika, du hast es besser / Als unser Kontinent, das alte, / Hast keine verfallene Schlösser / Und keine Basalte.* Goethe, *Den Vereinigten Staaten.*)

tibly small. The noble discovery of the genetic role of DNA was followed by innumerable instances of induction, deduction, expansion, and application. The recognition that the genes, instructing the formation of enzymes and other proteins, were partial DNA sequences, was followed by an understanding of the mode of their action, and by successful attempts to map the positions of individual genes on the genome. The discovery of highly specific enzymes, breaking a DNA chain at definite spots of known nucleotide composition, made it possible to envisage the isolation of DNA fragments comprising only one gene or a few. Methods became available—I do not want to go into the depressive details—to introduce such fragments into a living *Escherichia coli* cell, which would then go on multiplying these newly added pieces of DNA as well as the products for which the intruders carried the information. This meant the construction of new forms of life; forms that living nature presumably never encountered in its long, long history.

When news of atrocities being perpetrated are dispensed in small homeopathic doses, one becomes inured, for the normal human mind is not capable of the sort of integration that would raise the misdeed in its full abominable flesh. For that, the flame of an Isaiah is required or a religious genius of the intensity of Kierkegaard, of whom I once wrote as follows[4]:

> It is the privilege of the great religious thinker to predict the impending Martyrdom of the Ten Thousand, the coming slaughter of the millions of innocents, after reading some newspaper gossip about what Frøken Gusta said last night in a theater box to Frue Waller.

In the absence of Biblical prophets, however, the reading of such writers as Kierkegaard, Kraus, Kafka, or Bernanos may help; that is, if you take them seriously, which is something very difficult to accomplish in our light-minded time. In any event, "Today," I said to myself, "the bacteriunculum, tomorrow the homunculus. Today the cure of the genetic diseases, tomorrow the experimental improvement of the human character. *Erimus sicut dei,* as someone promised to my ancestress. The poor fool bought death instead." And to think that Adam and Eve could still live in Paradise, entirely unimproved genetically, reading as a mystery story, before going to sleep, the latest issue of the *Journal of Molecular Biology!*

If, according to Mallarmé, poems are made with words, scientific papers are made with acronyms. But in the following letter to the editor of *Science* I was far from cryptic.[11]

On the Dangers of Genetic Meddling

A bizarre problem is posed by recent attempts to make so-called genetic engineering palatable to the public. Presumably because they were asked to establish "guidelines," the National Institutes of Health have permitted themselves to be dragged into a controversy with which they should not have had anything to do. Perhaps such a request should have been addressed to the Department of Justice. But I doubt that they would have wanted to become involved with second-degree molecular biology.

Although I do not think that a terrorist organization ever asked the Federal Bureau of Investigation to establish guidelines on the proper conduct of bombing experiments, I do not doubt what the answer would have been; namely, that they ought to refrain from doing anything unlawful. This also applies to the case under discussion: no smoke-screen, neither P3 nor P4 containment facilities, can absolve an experimenter from having injured a fellow being. I set my hope in the cleaning women and the animal attendants employed in laboratories playing games with "recombinant DNA"; in the law profession, which ought to recognize a golden opportunity for biological malpractice suits; and in the juries that dislike all forms of doctors.

In pursuing my quixotic undertaking—fighting windmills with an M.D. degree—I shall start with the cardinal folly, namely, the choice of *Escherichia coli* as the host. Permit me to quote from a respected textbook of microbiology: "*E. coli* is referrred to as the 'colon bacillus' because it is the predominant facultative species in the large bowel." In fact, we harbor several hundred different varieties of this useful microorganism. It is responsible for few infections but probably for more scientific papers than any other living organism. If our time feels called upon to create new forms of living cells—

forms that the world has presumably not seen since its onset—why choose a microbe that has cohabited, more or less happily, with us for a very long time indeed? The answer is that we know so much more about *E. coli* than about anything else, including ourselves. But is this a valid answer? Take your time, study diligently, and you will eventually learn a great deal about organisms that cannot live in men or animals. There is no hurry, there is no hurry whatever.

Here I shall be interrupted by many colleagues who assure me that they cannot wait any longer, that they are in a tremendous hurry to help suffering humanity. Without doubting the purity of their motives, I must say that nobody has, to my knowledge, set out clearly how he plans to go about curing everything from alkaptonuria to Zenker's degeneration, let alone replacing or repairing our genes. But screams and empty promises fill the air. "Don't you want cheap insulin? Would you not like to have cereals get their nitrogen from the air? And how about green man photosynthesizing his nourishment: 10 minutes in the sun for breakfast, 30 minutes for lunch, and 1 hour for dinner?" Well, maybe Yes, maybe No.

If Dr. Frankenstein must go on producing his little biological monsters—and I deny the urgency and even the compulsion—why pick *E. coli* as the womb? This is a field where every experiment is a "shotgun experiment," not only those so designated; and who knows what is really being implanted into the DNA of the plasmids which the bacillus will continue multiplying to the end of time? And it will eventually get into human beings and animals despite all the precautions of containment. What is inside will be outside. Here I am given the assurance that the work will be done with enfeebled lambda and with modified, defective *E. coli* strains that cannot live in the intestine. But how about the exchange of genetic material in the gut? How can we be sure what would happen once the little beasts escaped from the laboratory? Let me quote once more from the respected textbook: "Indeed, the possibility cannot be dismissed that genetic recombination in the intestinal tract may even cause harmless enteric bacilli occasionally to become virulent." I am thinking, however, of something much more worse than virulence. We are playing with hotter fires.

It is not surprising, but it is regrettable that the groups that entrusted themselves with the formulation of "guidelines," as well as the several advisory committees, consisted exclusively, or almost exclusively, of advocates of this form of genetic experimentation. What seems to have been disregarded completely is that we are dealing here much more with an ethical problem than with one in public health, and that the principal question to be answered is whether we have the right to put an additional fearful load on generations that are not yet born. I use the adjective "additional" in view of the unresolved and equally fearful problem of the disposal of nuclear waste. Our time is cursed with the necessity for feeble men, masquerading as experts, to make enormously far-reaching decisions. Is there anything more far-reaching than the creation of new forms of life?

Recognizing that the National Institutes of Health are not equipped to deal with a dilemma of such import, I can only hope against hope for congressional action. One could, for instance, envision the following steps: (i) a complete prohibition of the use of bacterial hosts that are indigenous to man; (ii) the creation of an authority, truly representative of the population of this country, that would support and license research on less objectionable hosts and procedures; (iii) all forms of "genetic engineering" remaining a federal monopoly; (iv) all research eventually being carried out in one place, such as Fort Detrick. It is clear that a moratorium of some sort will have to precede the erection of legal safeguards.

But beyond all this, there arises a general problem of the greatest significance, namely, the awesome irreversibility of what is being contemplated. You can stop splitting the atom; you can stop visiting the moon; you can stop using aerosols; you may even decide not to kill entire populations by the use of a few bombs. But you cannot recall a new form of life. Once you have constructed a viable *E. coli* cell carrying a plasmid DNA into which a piece of eukaryotic DNA has been spliced, it will survive you and your children and your children's children. An irreversible attack on the biosphere is something so unheard-of, so unthinkable to previous generations, that I could only wish that mine had not been guilty of it. The hybridization of Prometheus with Herostratus is bound to give evil results.

Most of the experimental results published so far in this field are actually quite unconvincing. We understand very little about eukaryotic DNA. The significance of spacer regions, repetitive sequences, and, for that matter, of heterochromatin is not yet fully understood. It appears that the recombination experiments in which a piece of animal DNA is incorporated into the DNA of a microbial plasmid are being performed without a full appreciation of what is going on. Is the position of one gene with respect to its neighbors on the DNA chain accidental or do they control and regulate each other? Can we be sure—to mention one fantastic improbability—that the gene for a given protein hormone, operative only in certain specialized cells, does not become carcinogenic when introduced naked into the intestine? Are we wise in getting ready to mix up what nature has kept apart, namely the genomes of eukaryotic and prokaryotic cells?

The worst is that we shall never know. Bacteria and viruses have always formed a most effective biological underground. The guerilla warfare through which they act on higher forms of life is only imperfectly understood. By adding to this arsenal freakish forms of life—prokaryotes propagating eukaryotic genes—we shall be throwing a veil of uncertainties over the life of coming generations. Have we the right to counteract, irreversibly, the evolutionary wisdom of millions of years, in order to satisfy the ambition and the curiosity of a few scientists?

This world is given to us on loan. We come and we go; and after a time we leave earth and air and water to others who come after us. My generation, or perhaps the one preceding mine, has been the first to engage, under the leadership of the exact sciences, in a destructive colonial warfare against nature. The future will curse us for it.

André Gide, that great repeater of himself, wrote several times that it was with beautiful sentiments that bad literature was made. I am not certain that he is right: there is nothing more insipid than the flippancy of bygone years. But the English language now has an aversion to the purple patch; it is no longer a celebratory language, as it was in Shakespeare's or Dryden's times, and as French and Italian still are. In any event, the last paragraph of the letter quoted here came from my heart; I hope the rest came from my head.

I consider the attempt to interfere with the homeostasis of nature as an unthinkable crime. Have they peeped into the Creation and found it wanting? We do not yet have a pathology of scientific imagination; but the urge to change the biosphere irreversibly could make an excellent object for such a study; an even better one than would the desire to hop on the moon. If, as is claimed, a fish begins to stink from its head, one could say that man begins to stink from his heart.

I am being assured by the experts that nothing untoward can happen. How do they know? Have they watched the web of eternity opening and closing its infinite meshes? Is their foresight surer now than a few weeks ago when I last met them? The American ideal of an expert is that he be "cold-nosed." What a cold nose signifies in a dog, I used to know; but in an expert?

I have not been alone in protesting; I am certain that all these warnings will pass unheeded, the more so since the irrevocable process was started before there was even time for an alert. As far as I am concerned, this is presumably the end of my career as Mrs. Partington. But she had an easier task. The Atlantic Ocean has no publicity offices, and the fishes that inhabit it are probably more farsighted than are our scientific experts. Since humanity has never listened to a warning, why should it — and how could it — have listened to mine? All that can happen will happen; and it will be a long time before it appears whether I was right or wrong, certainly a longer time than it took for the DC-10 airplane to split up on March 3, 1974, in the forest of Ermenonville, shortly after the experts had certified its airworthiness.

Vanishing into Dust

IN JOSEPH HAYDN'S miraculous oratorio *The Creation*, one of his many "greatest works," I have always found three passages particularly moving: the chaos of the beginning, the coming of the sun, and the creation of the first man, or, as modern nondiscriminatory usage would make me say, the production of the primordial person.* Not all that

---

* In a recent reprinting of one of my articles in book form, a sentence of mine reading: " . . . it is not the men that make science; it is science that makes the men" was changed by the copy editor to read: " . . . it is not the person that makes science; it is science that makes the person." This was one of the few of her numerous alterations that I was able to reverse.

has a happy beginning has a happy end, but in Haydn's work this is the case, for it ends shortly before the advent of the snake: an additional proof of the well-known fact that every historical account can, by choosing its end-point properly, terminate in bliss and order. Most historians, and I among them, reject, however, this easy solution.

It seems that the libretto of *The Creation*, heavily dependent upon *Paradise Lost*, was written originally in English by a Mr. Linley or a Mrs. Delany for use by Handel, but the great composer did not set it to music. When, many years later, the text was offered to Haydn, he asked the Austrian diplomat and writer Baron Gottfried van Swieten to shorten and adapt the English version and to prepare a German translation, and these are the words to which the immortal music is sung.

After the ill-fated pair has been brought forth, the archangels have some comment.

Gabriel and Uriel:
> On Thee each living soul awaits;
> From Thee, O Lord, all seek their food;
> Thou openest Thy hand,
> And fillest all with good:

Raphael:
> But when Thy face, O Lord, is hid,
> With sudden terror they are struck;
> Thou tak'st their breath away,
> They vanish into dust:

And then the three angels unite and sing together most sweetly. Death was not invented at the time of action of the oratorio, but listening to Raphael's deep voice many hearers must have thought of it. I, however, was thinking of my retirement. The time of my vanishing into professional dust was approaching rapidly. The historian, unfortunately, must continue beyond the point of general jubilation; and real ends are rarely happy.

Among many other things, I have sometimes been called

gloomy. This may be so, although much of my gloom is actually brought on by my looking at the people who call me gloomy. Dealing with a somber subject, I feel it, therefore, incumbent upon me to assure the reader that my tone will be as light-hearted as that of a speculator in Florida real estate inviting the senior citizen to walk into his parlor. All glasses will be half full, wormwood will be called vermouth, bitterness will be semisweet, people will not die but pass on, Gehenna will be sanitized. Above all, I shall not be talking of myself, except at the conclusion of the chapter.

From a biography of Arnold Schönberg[12] I learned that the eminent composer, when he retired from the University of Southern California in 1944, received a pension of thirty-eight dollars per month. (From the same source I gather the interesting fact that when Schönberg, after his retirement, applied for a Guggenheim Fellowship, his request was rejected.) As an old admirer of American mythology, I always used to tell students complaining about various hardships: "This will look good in your biography." But even to one who believes more strongly than I do in the Protestant work ethic, the profit motive, and free enterprise, the account of the last years of this "Austrian-born American composer," as the dictionaries called him, may not have made joyful reading. It did not look good in the biography.

The difficulty that Juvenal experienced was spurious. If there is one thing more difficult than not to write a satire, it is to write one. I shall not even try. Probably because I do not own a television set, my collection of atrocities is rather old-fashioned, and there ought to be bitterer bile around. I do, however, concede that the attitudes of our times to old age, retirement, and death would deserve a far from swift, but thoroughly Swiftian, treatment of which I feel incapable. In choosing, for brief consideration, the least metaphysical of the three afflictions, retirement, I become aware of one curious shift in the prevailing climate. When I was young, I was supposed to genuflect before old age. Now that I am old, I am called upon to venerate youth and to feel ashamed about not having made room for them earlier. Nevertheless, I do not complain about being robbed of the prostrations for which I had been waiting so long. I only wish to point out that the concept of retirement has shifted concomitantly with the newly arisen cult of youth and vigor. Out of a procedure designed to relieve old people of burdens they could no longer carry, retirement has become a Tarpeian practice of *ôte-toi que je m'y mette*. But never mind: just as the only purpose of nature now is to support the natural scientist, life has become a machine to keep alive.

In any event, I should like to say a few words about the question of retirement as it confronts the university teacher. This is not meant as a critique of the concept of retirement itself, which, were it not foreseen by custom or by law, would earlier or later be enforced by nature. Under all circumstances, the difference can be only a few years.

As has been so spiritually stated by one of its presidents, the business of America is business. Given a relatively stable currency, and in the absence of severe economic upheavals, a nation consisting of, and made for, merchants, did not find it difficult, conceptionally or practically, to include a provision for old age among the profits accumulated in the business of the day. A large proportion owned homesteads to which they could retire. The rapid industrialization created a tremendous demand for cheap labor, which was satisfied by the importation and the immigration of the exploitable, and heavily exploited, poor of Europe. These succeeded, after bloody and heart-rending struggles, to get organized into unions which, at any rate at the beginning presumably honest, eventually set up pension funds of varying efficacy. These, together with the nation-wide Social Security System, guaranteed to many workers some degree of stability. The retirement incomes of federal, state, or city employees have also reached some form of sufficiency, if a pension rate around 60 percent of the working income is assumed as the minimum.

The great exception to this at least tolerable, if not satisfactory, state is represented by the employees of private enterprises, of which the private universities and colleges form an important, although chronically insolvent, part. The low esteem in which education is held by the people has baffled me from the very time I first came here. The schoolmarm in the little red schoolhouse may look good as staffage in political speeches, but nobody cares much about how she lives or, rather, starves. When I first began to think about these matters, I came to the conclusion that the degree of civilization of a country can be gauged from three things: how the people behave toward their children, their old, and their teachers. America fails in all three respects; and the Turks, for instance, appear to represent a much higher level, despite inferior plumbing and less competence in automobile repair.

Most private universities belong to a pension scheme that is administered by the Teachers Insurance and Annuity Association—an institution whose workings everybody who finds his way through Kafka's castle will understand readily. Each month, a certain proportion of the professor's salary is deducted, and the university contributes the same share or even twice as much toward the eventual pension. (This being a free-for-all country, there is a great deal of elegant variation among the ways in which different universities handle the arrangement.) Once a year, the professor receives a piece of paper on which various mysterious and highly tentative figures are inscribed, intimating a far from rosy future. He is only forty-eight or fifty, and the future seems far away. But suddenly, in a flash, he is sixty-five or sixty-eight or seventy, whatever the mandatory retirement age is; and the time has come for him to sit in the shade of a tree and enjoy the golden years. The plating is actually very thin, and probably not even gold, but there are many other things that he discovers at the same time. He finds, for instance, that the retirement pay dangled before him by the uninformative colored slips of the year corresponded to an entirely unrealistic option that, for reasons of family and obligations, he cannot accept, and that the pension he will receive will be much smaller than he thought. He also discovers, or his sharp scientific mind knew it before, that in the meantime the dollar has fallen to less than one-fifth of the value it had when he contributed the bulk of his contributions; and he may come to the paradoxical conclusion that the longer he has paid in, the less he will get. Moreover, because university salaries were in most cases incredibly low until the late nineteen-fifties, older colleagues, who retired ten years before I did, found — and if God spared them, still find — themselves with a pittance. This must be compared with the situation in most of Europe, where the retirement pay ranges between 80 and 100 percent.

The things I am discussing here transcend by far my own example. When I spoke about them with others, their faces often assumed an empty, glassy-eyed appearance, as happens when people try to become philosophical, and they said to me: "Well, you know, the philosophy of America is that everybody provides for himself. Nobody likes to be on the dole." And then I remembered how struck I was to notice, when I first came to this country, that poverty seemed to be considered as a shame or even a crime. I said to myself, "What a shabby philosophy!" My reading of the great writers of the past — Dostoevsky, Tolstoy, Hamsun — had taught me different values.

In any event, few university professors will find it easy to save enough money to supplement their outrageously small pensions. A professor of Chinese, with perhaps one-fourth of the salary of a fourth-rate pathologist, will hardly be able to "provide for himself"; nor will he, during the first and hardest years of retirement, be able to receive his Social Security benefits if he attempts to add to his pension by part-time work. Nevertheless, I believe that retirement is a necessary social institution, which, however, should not be applied in the present haphazard manner. What is very regrettable is the absence of satisfactory financial provisions for retirement.

The problems, of course, are not only monetary. If we limit ourselves to university people, professors or researchers, great differences can be seen in the way retirement affects an experimental scientist and a historian or a philologist. Provided the latter is permitted to keep his office or is able to continue his work at home, there need not be an abrupt break in the continuity of his research efforts. How different is the case of a laboratory scientist—a physicist, a chemist, a geneticist, or, to take the discipline that I know most about, a biochemist. Unless we happen to come upon the rare, humble, and happy man who is forever content with his simple colorimeter, Kjeldahl apparatus, or phase microscope, there is a costly, bulky, heavy, and complex array of machines and contraptions, all prone to go out of service at the shortest of notices and requiring an entire staff of assistants that are both—the machines and the assistants—not easily kept in good humor. Much space is needed, much help, and much money. All three are abolished or severely curtailed, and with explosive suddenness, at the time of retirement.

There is more to it. As he grows old, the scientist in his familiar laboratory feels more alone than is realized. A wall of ice has grown between him and the younger people who are around. Their language is no longer his, but it is the only language he hears. Their standards are different, but they are those by which he, too, will be judged. The editors of the scientific journals and their referees are the graduate students of his graduate students; and so are the so-called peers who sit in judgment on his research proposals. Change or, as the optimists may call it, progress has overtaken the old scientist. What still holds him upright—the young voices, the old rooms, the daily trip to laboratory and office, the letters he gets, the journals he reads, the view from his window, even the dust on his windowsill—all this has formed a framework of habit and repeat, a skeleton on which he has put the flesh of his own long years, of his sorrows and his joys; and then, suddenly and cruelly, all this collapses. From one day to the next he is told to clear out, to flutter away, do as if nothing had happened, fade. And so he is gone.

This has been, more or less and with a minimum of poetic freedom, my own story. I got into this situation, as happened always in my life, without any doing on my part or, rather, because I had not done anything. Originally, I had hoped to retire from the University in 1970, when I was sixty-five, and to move to Europe. Life in New York had become unpleasant, and the outrageous Vietnam war made symbolic separation advisable. Some nebulous interest in having me had even been expressed in several places: Bordeaux, Montpellier, Lausanne, Naples. But the collapse of the value of the dollar, the inflation, and the concomitant shrinkage of my savings and of the pension I could expect rendered such a move impossible. And so, an old practitioner of the Taoist principle *wu wei* (do nothing), I stayed.

As I had been told repeatedly that I was to move out as soon as my current research grant was terminated, I no longer accepted graduate students during the last active years, since I did not want to involve young people in the decline and fall. Although retirement itself has some ludicrous features, I was dismayed to find that my pension amounted to less than 30 percent of my last regular salary. As to the rites of passage that lead to becoming an emeritus professor, they have obviously been designed by someone who fell in love with the old films depicting the degradation of Captain Dreyfus. It is true that the muffled drums are barely audible, no epaulets are ripped off, no sabers broken. But the spirit, and especially the hypocrisy, are the same. The sudden transition also brings with it something else: one day you are in the middle of almost too much activity, and there is a lot of noise; the next day it gets so still that you can hear the dollar drop.

I had a very well-equipped laboratory, a large scientific library, and a considerable quantity of papers and correspondence, as is bound to accumulate in more than forty years. And, besides, research cannot be turned off like a tap; there was quite a bit of scientific activity still going on and a heap of half-written and unwritten articles. I sent my papers to the library of the American Philosophical Society in Philadelphia; I gave most of my books to the library of Columbia Medical School. All the rest I had to transfer in an incredible hurry to a hospital in another part of New York where there was some space.

On November 20, 1975, the movers came. Certain things had to be left behind because they required individual attention, especially a cupboard full of my own old preparations. When we returned, we could not get into the laboratories. We were told that all locks had been changed at somebody's order.

Were I given to metaphorical writing, I should say that what happened, and especially the way in which it happened, has broken my heart. If I refrain from saying so, it is because the sardonic delight in seeing events occur exactly as I had predicted them outweighed all else. I have always had a sense of the fittingness of things. And since at Columbia one left hand never knows what the other does, it was quite fitting that less than six months after they had changed the locks on me at the Medical School, the University gave me an honorary doctorate.

While the movers were busy I stayed at home and browsed around. My eyes fell on a page of Heraclitus, and there he said: "The way up and the way down is one and the same." I concluded that Heraclitus was wrong.

Liber Scriptus Proferetur

"EC," said the Voiceless Voice, "would you mind telling me what you consider your greatest sin?"

"VV," said EC, "I am surprised. Do you really expect confessions? After all, I am not Jean-Jacques; and if there had been a Madame de Warens around, which really was not the case, she would not have found a place in this book. And as for the other, the greatest writer of confessions, Monica's son, where would he have been able now to find a publisher, with all this stuff about the soul longing for God? Dr. Freud's flea circus had not yet opened in Augustine's time. He could not even show a good identity crisis or at least an Oedipus complex. Who has a soul anyway? Now we have psyches, and they are sick, but analyzable."

vv: Would you mind answering my question?

ec: I was only trying to gain time, so that I could collect my wits. I did not realize that this was serious. Scientists are not wont to deal with sins or with virtues. They collect data, and once they have enough data, they fashion them into facts; when they have enough facts, they arrange them into a system. When they have enough systems, they forget about them and start all over again.

vv: You talk too much. Please answer my question.

ec: My greatest sin has been indolence. As I began, nature had endowed me —

vv: Please use the proper term. Who had endowed you?

ec: All right, life had endowed me —

vv: I shall have to say it for you. God had endowed you —

ec: . . . had endowed me with some gifts, not many, but a few; and through my entire life I have had the feeling that I did not make good use of them. It may well be that I was what one now calls mediocre, although I do not much like that kind of rating humanity. To me all men are the best; I still believe in the dignity of man. But during all my life I have been trying to cry out: "Wake up, wake up!"

vv: Have you been successful?

ec: No. I dreamed away my birthright for a mess of foam. I was never one of those who find without searching. So I searched, but always with one hand tied to my back. I never burned my way through the rocks. I was too tepid for that. When I found something, I picked it up, but next day I had often mislaid it.

vv: Tepidity and indolence are not the same. Which is it?

EC: I should say I was almost too indolent to be tepid. I was never wholly one thing. In the sad I saw the ridiculous, and in the ridiculous I saw the sad. My ancestress had been misled by the serpent, that most double-tongued of dialecticians, and I must have inherited from her my love of dialectics. And so I often dream of the horrible one, the great Scaretruth.

vv: Do I understand you to say that truth and dialectics are incompatible?

EC: Is this the Last Judgment or a placement exam?

vv: You wouldn't ask if you didn't know. Or do I hear again the lukewarm dialectician?

EC: Truth and dialectics are not incompatible, but dialectics without mercy will only yield a high degree of probability. Truth is more, and it comes from the heart—may I quote Vauvenargues?

vv: You may not. The library is burned.

EC: And still, it is so cold here.

vv: Would you then say that dialectical thinking was your greatest sin, that you always saw both faces of the coin at the same time?

EC: No, I was looking for the third face of the coin. But whatever I did was done hesitatingly, halfheartedly. I was poisoned by Ecclesiastes: *vanitas, vanitatum vanitas!* I would still say my greatest sin was indolence. At the same time, I seem to have been born a wrong kind of King Midas: whatever I touched turned into a fake. And while gold, in moderation, has some uses, fakes have not.

vv: No nasty remarks about your former surroundings,

please. Would you then be inclined to modify your statement and agree that arrogance was your greatest sin?

EC: No, indolence always broke through. The Russians have a marvelous word for my situation: *oblomovshchina*. It is taken from the greatest personification of metaphysical sloth, Oblomov, in Goncharov's beautiful novel.

VV: The library is burned. But I shall have to accept your statement, which you don't like to call a confession, although I suspect a little bit of affectation. Let me then ask you another question: What would you consider as your best quality or your most redeeming one?

EC: Blushing is useless in this night. I should again say, indolence.

VV: This is ridiculous. The time for paradoxes has passed. Stop pretending that you are "The Man Without Qualities."

EC: But I have always lived in a world of paradoxes. It is a world long like eternity and short like the life of a fly. Indolence is really the only response to an absurd universe. It is a sin, if it creates the inability to recognize that there are riddles; it is redeeming, if it produces a hesitancy to proclaim those riddles solved, when nothing of the sort has happened, for the great riddles probably have no solution. Indolence is a virtue if it prevents you from stirring the pot just for the sake of stirring. The do-gooders have done so much evil that not to do this kind of good has become a virtue.

VV: Thank you for the eloquence, but I repeat my question.

EC: I shall then have to look among my second-best qualities, which is difficult: there are so many of them. Perhaps it is my ability to put myself in other people's places, a modest form of imagination; perhaps it is my weightlessness.

VV: I didn't know you had dabbled — or should I say moon-lighted? — as a cosmonaut.

EC: No, no; not that kind. I mean my unwillingness to throw my weight around, a sort of congenital inconspicuousness, a form of detached anonymity. How many scientists will you find who, in fifty years, did not get a single offer? Except, of course, introductory offers to subscribe to the *Scientific American*.

vv: What you describe is really an extreme form of unpopularity. Would you call this one of your best qualities?

ec: Yes.

vv: You seem to have the mistaken belief that I am the one who can see into your heart. I am neither omniscient nor omnipotent. I am merely omniquaerent, if there were such a word: I am the one who asks all questions. So don't count on my understanding; if you can answer my question more fully, please do so.

ec: If you keep on squeezing me for desirable qualities, you will soon force me to say that I like to eat cherries. But there may be a few other things. For instance, I suffer from logophilia: I love little words and have a deep pity for them when they are mistreated. I consider them one of the greatest wonders of the world, these thought-creators, these crystalline tears and peals. They are the last witnesses of the Creation, the only tokens of a humanity that is disappearing fast.

vv: If you really loved words so much, why did you not make them the object of your studies?

ec: Well, once I had that plan. But I came soon to the conclusion that one ought not to study what one loves. One gets the wrong sort of familiarity.

vv: But didn't I often hear you assert that you loved nature? And yet, you became a scientist.

ec: It took me a long time to find out, but now I am convinced that our present natural sciences have nothing to do with nature. Therefore, one can be a scientist and still love nature. These are two different categories, like selling insurance and playing the recorder. Incidentally, I forgot one more redeeming feature: I always liked young people, and I believe I was a pretty good teacher. By the way, may I make a confession?

vv: That's what you are here for.

ec: Then I must say that, when I look at what now is called a scientist, I begin to wonder whether I ever was one. I may have started with a wrong conception, or it was really different. I belonged probably to the last generation of nonexperts, before the sciences began to divide into innumerable specialties. I have the impression that scientific research as a profession barely existed when I began. One got into science as a cobbler gets into shoe-making; or, rather, it was as a teacher that one started, and research was an avocation. It is, therefore, possible that I began as a scientist, at the terms then prevailing, but do not end up as one now.

vv: Never fear—as you came into this world, so will you go out, entirely without diploma. Are you satisfied with your life?

ec: What can I say? It may not be the best, but it is all I have. And there are certain delectable features that do not fit into this peculiar conversation.

vv: And the time in which you lived?

ec: Again, I had remarkably little choice. I will say, however, that the present century is among the beastliest that human history has known, although it will probably be surpassed by the next. Whether mankind will ever again wake up between two nightmares is more than I can say.

vv: If you had to describe your character in five words, what would they be?

ec: Shyness, exaltation, desperation, irascibility, pity.

vv: Would another set be equally descriptive? For instance, arrogance, ambition, irritability, resentment, intransigence.

ec: I am afraid, yes. But since man is constructed antonymically, also modesty, placidity, apathy, compassion, laxness. But have not the scholastics said that the individual is ineffable? Why insist? I used to say of myself: every day I am a different man, but I always wear the same overcoat. And that is what the others see. As you say, the library is burned; but I have here in my pocket a piece of paper with a passage from Meister Eckhart, the great Dominican mystic. Here is my own very poor translation from his *Book of Divine Consolation*.

> For this teaching we have a clear proof in the stone. Its outward deed is to fall and lie on the earth. The deed can be hindered, and the stone does not fall at all times nor incessantly. But another deed is innate in the stone; that is its continuous inclination downward. Neither God nor man can take it away. This deed the stone does incessantly day and night. And if it lay a thousand years up there, it would incline downward no less than on the first day.

vv: Very nice, but what does it mean?

EC: Well, apart from the bold assertion that even God cannot abolish the laws of gravity—something I should not have dared say—it seems to tell me that, whether we stones have fallen to earth or not yet, we all want to fall. We are what we were born, not what we have become. This "continuous inclination downward," this blind urge to an unknown goal, is what makes us fall while resting, and it also makes us rest while falling. "As you began, so will you remain," Hölderlin wrote in one of his late poems.

vv: If that is meant as an apology, it is useless. You seem to hint at predestination. Are you, by any chance, a Calvinist?

EC: God forbid. The supreme wisdom is, in Dante's words, also the first love. Redemption is a beautiful word, and salvation is even better. God can make all stones fly to heaven. He is the great suspender of the laws of nature.

vv: Have you ever witnessed a miracle?

EC: No; except that one can become a great man in this world without having had a single thought in the head.

vv: What have you learned from science?

EC: Only one thing: that one ought to wash one's hands before touching nature.

vv: You want to imply that most scientists don't deserve science?

EC: Yes. But they have made science into something that they deserve.

VV: What is the remedy?

EC: There is no remedy.

VV: At the place where you are now it is not for you to blow the trumpet of the Apocalypsis. Another tuba will spread its miraculous sound. I repeat my question.

EC: The first step would have to be to make science small again and to disengage it from technology and from the pursuit of power.

VV: How would you do this?

EC: I don't think it can be done according to a blueprint, and it will not take place without a series of catastrophes of a dimension that would make mankind stop and look. Our kind of science has become a disease of the Western mind. We were taught that by digging deeper and deeper we should reach the center of our world. But all we find is rock and fire. So we take the stone as our heart and the flame as our hope.

VV: Is that all that has been found?

EC: We have been lured into a search for the ever-diminishing dimensions. Each new decimal opens a new grotto of delights. Drowning in precision, drunk with controls of controls, we lose ourselves in the quick and dead sands of eternity. It will be too late when we finally become aware of our error. The center of our world is not where we have been looking for it.

VV: Where is the center of our world?

EC: If I had known where it is, I should not be here.

VV: Do you really believe there are exceptions? Do you think it makes a difference whether the candidates are led or dragged to the checkpoint?

EC: Yes, I do. But I shall try to answer your question. When I was young, the center of my world was hope. It was not hope for something definite, definable. It was the hope that above the clouds, or even the blue summer sky, there was an incredible essence, an eternal beyond of unimaginable possibilities. It was the certainty that, if my soul was in a dark night, the only thing that could come to the blackness was light; and that this would happen.

vv: Did it happen?

ec: Yes.

vv: How about a little more information?

ec: Do you expect me to compete with San Juan de la Cruz? Really, I cannot answer. But I can say that I was in the position of a young sculptor who found what he hoped was a block of marble. The stone was all covered with mud and filth; one could not even be sure that it was a piece of marble. And he began to clear and clean, and later he took a chisel or a hammer, but still he did not know what the material was and what he was shaping. Suddenly there sprang a form at him out of the stone. Was it what he had hoped for, was it the marble figure he had set out to find? He could not say. As he went on working, the form vanished, the figure crumbled. There were shapes, but they kept changing; there was some stone, but was it marble? Standing on a windy plain, he found himself among many thousands who were doing as he did. "So many idols," he said, "but where is Easter Island?" New people came with new tools; the number of images grew enormously; they filled every available space, and most of them looked half-finished. He was told that this was good for the soul and the mind of man.

vv: Did you find it so?

ec: No. I became frightened by the mass of what was offered. There was nothing I could do with it, except to register its existence. While the frenzy of the sculptors grew, most others seemed to take no notice.

vv: Would you mind leaving the charming allegory? Will all this go on, or what is the future of science?

ec: In my opinion, our kind of science will not exist for very much longer. I give it less than a hundred years.

vv: Will there be anything taking its place?

EC: Science has actually never had a place in our world; just as little as have the arts, writing, music, and so on. But the other things of the mind did not grow into such mass occupations as did science. At the moment, everything looks absurd; but it will look less so to the few survivors, feeding on radioactive ants, whom I imagine inhabiting the earth in future.

vv: Don't you know that the end of time has come, that space is abolished, that there is no Here, no Now, that there is no future?

EC: I do know it. But I thought you were questioning me about the past; and there is always a past. Of my time I could say that the world had grown much too complicated for the people who lived in it. It was not due to the great achievements in biology that human life lost all its value; but those events went in parallel. Whenever I saw an interesting paper in a scientific journal, I also read of a horrible murder in the newspaper. A society that had the means to visit the moon could not maintain the humanity of its own people, and it broke to pieces even while it invaded the universe. It made its own surroundings unlivable while speculating about life on Mars. I am sure the dinosaurs also had their biohazards committees, and they were as effective as ours.

vv: Would you say that the natural sciences were the causes of the decline?

EC: I have stopped distinguishing between cause and symptom. Rottenness follows upon ripeness as night upon day.

vv: In the beginning was the word, and in the end is silence. The interrogation is adjourned.

With a Tear for Johann Peter Hebel *

IN THE MEANTIME, four years of war took millions of young lives, ancient empires collapsed, and the nations were impoverished. The tsardom of the Romanovs fell and was replaced by a soviet republic; the monarchy of the Habsburgs broke to pieces; Germany became an uneasy republic. Science swelled and became powerful through its applications. Fascism took over Italy, Germany, Spain. The opinion industry learned how to manipulate the human brain. Hitler attempted to spread German domination over the whole of Europe and failed. The atom was split. Untold millions of Jews, Gypsies, communists, lunatics, and insurgents were killed by the Germans. Other millions perished in a second war which lasted nearly six years. Atom bombs were thrown on Hiroshima and Nagasaki. The discovery of the nature of the gene opened the way to its manipulation. Victory over the fascist powers was followed by the ostensible end of the colonial empires. China became a people's republic; the state of Israel was proclaimed. The Americans devastated Southeast Asia and visited the moon. Poverty and unemployment spread; the treasures of the earth were wasted; the entire world was polluted; murder and crime became abundant; organized religion retreated; drug addiction advanced.

While all this happened, I grew up, became old, and wrote this book.

* In the writings of the great Alemannic writer Johann Peter Hebel (1760–1826), there occurs one remarkable passage in which on the *cantus firmus* of a miserable private life the great events of more than half a century are counterpointed. This passage — one of the most beautiful known to me in all German literature — beginning with the adverb *Unterdessen,* will be found in his short story entitled *Unverhofftes Wiedersehen* (Unexpected Reunion).

REFERENCES

I

A FEVER OF REASON

Portions of this section were published under the same title in *Annual Review of Biochemistry*, Vol.44 (1975), and are used here with the permission of the editor.

White Blood, Red Snow

1. Bloy, L. 1902. *Exégèse des lieux communs*, lère série. CXXIV. Paris: Mercure de France.
2. Chargaff, E. 1931. Über den gegenwärtigen Stand der chemischen Erforschung des Tuberkelbazillus. *Naturwissenschaften* 19: 202–206.
3. Chargaff, E. 1944. Lipoproteins. *Adv. Protein Chem.* 1: 1–24.

The Outsider on the Inside

4. Chargaff, E. 1973. Bitter fruits from the tree of knowledge: Remarks on the current revulsion from science. *Perspect. Biol. Med.* 16: 486–502.

Experimental Station for the End of the World

5. Chargaff, E. 1963. *Essays on Nucleic Acids*. Amsterdam, London, New York: Elsevier.
6. Fuchs, A. 1949. *Geistige Strömungen in Österreich, 1867–1918*. Wien: Globus-Verlag.

No Hercules, No Crossroads

7. Feigl, F., and Chargaff, E. 1928. Über die Reaktionsfähigkeit von Jod in organischen Lösungsmitteln (I.). *Monatsh. Chem.* 49: 417–428.
8. Feigl, F., and Chargaff, E. 1928. Über die analytische Auswertung einer durch CS_2 bewirkten Katalyse zur jodometrischen Bestimmung von Aziden und zum Nachweis von CS_2. *Z. anal.*

Chem. 74: 376–380.

9. Chargaff, E., Levine, C., and Green, C. 1948. Techniques for the demonstration by chromatography of nitrogenous lipide constituents, sulfur-containing amino acids, and reducing sugars. *J. Biol. Chem.* 175: 67–71.

Il Gran Rifiuto

10. Chargaff, E. 1974. Building the Tower of Babble. *Nature* 248: 776–779.

Sunrise in New Haven

11. Anderson, R.J., and Chargaff, E. 1929. The chemistry of the lipoids of tubercle bacilli. V. Analysis of the acetone-soluble fat. *J. Biol. Chem.* 84: 703–717.

12. Anderson, R.J., and Chargaff, E. 1929. The chemistry of the lipoids of tubercle bacilli. VI. Concerning tuberculostearic acid and phthioic acid from the acetone-soluble fat. *J. Biol. Chem.* 85: 77–88.

13. Chargaff, E., and Anderson, R.J. 1930. Ein Polysaccharid aus den Lipoiden der Tuberkelbakterien. *Z. physiol. Chem.* 191: 172–178.

14. Chargaff, E. 1928. The reactivity of iodine cyanide in different organic solvents. *J. Am. Chem. Soc.* 51: 1999–2002.

15. Chargaff, E. 1929. Über die katalytische Zersetzung einiger Jodverbindungen. *Biochem. Z.* 215: 69–78.

16. Chargaff, E. 1930. Zur Kenntnis der Pigmente der Timotheegrasbakterien. *Zentralbl.f.Bakt.* 119: 121–123.

Late Evening in Berlin

(This is an expanded version of an article of the same title that appeared in *Trends in Biochemical Sciences* 1: 171-172, 1976, published by Elsevier/North Holland Biomedical Press for the International Union of Biochemistry, used here by permission.)

17. Chargaff, E. 1933. Über die Lipoide des Bacillus Calmette-Guérin (BCG). *Z. physiol. Chem.* 217: 115–137.

18. Chargaff, E. 1933. Über das Fett und das Phosphatid der Diphtheriebakterien. *Z. physiol. Chem.* 218: 223–240.

The End of the Beginning

19. Chargaff, E., and Dieryck, J. 1932. Über den Lipoidgehalt verschiedener Typen von Tuberkelbazillen. *Biochem. Z.* 255:319–329.

The Silence of the Heavens

20. Chargaff, E.   1970. Vorwort zu einer Grammatik der Biologie. Hundert Jahre Nukleinsäureforschung. *Experientia* 26: 810–816.

21. Chargaff, E.   1971. Preface to a grammar of biology. A hundred years of nucleic acid research. *Science* 172: 637–642.

II

MORE FOOLISH AND MORE WISE

A Bouquet of Mortelles

1. Chargaff, E.   1945. The Coagulation of Blood. *Adv. Enzymol.* 5: 59.

2. Chargaff, E.   1944. Lipoproteins. *Adv. Protein Chem.* 1: 1–24.

3. Chargaff, E.   1938. Synthesis of a radioactive organic compound: alpha-glycerophosphoric acid. *J. Am. Chem. Soc.* 60: 1700–1701.

"The Hereditary Code-Script"

4. Avery, O.T., MacLeod, C.M., and McCarty, M.   1944. Studies on the chemical nature of the substance inducing transformation of pneumococcal types. *J. Exp. Med.* 79: 137–158.

5. Chargaff, E.   1971. Preface to a grammar of biology. A hundred years of nucleic acid research. *Science* 172: 639.

6. Schrödinger, E.   1945. *What Is Life? The Physical Aspect of the Living Cell.* New York: Cambridge University Press, pp. 20–21.

The Exquisiteness of Minute Differences

7. Chargaff, E.   1963. *Essays on Nucleic Acids.* Amsterdam, London, New York: Elsevier, p. vii.

8. Chargaff, E.   1976. Triviality in science: A brief meditation on fashions. *Perspect. Biol. Med.* 19: 324–333.

9. Chargaff, E.   1932. Über höhere Fettsäuren mit verzweigter Kohlenstoffkette. *Ber. Chem. Ges.* 65: 745–754.

10. Vischer, E., and Chargaff, E.   1947. The separation and characterization of purines in minute amounts of nucleic acid hydrolysates. *J. Biol. Chem.* 168: 781–782.

11. Chargaff, E.   1947. On the nucleoproteins and nucleic acids of microorganisms. *Cold Spring Harbor Symp. Quant. Biol.* 12: 33.

12. Chargaff, E. 1950. Chemical specificity of nucleic acids and mechanism of their enzymatic degradation. *Experientia* 6: 201–209.

13. Chargaff, E. 1951. Some recent studies on the composition and structure of nucleic acids. *J. Cell. Comp. Physiol.* 38 (Suppl. 1): 41–59.

14. Chargaff, E. 1951. Structure and function of nucleic acids as cell constituents. *Fed. Proc.* 10: 654–659.

15. Olby, R. 1974. *The Path to the Double Helix.* Seattle: University of Washington Press.

Gullible's Troubles

16. Watson, J.D. 1968. *The Double Helix.* New York: Atheneum.

17. Chargaff, E. 1974. Building the Tower of Babble. *Nature* 248: 776–779.

18. Watson, J.D., and Crick, F.H.C. 1953. Molecular structure of nucleic acids. *Nature* 171: 737–738.

19. Chargaff, E. 1976. Review of *The Path to the Double Helix*, by R. Olby. *Perspect. Biol. Med.* 19: 289–290.

Matches for Herostratos

20. Chargaff, E. 1965. On some of the Biological Consequences of Base-pairing in the Nucleic Acids. In: M.D. Anderson (Ed.), *Developmental and Metabolic Control Mechanisms and Neoplasia.* Baltimore: Williams and Wilkins, pp. 7–25.

21. Chargaff, E. 1957. Nucleic Acids as Carriers of Biological Information. In: *Symposium on the Origin of Life*, Acad. Sci. USSR, Moscow, pp. 188–193. Reprinted in *The Origin of Life on Earth*, Pergamon Press, London, 1959, pp. 297–302.

22. Chargaff, E. 1959. First steps towards a chemistry of heredity. *4th International Congress of Biochemistry.* London: Pergamon Press, 14: 21–35.

In the Light of Darkness

23. Chargaff, E. 1970. Vorwort zu einer Grammatik der Biologie. Hundert Jahre Nukleinsäureforschung. *Experientia* 26: 810–816.

24. Chargaff, E. 1977. Kommentar im Proszenium. *Scheidewege* 7: 131–152.

25. Plotinus. *Enneads.* I.6.2. Taken from A.H. Armstrong, 1953, *Plotinus*, p. 147. London: Allen & Unwin.

III

THE SUN AND THE DEATH

Coping under Hot and Gray

1. Chargaff, E. 1973. Bitter fruits from the tree of knowledge: Remarks on the current revulsion from science. *Perspect. Biol. Med.* 16: 501.

2. Chargaff, E., and Davidson, J.N. (Eds.). 1955 and 1960. *The Nucleic Acids*. 3 vols. New York, London: Academic Press.

3. Chargaff, E. 1963. *Essays on Nucleic Acids*. Amsterdam, London, New York: Elsevier.

4. Chargaff, E. 1975. Voices in the labyrinth: Dialogues around the study of nature. *Perspect. Biol. Med.* 18: 251–285; 313–330.

Science as a Profession

5. Liebig, J., and Wöhler, F. 1958. *Briefwechsel 1829–1873*. Weinheim: Verlag Chemie.

Science as an Obsession

6. Chargaff, E. 1965. On Some of the Biological Consequences of Base-pairing in the Nucleic Acids. In: M.D. Anderson (Ed.), *Developmental and Metabolic Control Mechanisms and Neoplasia*. Baltimore: Williams and Wilkins, p. 19.

7. Chargaff, E. 1976. Triviality in science: A brief meditation on fashions. *Perspect. Biol. Med.* 19: 324–333.

8. See reference 3, above (*Essays on Nucleic Acids*), p. 83.

The Trembling of the Balance

9. *Ibid.*, p. 110.

Mrs. Partington's Mop, or the Third Face of the Coin

10. Chargaff, E. *Voices in the Labyrinth: Essays and Dialogues on the Study of Nature*. In preparation.

11. Chargaff, E. 1976. On the dangers of genetic meddling. *Science* 192: 938–940.

Vanishing into Dust

12. Freitag, E. 1973. *Schönberg*. Reinbeck: Rowohlt, p. 149.

NAME INDEX

Adams, Henry B.
U.S. historian 130

Adler, Alfred
Austrian psychoanalyst 26

Aeschylus
Greek tragic poet 182

Altenberg, Peter
Austrian writer 17

Anderson, Rudolph J.
U.S. chemist 37, 45–47, 70

Angelico, Fra
Italian painter 133

Arcimboldi, Giuseppe
16th century Italian painter 106

Aristotle
Greek philosopher 122, 163, 168

Artom, Camillo
U.S. biochemist 79

Aschoff, Ludwig
German pathologist 74

Astbury, W. T.
British biophysicist 99

Augustinus, St. Aurelius
Father of the Church 62, 155, 200

Ausonius, Decimus Magnus
late Roman poet 137

Avery, Oswald T.
U.S. microbiologist 82–84, 86, 88–89,
105, 134, 156

Bach, Johann Sebastian
German composer 175

Bacon, Francis
British philosopher 168

Bacon, Roger
British philosopher and scientist 4

Baldwin, Stanley
British statesman 136

Bancroft, Frederic W.
U.S. surgeon 70

Baudelaire, Charles
French poet 135

Beerbohm, Max
British caricaturist and writer 135

Belozersky, Andrei
Russian biochemist 144

Berg, Alban
Austrian composer 16, 26

Bergmann, Ernst
Israeli chemist 50

Bergmann, Max
German-American chemist 75

Bernal, J. D.
British physicist 99

Bernanos, Georges
French writer 18, 186

Blake, William
British poet and artist 17, 44

Bleibtreu, Hedwig
Austrian actress 16

Bloch, Konrad E.
U.S. biochemist 75

Bloy, Léon
French writer 4

Bodenstein, Max
German chemist 50

Böhme, Jakob
German philosopher 112

Borek, Ernest
U.S. biochemist 75

Botticelli, Sandro
Italian painter 94

Brahe, Tycho
Danish astronomer 104

FIFTY YEARS

BIBLIOGRAPHY · 1928-1977

FIFTY YEARS

BIBLIOGRAPHY · 1928-1977

KEY TO CLASSIFICATION

B	Book	**R**	Review article
C	Contribution to book	**S**	Survey of own work
G	General	**T**	Translation
L	Literary		

Scientific papers published in journals are not keyed. Preliminary publications are listed, but not abstracts of papers read at scientific meetings. In a few cases, two symbols are combined; e.g., **C-R** signifies a review article forming part of a book. When an article is a translation of one previously published in another language, this is indicated, together with the year in which the original article appeared; e.g., **T**/70 means that it is the translation of a text listed under 1970.

1928

[WITH] F. Feigl. Über die Reaktionsfähigkeit von Jod in organischen Lösungsmitteln (I.). *Monatshefte für Chemie 49:* 417–428.

[WITH] F. Feigl. Über die analytische Auswertung einer durch CS_2 bewirkten Katalyse zur jodometrischen Bestimmung von Aziden und zum Nachweis von CS_2. *Zeitschrift für analytische Chemie 74:* 376–380.

1929

The Reactivity of Iodine Cyanide in Different Organic Solvents. *J. Am. Chem. Soc. 51:* 1999–2002.

Über die katalytische Zersetzung einiger Jodverbindungen. *Biochemische Zeitschrift 215:* 69–78.

[WITH] R. J. Anderson. The Chemistry of the Lipoids of Tubercle Bacilli. V. Analysis of the Acetone-Soluble Fat. *J. Biol. Chem. 84:* 703–717.

[WITH] R. J. Anderson. The Chemistry of the Lipoids of Tubercle Bacilli. VI. Concerning Tuberculostearic Acid and Phthioic Acid from the Acetone-Soluble Fat. *J. Biol. Chem. 85:* 77–88.

1930

[WITH] R. J. Anderson. Über die Zusammensetzung des gesamten extrahierbaren Fettes der Tuberkelbakterien. Hoppe-Seyler's *Zeitschrift für Physiologische Chemie 191:* 157–165.

[WITH] R. J. Anderson. Über das Vorkommen einer ungesättigten Hexakosansäure im Fett der Tuberkelbakterien. *Ibid.,* 166–171.

[WITH] R. J. Anderson. Ein Polysaccharid aus den Lipoiden der Tuberkelbakterien. *Ibid.,* 172–178.

Zur Kenntnis der Pigmente der Timotheegrasbakterien. *Zentralblatt für Bakteriologie, Parasitenkunde und Infektionskrankheiten 119:* 121–123.

1931

[WITH] M. C. Pangborn and R. J. Anderson. The Chemistry of the Lipoids of Tubercle Bacilli. XXIII. Separation of the Lipoid Fractions from the Timothy Bacillus. *J. Biol. Chem. 90:* 45–55.

Über den gegenwärtigen Stand der chemischen Erforschung des Tuberkelbazillus. *Naturwissenschaften 19:* 202–206. **R**

Neuere Arbeiten über die chemischen und biologischen Eigenschaften der einzelnen Fraktionen der Tuberkelbazillen. *Zeitschrift für Tuberkulose 61:* 142–148. **R**

Über die Charakterisierung von Fetten in geringen Substanzmengen. Hoppe-Seyler's *Zeitschrift für Physiologische Chemie 199:* 221–224.

Zur Chemie der Bakterien. 1. Mitteilung: Über die Lipoide der Diphtheriebakterien. Hoppe-Seyler's *Zeitschrift für Physiologische Chemie 201:* 191–198.

Zur Chemie der Bakterien. 2. Mitteilung: Über die Lipoidverteilung in säurefesten Bakterien. *Ibid.,* 198–207.

1932

Über höhere Fettsäuren mit verzweigter Kohlenstoffkette. *Berichte der Deutschen Chemischen Gesellschaft 65:* 745–754.

[WITH] M. C. Pangborn and R. J. Anderson. The Chemistry of the Lipids of Tubercle Bacilli. XXXI. The Composition of the Acetone-Soluble Fat of the Timothy Bacillus. *J. Biol. Chem. 98:* 43–55.

[WITH] J. Dieryck. Die Pigmente der Sarcina lutea. *Naturwissenschaften 20:* 872–873.

[WITH] J. Dieryck. Über den Lipoidgehalt verschiedener Typen von Tuberkelbazillen. III. Mitteilung: Zur Chemie der Bakterien. *Biochemische Zeitschrift 255:* 319–329.

1933

Über die Lipoide des Bacillus Calmette-Guérin (BCG). Hoppe-Seyler's *Zeitschrift für Physiologische Chemie 217:* 115–137.

Über das Fett und das Phosphatid der Diphtheriebakterien. Hoppe-Seyler's *Zeitschrift für Physiologische Chemie 218:* 223–240.

Sur les carotinoides des bactéries. *Compt. Rend. Acad. Sci. 197:* 946.

Methoden zur Untersuchung der chemischen Zusammensetzung von Bakterien. *Handbuch der biologischen Arbeitsmethoden* (hrsg. E. Abderhalden), Abt. XII, 2, 79–136. **C-R**

1934

Étude des Pigments Caroténoides de Quelques Bactéries. *Annales de l'Institut Pasteur 52:* 415–423.

[WITH] G. Abel. On the Mechanism of the Formation of Choleic Acids. *Biochem. J. 28:* 1901–1906.

1935

[WITH] E. Lederer. Sur les Pigments Caroténoides de Deux Bactéries Acido-Résistantes. *Annales de l'Institut Pasteur 54:* 383–388.

[WITH] W. Schaefer. Analyse Sérologique des Différentes Fractions Lipoidiques du BCG. *Ibid.*, 708–714.

The Chemistry of the Acyclic Constituents of Natural Fats and Oils. *Annual Review of Biochemistry 4:* 79–92. **C-R**

[WITH] W. Schaefer. A Specific Polysaccharide from the Bacillus Calmette-Guérin (BCG). *J. Biol. Chem. 112:* 393–405.

1936

[WITH] M. Levine. Chemical Composition of *Bacterium Tumefaciens. Proc. Soc. Exp. Biol. Med. 34:* 675–677.

[WITH] F. W. Bancroft and M. Stanley-Brown. Studies on the Chemistry of Blood Coagulation. I. The Measurement of the Inhibition of Blood Clotting. Methods and Units. *J. Biol. Chem. 115:* 149–154.

[WITH] F. W. Bancroft and M. Stanley-Brown. Studies on the Chemistry of Blood Coagulation. II. On the Inhibition of Blood Clotting by Substances of High Molecular Weight. *Ibid.*, 155–161.

[WITH] F. W. Bancroft and M. Stanley-Brown. Studies on the Chemistry of Blood Coagulation. III. The Chemical Constituents of Blood Platelets and Their Role in Blood Clotting, with Remarks on the Activation of Clotting by Lipids. *J. Biol. Chem. 116:* 237–251.

1937

The Separation of Choline and Ethanolamine. *J. Biol. Chem. 118:* 417–419.

[WITH] M. Bovarnick. A Method for the Isolation of Glucosamine. *Ibid.*, 421–426.

The Occurrence in Mammalian Tissue of a Lipid Fraction Acting as Inhibitor of Blood Clotting. *Science 85:* 548–549.

[WITH] M. Levine. The Response of Plants to Chemical Fractions of Bacterium Tumefaciens. *American Journal of Botany 24:* 461–472.

Studies on the Chemistry of Blood Coagulation. IV. Lipid Inhibitors of Blood Clotting Occurring in Mammalian Tissue. *J. Biol. Chem. 121:* 175–186.

Studies on the Chemistry of Blood Coagulation. V. Synthetic Cerebroside Sulfuric Acids and Their Action in Blood Clotting. *Ibid.*, 187–193.

[WITH] K. B. Olson. Studies on the Chemistry of Blood Coagulation. VI. Studies on the Action of Heparin and Other Anticoagulants. The Influence of Protamine on the Anticoagulant Effect in Vivo. *J. Biol. Chem. 122:* 153–167.

1938

[WITH] M. Levine. The Lipids of Bacterium Tumefaciens. *J. Biol. Chem. 124:* 195–205.

Synthesis of a Radioactive Organic Compound: Alpha-Glycerophosphoric Acid. *J. Am. Chem. Soc. 60:* 1700.

The Protamine Salts of Phosphatides, with Remarks on the Problem of Lipoproteins. *J. Biol. Chem. 125:* 661–670.

Studies on the Chemistry of Blood Coagulation. VII. Protamines and Blood Clotting. *Ibid.*, 671–676.

Studies on the Chemistry of Blood Coagulation. VIII. Isolation of a Lipid Inhibitor of Blood Clotting from the Spleen in a Case of Niemann-Pick's Disease. *Ibid.*, 677–680.

1939

Unstable Isotopes. I. The Determination of Radioactive Isotopes in Organic Material. *J. Biol. Chem. 128:* 579–585.

Unstable Isotopes. II. The Relative Speed of Formation of Lecithin and Cephalin in the Body. *Ibid.*, 587–595.

[WITH] S. S. Cohen. On Lysophosphatides. *J. Biol. Chem. 129:* 619–628.

The Configuration of Glutamic and Aspartic Acids from Pathogenic Bacteria (Phytomonas Tumefaciens and Corynebacterium Diphtheriae). *J. Biol. Chem. 130:* 29–33.

A Study of the Spleen in a Case of Niemann-Pick Disease. *Ibid.*, 503–511.

[WITH] M. Ziff. The Compounds Between Phosphatides and Basic Proteins. *J. Biol. Chem. 131:* 25–34.

[WITH] M. Ziff and B. M. Hogg. The Reaction Between Cephalin and Hemoglobins. *Ibid.*, 35–44.

1940

[WITH] M. Ziff. The Mechanism of Action of Heparin. *Proc. Soc. Exp. Biol. Med. 43:* 740–742.

[WITH] K. B. Olson and P. F. Partington. The Formation of Phosphatides in the Organism under Normal and Pathological Conditions. *J. Biol. Chem. 134:* 505–514.

[WITH] A. S. Keston. The Metabolism of Aminoethylphosphoric Acid, Followed by Means of the Radioactive Phosphorus Isotope. *Ibid.*, 515–522.

[WITH] M. Ziff and S. S. Cohen. The Conversion of Prothrombin to Thrombin, Followed by Means of the Radioactive Phosphorus Isotope. *J. Biol. Chem. 135:* 351–352.

[WITH] S. S. Cohen. Studies on the Chemistry of Blood Coagulation. IX. The Thromboplastic Protein from Lungs. *J. Biol. Chem. 136:* 243–256.

[WITH] M. Ziff and S. S. Cohen. Studies on the Chemistry of Blood Coagulation. X. The Reaction Between Heparin and the Thromboplastic Factor. *Ibid.*, 257–264.

[WITH] M. Ziff. Studies on the Chemistry of Blood Coagulation XI. The Mode of Action of Heparin. *Ibid.*, 689–695.

1941

[WITH] M. Ziff and D. Rittenberg. Determination of the Bases of Phospholipids by the Isotope Dilution Method. *J. Biol. Chem. 138:* 439–440.

[WITH] M. Ziff. Coagulation of Fibrinogen by Simple Organic Substances as a Model of Thrombin Action. *Ibid.*, 787–788.

[WITH] M. Ziff and D. H. Moore. Studies on the Chemistry of Blood Coagulation. XII. An Electrophoretic Study of the Effect of Anticoagulants on Human Plasma Proteins, with Remarks on the Separation of the Heparin Complement. *J. Biol. Chem. 139:* 383–405.

[WITH] S. S. Cohen. Studies on the Chemistry of Blood Coagulation. XIII. The Phosphatide Constituents of the Thromboplastic Protein from Lungs. *Ibid.*, 741–752.

[WITH] K. J. Palmer and F. O. Schmitt. X-ray Diffraction Studies of Certain Lipide-Protein Complexes. *J. Cell. Comp. Physiol. 18:* 43–47.

[WITH] S. S. Cohen. The Electrophoretic Properties of the Thromboplastic Protein from Lungs. *J. Biol. Chem. 140:* 689–695.

[WITH] M. Ziff. Note on the Isolation of Serine from Beef Brain Phosphatides. *Ibid.*, 927–929.

1942

A Study of Lipoproteins. *J. Biol. Chem.* 142: 491–504.

The Formation of the Phosphorus Compounds in Egg Yolk. *Ibid.*, 505–512.

Fat Metabolism. *Annual Review of Biochemistry 11:* 235–256. **C-R**

[WITH] M. Ziff and D. Rittenberg. A Study of the Nitrogenous Constituents of Tissue Phosphatides. *J. Biol. Chem.* 144: 343–352.

Note on the Mechanism of Conversion of β-Glycerophosphoric Acid into the α Form. *Ibid.*, 455–458.

[WITH] D. H. Moore and A. Bendich. Ultracentrifugal Isolation from Lung Tissue of a Macromolecular Protein Component with Thromboplastic Properties. *J. Biol. Chem.* 145: 593–603.

1943

[WITH] D. B. Sprinson. The Mechanism of Deamination of Serine by Bacterium Coli. *J. Biol. Chem.* 148: 249–250.

[WITH] A. Bendich. On the Coagulation of Fibrinogen. *J. Biol. Chem.* 149: 93–110.

[WITH] A. Bendich. Synthesis of 2-Methyl-1,4-naphthoquinone-8-sulfonic Acid. *J. Am. Chem. Soc.* 65: 1568–1569.

[WITH] D. B. Sprinson. Studies on the Mechanism of Deamination of Serine and Threonine in Biological Systems. *J. Biol. Chem.* 151: 273–280.

1944

[WITH] A. Bendich. The Disintegration of Macromolecular Tissue Lipoproteins. *Science 99:* 147–148.

[WITH] S. S. Cohen. Studies on the Composition of Rickettsia Prowazeki. *J. Biol. Chem.* 154: 691–704.

Lipoproteins. *Advances in Protein Chemistry 1:* 1–24. **C-R**

The Thromboplastic Activity of Tissue Phosphatides. *J. Biol. Chem.* 155: 387–399.

[WITH] D. H. Moore. On Bacterial Glycogen: The Isolation from Avian Tubercle Bacilli of a Polyglucosan of Very High Particle Weight. *Ibid.*, 493–501.

[WITH] A. Bendich and S. S. Cohen. The Thromboplastic Protein: Structure, Properties, Disintegration. *J. Biol. Chem.* 156: 161–178.

1945

The Coagulation of Blood. *Advances in Enzymology 5:* 31–65. **C-R**

Cell Structure and the Problem of Blood Coagulation. *J. Biol. Chem.* 160: 351–359.

The Isolation of Preparations of Thromboplastic Protein from Human Organs. *J. Biol. Chem. 161:* 389–394.

[WITH] L. Recant and F. M. Hanger. Comparison of the Cephalin-Cholesterol Flocculation with the Thymol Turbidity Test. *Proc. Soc. Exp. Biol. Med. 60:* 245–247.

1946

[WITH] D. B. Sprinson. The Occurrence of Hydroxypyruvic Acid in Biological Systems. *J. Biol. Chem. 164:* 411–415.

[WITH] D. B. Sprinson. A Study of β-Hydroxy-α-Keto Acids. *Ibid.*, 417–432.

[WITH] D. B. Sprinson. On Oxidative Decarboxylations with Periodic Acid. *Ibid.*, 433–449.

[WITH] B. Magasanik. Oxidation of Stereoisomers of the Inositol Group of Acetobacter Suboxydans. *J. Biol. Chem. 165:* 379–380.

[WITH] R. West. The Biological Significance of the Thromboplastic Protein of Blood. *J. Biol. Chem. 166:* 189–197.

[WITH] A. Bendich. The Isolation and Characterization of Two Antigenic Fractions of Proteus OX-19. *Ibid.*, 283–312.

1947

[WITH] S. Zamenhof. Highly Polymerized Desoxypentose Nucleic Acid from Yeast. *J. Am. Chem. Soc. 69:* 975.

[WITH] E. Vischer. The Separation and Characterization of Purines in Minute Amounts of Nucleic Acid Hydrolysates. *J. Biol. Chem. 168:* 781–782.

[WITH] B. Magasanik. The Action of Periodic Acid on Glucose Phenylosazone. *J. Am. Chem. Soc. 69:* 1459–1461.

On the Nucleoproteins and Nucleic Acids of Microorganisms. *Cold Spring Harbor Symposia on Quantitative Biology 12:* 28–34. **C-R**

Studies on the Mechanism of the Thromboplastic Effect. *J. Biol. Chem. 173:* 253–262.

[WITH] C. Green. On the Inhibition of the Thromboplastic Effect. *Ibid.*, 263–270.

1948

[WITH] S. Zamenhof. The Isolation of Highly Polymerized Desoxypentosenucleic Acid from Yeast Cells. *J. Biol. Chem. 173:* 327–335.

[WITH] B. Magasanik. The Stereochemistry of an Enzymatic Reaction: The Oxidation of *l*-, *d*-, and *epi*-Inositol by Acetobacter Suboxydans. *J. Biol. Chem. 174:* 173–188.

[WITH] B. Magasanik. The Action of Periodic Acid on a Cyclohexose Osazone. *J. Am. Chem. Soc. 70:* 1928–1929.

Recent Work on Lipoproteins as Cellular Constituents. *Proc. 6th Internatl. Congr. Exp. Cytol.* 24–31. **C-S**

[WITH] Ernst Vischer. Nucleoproteins, Nucleic Acids, and Related Substances. *Annual Review of Biochemistry,* 201–226. **C-R**

[WITH] C. Levine and C. Green. Techniques for the Demonstration by Chromatography of Nitrogenous Lipide Constituents, Sulfur-Containing Amino Acids, and Reducing Sugars. *J. Biol. Chem. 175:* 67–71.

Le Rôle des Lipides et des Lipoprotéines dans la Structure Cellulaire. *Archives des Sciences Physiologiques 2:* 157–167. **S**

Remarks on the Role of Lipids in Blood Coagulation. *Ibid.,* 269–271. **S**

[WITH] B. Magasanik. The Structure of a New Cyclohexose Produced from *d*-Inositol by Biological Oxidation. *J. Biol. Chem. 175:* 929–937.

[WITH] B. Magasanik. The Oxidation of *d*-Quercitol by Acetobacter Suboxydans. *Ibid.,* 939–943.

[WITH] J. Kream. Procedure for the Study of Certain Enzymes in Minute Amounts and its Application to the Investigation of Cytosine Deaminase. *Ibid.,* 993–994.

[WITH] E. Vischer. The Separation and Quantitative Estimation of Purines and Pyrimidines in Minute Amounts. *J. Biol. Chem. 176:* 703–714.

[WITH] E. Vischer. The Composition of the Pentose Nucleic Acids of Yeast and Pancreas. *Ibid.,* 715–734.

[WITH] R. N. Stewart and B. Magasanik. Inhibition of Mitotic Poisoning by meso-Inositol. *Science 108:* 556–558.

[WITH] S. Zamenhof. Desoxypentosenuclease in Yeast and Specific Nature of Its Cellular Regulation. *Ibid.,* 628–629.

1949

[WITH] E. Vischer, R. Doniger, C. Green, and F. Misani. The Composition of the Desoxypentose Nucleic Acids of Thymus and Spleen. *J. Biol. Chem. 177:* 405–416.

[WITH] H. F. Saidel. On the Nucleoproteins of Avian Tubercle Bacilli. *Ibid.,* 417–428.

[WITH] E. Vischer and S. Zamenhof. Microbial Nucleic Acids: The Desoxypentose Nucleic Acids of Avian Tubercle Bacilli and Yeast. *Ibid.,* 429–438.

[WITH] S. Zamenhof. Evidence of the Existence of a Core in Desoxyribonucleic Acids. *J. Biol. Chem. 178:* 531–532.

[WITH] B. Magasanik, R. Doniger and E. Vischer. The Nucleotide Composition of Ribonucleic Acids. *J. Am. Chem. Soc. 71:* 1513.

[WITH] S. Zamenhof. Studies on the Desoxypentose Nuclease of Yeast and its Specific Cellular Regulation. *J. Biol. Chem. 180:* 727–740.

[WITH] A. Nyman. On the Lipoprotein Particles of Yeast Cells. *Ibid.*, 741–746.

Recent Studies on Cellular Lipo-Proteins. *Faraday Society Discussion*, No. 6, 118–124. **S**

[WITH] M. Goldenberg, M. Faber, and E. J. Alston. Evidence for the Occurence of Nor-Epinephrine in the Adrenal Medulla. *Science 109:* 534–535.

New Yorker Satiren (I. Krieg; II. Die bösen Elemente; III. Radio), *Die Wandlung 4:* 498–500. **L**

1950

[WITH] S. Zamenhof and L. B. Shettles. Human Desoxypentose Nucleic Acid; Isolation of Desoxypentose Nucleic Acid from Human Sperm. *Nature 165:* 756.

[WITH] S. Zamenhof and C. Green. Composition of Human Desoxypentose Nucleic Acid. *Ibid.*, 756–757.

Chemical Specificity of Nucleic Acid and Mechanism of their Enzymatic Degradation. *Experientia 6:* 201–209. **S**

[WITH] C. Levine, C. Green, and J. Kream. Study of Some Constituents of Vitamin B_{12}. *Ibid.*, 229.

[WITH] B. Magasanik, E. Vischer, R. Doniger, and D. Elson. The Separation and Estimation of Ribonucleotides in Minute Quantities. *J. Biol. Chem. 186:* 37–50.

[WITH] B. Magasanik, E. Vischer, C. Green, R. Doniger, and D. Elson. Nucleotide Composition of Pentose Nucleic Acids from Yeast and Mammalian Tissues. *Ibid.*, 51–67.

[WITH] S. Zamenhof. Studies on the Diversity and the Native State of Desoxypentose Nucleic Acids. *Ibid.*, 207–219.

[WITH] S. Zamenhof. Dissymmetry in Nucleotide Sequence of Desoxypentose Nucleic Acids. *J. Biol. Chem. 187:* 1–14.

[WITH] S. Zamenhof, G. Brawerman, and L. Kerin. Bacterial Desoxypentose Nucleic Acids of Unusual Composition. *J. Am. Chem. Soc. 72:* 3825.

1951

[WITH] M. R. Murray and H. H. de Lam. Specific Inhibition by meso-Inositol of the Colchicine Effect on Rat Fibroblasts. *Experimental Cell Research 2:* 165–177.

Some Recent Studies on the Composition and Structure of Nucleic Acids. *J. Cell. Comp. Physiol. 38* (suppl. 1): 41–59. **S**

[WITH] B. Magasanik. Studies on the Structure of Ribonucleic Acids, *Biochim. Biophys. Acta 7:* 396–412.

[WITH] R. Lipshitz, C. Green, and M. E. Hodes. The Composition of the Desoxyribonucleic Acid of Salmon Sperm. *J. Biol. Chem. 192:* 223–230.

[WITH] C. Levine. Procedures for the Microestimation of Nitrogenous Phosphatide Constituents. *Ibid.*, 465–479.

[WITH] C. Levine. Chromatographic Behavior of Analogues of the Nitrogenous Lipide Constituents. *Ibid.*, 481–483.

Structure and Function of Nucleic Acid as Cell Constituents. *Federation Proceedings 10:* 654–659. **S**

[WITH] G. Brawerman. Enzymatic Disintegration of Wheat Germ Desoxypentose Nucleic Acid. *J. Am. Chem. Soc. 73:* 4052.

[WITH] S. Zamenhof. Separation of Desoxypentose and Pentose Nucleic Acids. *Nature 168:* 604–605.

[WITH] C. Tamm. Specific Requirements for the Action of Deoxyribonuclease. *Ibid.*, 916–917.

[WITH] R. E. Franzl. Bacterial Enzyme Preparations Oxidizing Inositol and Their Inhibition by Colchicine. *Ibid.*, 955–957.

1952

[WITH] C. Levine. Phosphatide Composition in Different Liver Cell Fractions. *Experimental Cell Research 3:* 154–162.

[WITH] C. Tamm and M. E. Hodes. The Formation of Apurinic Acid from the Desoxyribonucleic Acid of Calf Thymus. *J. Biol. Chem. 195:* 49–63.

[WITH] R. Lipshitz and C. Green. Composition of the Desoxypentose Nucleic Acids of Four Genera of Sea-Urchin. *Ibid.*, 155–160.

[WITH] B. Magasanik and R. E. Franzl. The Stereochemical Specificity of the Oxidation of Cyclitols by *Acetobacter Suboxydans. J. Am. Chem. Soc. 74:* 2618–2621.

[WITH] D. Elson. On the Desoxyribonucleic Acid Content of Sea Urchin Gametes. *Experientia 8:* 143.

[WITH] J. Kream. Procedures for the Study of Purine and Pyrimidine Deaminases in Small Amounts. *J. Am. Chem. Soc. 74:* 4274–4277.

[WITH] J. Kream. On the Cytosine Deaminase of Yeast. *Ibid.*, 5157–5160.

The Nucleic Acids of Microorganisms. *Symposium sur le Métabolisme Microbien, 2ᵉ Congrès International de Biochimie*, Paris, 41–46. **R**

[WITH] B. Gandelman and S. Zamenhof. The Desoxypentose Nucleic Acids of Three Strains of *Escherichia coli*. *Biochim. Biophys. Acta 9:* 399–401.

[WITH] S. Zamenhof and G. Brawerman. On the Desoxypentose Nucleic Acids from Several Microorganisms. *Ibid.*, 402–405.

[WITH] S. Zamenhof, G. Leidy, H. E. Alexander, and P. L. Fitz-Gerald. Purification of the Desoxypentose Nucleic Acid of *Hemophilus influenzae* Having Transforming Activity. *Archives Biochem. Biophys. 40:* 50–55.

[WITH] C. Tamm and H. S. Shapiro. Correlation Between the Action of Pancreatic Desoxyribonuclease and the Nature of its Substrates. *J. Biol. Chem. 199:* 313–327.

[WITH] D. Elson. Observations on Pentose Nucleic Acid Composition in Sea Urchin Embryos and in Mammalian Cell Fractions. *Phosphorus Metabolism*, Vol. 2. The Johns Hopkins Press, Baltimore, 329–335. **C-S**

1953

[WITH] C. Tamm, H. S. Shapiro, and R. Lipshitz. Distribution of Nucleotides Within a Desoxyribonucleic Acid Chain. *J. Biol. Chem. 203:* 673–688.

[WITH] C. Tamm. Physical and Chemical Properties of the Apurinic Acid of Calf Thymus. *Ibid.*, 689–694.

[WITH] S. Zamenhof, G. Leidy, P.L. FitzGerald, and H. E. Alexander. Polyribophosphate, the Type-Specific Substance of Hemophilus Influenzae, Type b. *Ibid.*, 695–704.

Introductory Remarks to the Symposium on Conjugated Proteins, in: Some Conjugated Proteins (ed. W. H. Cole), Rutgers University Press, New Brunswick, N.J., p.1. **G**

On the Problem of Nucleoproteins, *Ibid.*, 36–42. **R**

[WITH] G. Brawerman. Enzymatic Phosphorylation of Nucleosides by Phosphate Transfer. *J. Am. Chem. Soc. 75:* 2020.

[WITH] R. Lipshitz. Composition of Mammalian Desoxyribonucleic Acids. *Ibid.*, 3658–3661.

[WITH] C. G. Crampton and R. Lipshitz. Separation of Calf Thymus Deoxyribonucleic Acid into Fractions of Different Composition. *Nature 172:* 289–292.

[WITH] H. H. Benitez and M. R. Murray. Antagonism between Tropolone and Colchicine in Rat Fibroblast Cultures. *Experientia 9:* 426.

[WITH] G. Brawerman. Nucleotide Synthesis by Malt and Prostate Phosphatases. *J. Am. Chem. Soc. 75:* 4113.

1954

[WITH] J. N. Hawthorne. A Study of Inositol-Containing Lipides. *J. Biol. Chem. 206:* 27–37.

[WITH] C. F. Crampton and R. Lipshitz. Studies on Nucleoproteins. I. Dissociation and Reassociation of the Deoxyribonucleohistone of Calf Thymus. *Ibid.,* 499–510.

[WITH] D. Elson and T. Gustafson. The Nucleic Acids of the Sea-Urchin During Embryonic Development. *J. Biol. Chem. 209:* 285–294.

[WITH] D. Elson. Regularities in the Composition of Pentose Nucleic Acids. *Nature 173:* 1037–1038.

Chemistry of Inositol, in: *The Vitamins,* (ed. W.H. Sebrell and R.S. Harris), Academic Press Inc., New York, N.Y., Vol. 2. 329–338. **C-R**

[WITH] G. Brawerman. On a Deoxyribonuclease from Germinating Barley. *J. Biol. Chem. 210:* 445–454.

[WITH] C. F. Crampton and R. Lipshitz. Studies on Nucleoproteins. II. Fractionation of Deoxyribonucleic Acids Through Fractional Dissociation of Their Complexes with Basic Proteins. *J. Biol. Chem. 211:* 125–142.

[WITH] G. Brawerman. On the Synthesis of Nucleotides by Nucleoside Phosphotransferases. *Biochim. Biophys. Acta 15:* 549–559.

[WITH] H. H. Benitez and M.R. Murray. Studies on Inhibition of the Colchicine Effect on Mitosis. *Annals N.Y. Acad. Sci. 58:* 1288–1302.

[WITH] S. Hörstadius and I. J. Lorch. The Effect of Deoxyribonucleic Acids Extracted from Sea Urchin Sperm on the Development of Sea Urchin Eggs. *Experimental Cell Research 6:* 440–452.

1955

[WITH] J. N. Davidson (editors). *The Nucleic Acids — Chemistry and Biology,* Academic Press, New York. Vol. 1, 692 pp.; Vol. 2, 576 pp. **B**

[WITH] J. N. Davidson. Introduction, in: *The Nucleic Acids.* Vol. 1, 1–8. **C-G**

Isolation and Composition of the Deoxypentose Nucleic Acids and of the Corresponding Nucleoproteins, in: *The Nucleic Acids.* Vol. 1, 307–371. **C-R**

[WITH] G. Brawerman. On the Distribution and Biological Significance of the Nucleoside Phosphotransferases. *Biochim. Biophys. Acta 16:* 524–532.

Deoxypentose Nucleoproteins and Their Prosthetic Groups, in: *Fibrous Proteins and Their Biological Significance. Symposia of the Society for Experimental Biology 9:* 32–48. **C-S**

Remarks on the Physiological Importance of the Nucleoside Phospho-transferases. *Ann. Acad. Scient. Fennicae*, A.II. *60:* 447–454. **s**

[WITH] P. Spitnik and R. Lipshitz. Studies on Nucleoproteins. III. Deoxyribonucleic Acid Complexes with Basic Polyelectrolytes and Their Fractional Extraction. *J. Biol. Chem. 215:* 765–775.

[WITH] D. Elson and L. W. Trent. The Nucleotide Composition of Pentose Nucleic Acids in Different Cellular Fractions. *Biochim. Biophys. Acta 17:* 362–366.

[WITH] D. Elson. Evidence of Common Regularities in the Composition of Pentose Nucleic Acids. *Ibid.*, 367–376.

[WITH] H. S. Shapiro. Remarks on Deoxyribonuclease. *Experimental Cell Research*, Suppl. 3, 64–71.

On the Chemistry and Function of Nucleoproteins and Nucleic Acids. *Istituto Lombardo (Red. Sc.) 89:* 101–115. **R**

Remarks on the Biochemistry of the Inositols. Society of Biological Chemists, India: Souvenir, 222–226. **s**

Mit heissen Wangen. *Du 15:* Nr.11, 70. **L**

1956

The Very Big and the Very Small—Remarks on Conjugated Proteins, in: *Essays in Biochemistry* (ed. S. Graff), Wiley, New York, 72–76. **C-G**

[WITH] R. Lipshitz. Studies on Nucleoproteins. IV. Preparation of the Deoxyribonucleoprotein and Fractionation of the Deoxyribonucleic Acid of Wheat Germ. *Biochim. Biophys. Acta 19:* 256–266.

[WITH] A. Rosenberg and C. Howe. Inhibition of Influenza Virus Haemagglutination by a Brain Lipid Fraction. *Nature 177:* 234–235.

[WITH] A. Lombard. The Pentose Nucleic Acid of Azotobacter Vinelandii. *Biochim. Biophys. Acta 20:* 585–586.

[WITH] M. Tunis. Separation of Nucleoside Phosphotransferase and Phosphatase Activities. *Biochim. Biophys. Acta 21:* 204–205.

[WITH] A. Rosenberg. Nitrogenous Constituents of an Ox Brain Mucolipid. *Ibid.*, 588–590.

[WITH] M. E. Hodes. The Apurinic Acids from Deoxyribonucleic Acid Fractions. *Biochim. Biophys. Acta 22:* 348–360.

[WITH] M. E. Hodes. Note on the Action of Deoxyribonuclease on Fractions of Calf Thymus Deoxyribonucleic Acid. *Ibid.*, 361–364.

[WITH] D. Elson and H. T. Shigeura. The Stoichiometric Relationship between Amino-Acid and Nucleotide Residues in a Ribonucleoprotein. *Nature 178:* 682–684.

1957

Base Composition of Deoxypentose and Pentose Nucleic Acids in Various Species, in: *The Chemical Basis of Heredity* (ed. W.D. McElroy and B. Glass), The Johns Hopkins Press, Baltimore, 521–527. **C-R**

[WITH] C. F. Crampton. Studies on Nucleoproteins. V. Interactions. *J. Biol. Chem. 226:* 157–164.

[WITH] H. S. Shapiro. Characterization of Nucleotide Arrangement in Deoxyribonucleic Acids Through Stepwise Acid Degradation. *Biochim. Biophys. Acta 23:* 451–452.

[WITH] M. Tunis. Nonparticipation of Inorganic Phosphate in the Enzymic Formation of Nucleotides by Nucleoside Phosphotransferases. *Archives of Biochemistry and Biophysics 69:* 295–299.

[WITH] H. T. Shigeura. Comparative Studies of Protein and Ribonucleic Acid Formation. *Biochim. Biophys. Acta 24:* 450–451.

[WITH] A. Lombard. Aspects of the Invariability of a Bacterial Ribonucleic Acid. *Biochim. Biophys. Acta 25:* 549–554.

[WITH] H. M. Schulman and H. S. Shapiro. Protoplasts of *E. Coli* as Sources and Acceptors of Deoxypentose Nucleic Acid: Rehabilitation of a Deficient Mutant. *Nature 180:* 851–852.

[WITH] H. S. Shapiro. Studies on the Nucleotide Arrangement in Deoxyribonucleic Acids. I. The Relationship between the Production of Pyrimidine Nucleoside 3′,5′-Diphosphates and Specific Features of Nucleotide Sequence. *Biochim. Biophys. Acta 26:* 596–608.

[WITH] H. S. Shapiro. Studies on the Nucleotide Arrangement in Deoxyribonucleic Acids. II. Differential Analysis of Pyrimidine Nucleotide Distribution as a Method of Characterization. *Ibid.*, 608–623.

1958

Of Nucleic Acids and Nucleoproteins. The Harvey Lectures, 1956–1957, Academic Press Inc., New York, 57–73. **C-S**

Novye Issledovaniya po Spetsifichnosti Nukleinovykh Kislot (Recent Studies on Nucleic Acid Specificity). *Bull. Acad. Sci. USSR*, Biol. Series, Nr.2, 144–148. **S**

[WITH] A. Rosenberg. A Study of a Mucolipide from Ox Brain. *J. Biol. Chem. 232:* 1031–1049.

[WITH] J. Horowitz and J. J. Saukkonen. Effect of 5-Fluorouracil on a Uracil-Requiring Mutant of *Escherichia coli*. *Biochim. Biophys. Acta 29:* 222–223.

[WITH] T. Tsumita. Studies on Nucleoproteins. VI. The Deoxyribonucleoprotein and the Deoxyribonucleic Acid of Bovine Tubercle Bacilli (BCG). *Ibid.*, 568–578.

[WITH] H. T. Shigeura. Fractionation of the "Soluble" Ribonucleic Acid of Rat-Liver Cytoplasm. *Biochim. Biophys. Acta 30:* 434–435.

[WITH] H. T. Shigeura. Studies of the Dynamics of Ribonucleic Acid Formation. *J. Biol. Chem. 233:* 197–202.

[WITH] A. Rosenberg. A Reinvestigation of the Cerebroside Deposited in Gaucher's Disease. *Ibid.*, 1323–1326

[WITH] J. Horowitz and A. Lombard. Aspects of the Stability of a Bacterial Ribonucleic Acid. *Ibid.*, 1517–1522.

1959

[WITH] A. Rosenberg. Some Observations on the Mucolipids of Normal and Tay-Sachs' Disease Brain Tissue. *A.M.A.J. of Diseases of Children*, Part II, *97:* 739–744.

[WITH] H. H. Benitez and M. R. Murray. Heteromorphic Change of Adult Fibroblasts by Ribonucleoproteins. *J. Biophys. Biochem. Cytology 5:* 25–34.

[WITH] G. Brawerman. Changes in Protein and Ribonucleic Acid During the Formation of Chloroplasts in *Euglena Gracilis. Biochim. Biophys. Acta 31:* 164–171.

[WITH] G. Brawerman. Relation of Ribonucleic Acid to the Photosynthetic Apparatus in *Euglena Gracilis. Ibid.*, 172–177.

[WITH] G. Brawerman. Factors Involved in the Development of Chloroplasts in *Euglena Gracilis. Ibid.*, 178–186.

First Steps Towards a Chemistry of Heredity, in: Fourth International Congress of Biochemistry, *14*, Transactions of the Plenary Sessions, Pergamon Press, 21–35. **C-G**

Aspects of Nucleic Acid Fractionation, Congress of the International Society of Hematology, Rome, 1958. *Haematologica Latina*, Suppl.2, 5–8. **C-G**

Nucleic Acids as Carriers of Biological Information, in: *The Origin of Life on the Earth*, Pergamon Press, 297–302. **C-S**

[WITH] Jack Horowitz. Massive Incorporation of 5-Fluorouracil into a Bacterial Ribonucleic Acid. *Nature 184:* 1213–1215.

1960

[WITH] G. Brawerman. A Self-Reproducing System Concerned With the Formation of Chloroplasts in *Euglena Gracilis. Biochim. Biophys. Acta 37:* 221–229.

[WITH] M. Tunis. Studies on the Nucleoside Phosphotransferase of Carrot. I. Partial Purification of the Nucleoside Phosphotransferase. *Ibid.*, 257–266.

[WITH] M. Tunis. Studies on the Nucleoside Phosphotransferase of Carrot. II. Separation of Transferase and Phosphatase Activities. *Ibid.*, 267–273.

[WITH] H. T. Shigeura. Action of Ribonuclease on a Microsomal Ribonucleoprotein. *Ibid.*, 347–349.

[WITH] H. S. Shapiro. Studies on the Nucleotide Arrangement in Deoxyribonucleic Acids. III. Identification of Methylcytidine Derivatives Among the Acid Degradation Products of Rye Germ DNA. *Biochim. Biophys. Acta 39:* 62–67.

[WITH] H. S. Shapiro. Studies on the Nucleotide Arrangement in Deoxyribonucleic Acids. IV. Patterns of Nucleotide Sequence in the Deoxyribonucleic Acid of Rye Germ and its Fractions. *Ibid.*, 68–82.

[WITH] M. Tunis. Studies on the Nucleoside Phosphotransferase of Carrot. III. On the Synthetic Ability of the Transfer Enzyme. *Biochim. Biophys. Acta 40:* 206–210.

[WITH] A. Rosenberg. Type of Attachment of Sialic Acid in Ox-Brain Mucolipid. *Biochim. Biophys. Acta 42:* 357–359.

[WITH] J. D. Karkas. Methylation Studies on Ox-Brain Mucolipid. *Ibid.*, 359–360.

[WITH] R. Lipshitz. Studies on the Fractionation of Ribonucleic Acid. *Ibid.*, 544–546.

[WITH] F. Goodman and J. J. Saukkonen. Patterns of Cellular Controls Operating in Bacteriophage Reproduction. I. Effect of 5-Fluorouracil on the Multiplication of Several Coliphages. *Biochim. Biophys. Acta 44:* 458–468.

[WITH] J. J. Saukkonen and F. Goodman. Patterns of Cellular Controls Operating in Bacteriophage Reproduction. II. Effect of 5-Fluorouracil on Metabolic Events in Bacteria Infected with Coliphage T_{2r+}. *Ibid.*, 469–477.

[WITH] G. Brawerman and C. A. Rebman. A Bleached Variant of *Euglena Gracilis* Showing a Doubling of the Content of Deoxyribonucleic Acid. *Nature 187:* 1037–1038.

[WITH] J. Horowitz and J. J. Saukkonen. Effects of Fluoropyrimidines on the Synthesis of Bacterial Proteins and Nucleic Acids. *J. Biol. Chem. 235:* 3266–3272.

[WITH] A. Rosenberg and B. Binnie. Properties of a Purified Sialidase and its Action on Brain Mucolipid. *J. Am. Chem. Soc. 82:* 4113–4114.

[WITH] H. S. Shapiro. Severe Distortion by 5-Bromouracil of the Sequence Characteristics of a Bacterial Deoxyribonucleic Acid. *Nature 188:* 62–63.

[WITH] J. N. Davidson (editors). *The Nucleic Acids — Chemistry and Biology*, Academic Press, New York and London. Vol. 3, XVI and 588 pp.

B

1961

[WITH] G. Brawerman and A. O. Pogo. Synthesis of Novel Ribonucleic Acids and Proteins During Chloroplast Formation in Resting *Euglena* Cells. *Biochim. Biophys. Acta 48:* 418–420.

[WITH] J. H. Spencer. Pyrimidine Nucleotide Sequences in Deoxyribonucleic Acids. *Biochim. Biophys. Acta 51:* 209–211.

1962

[WITH] G. Brawerman and A. O. Pogo. Induced Formation of Ribonucleic Acids and Plastid Protein in *Euglena Gracilis* under the Influence of Light. *Biochim. Biophys. Acta 55:* 326–334.

[WITH] R. Rudner. Sequential Arrangement of 5-Bromouracil as a Tool for the Study of the Replication of Deoxyribonucleic Acid. *Ibid.*, 997–999.

[WITH] A. O. Pogo and G. Brawerman. New Ribonucleic Acid Species Associated with the Formation of the Photosynthetic Apparatus in *Euglena Gracilis*. *Biochem. 1:* 128–131.

The Problem of the Primary Structure of the Deoxyribonucleic Acids, in: *Semaine d'Étude sur le Problème des Macromolécules d'Intérêt Biologique*. Pontificiae Academiae Scientiarum Scripta Varia 22, 39–52.

S

[WITH] N. Z. Stanacev. Icosisphingosine, a Long-Chain Base Constituent of Mucolipids. *Biochim. Biophys. Acta 59:* 733–734.

Calculated Composition of a 'Messenger' Ribonucleic Acid. *Nature 194:* 86–87.

[WITH] R. Rudner and H. S. Shapiro. Distribution of 5-Bromouracil Among the Pyrimidine Clusters of the Deoxyribonucleic Acid of *E. Coli*. *Nature 195:* 143–146.

[WITH] G. Brawerman and D. A. Hufnagel. On the Nucleic Acids of Green and Colorless *Euglena Gracilis*: Isolation and Composition of Deoxyribonucleic Acid and of Transfer Ribonucleic Acid. *Biochim. Biophys. Acta 61:* 340–345.

[WITH] A. M. Haywood and E. D. Gray. Pulse-Labeled Ribonucleic Acid of *Rhodopseudomonas Spheroides* in the Presence and Absence of Massive Catalase Formation. *Ibid.*, 155–156.

1963

Essays on Nucleic Acids, Elsevier, Amsterdam, London, New York, IX and 211 pp. **B**

The Problem of Nucleotide Sequence in Deoxyribonucleic Acids. *Ibid.*, 126–160. **C-S**

A Few Remarks on Nucleic Acids, Decoding, and the Rest of the World. *Ibid.*, 161–173. **C-G**

Amphisbaena. *Ibid.*, 174–199. **C-G**

[WITH] J. H. Spencer. Studies on the Nucleotide Arrangement in Deoxyribonucleic Acids. V. Pyrimidine Nucleotide Clusters: Isolation and Characterization. *Biochim. Biophys. Acta 68:* 9–17.

[WITH] J. H. Spencer. Studies on the Nucleotide Arrangement in Deoxyribonucleic Acids. VI. Pyrimidine Nucleotide Clusters: Frequency and Distribution in Several Species of the AT-Type. *Ibid.*, 18–27.

[WITH] S. Morisawa. 2'-O-Methylribonucleosides Participating in Alkali-Resistant Sequences of Ribonucleic Acid. *Ibid.*, 147–149.

[WITH] O. W. Garrigan. Studies on the Mucolipids and the Cerebrosides of Chicken Brain During Embryonic Development. *Biochim. Biophys. Acta 70:* 452–464.

[WITH] H. S. Shapiro. Studies on the Nucleotide Arrangement in Deoxyribonucleic Acids. VII. Direct Estimation of Pyrimidine Nucleotide Runs. *Biochim. Biophys. Acta 76:* 1–8.

[WITH] P. Rüst, A. Temperli, S. Morisawa, and A. Danon. Investigation of the Purine Sequences in Deoxyribonucleic Acids. *Ibid.*, 149–151.

[WITH] R. Lipshitz-Wiesner. An Investigation of the Fractionation and Sequential Characterization of the Ribonucleic Acids of Rat Liver. *Ibid.*, 372–390.

1964

Dialog o Molekulyarnoy Biologii. *Agrobiologiya*, Nr.5, 665–681. T/63.

Nekotorye Zamechaniya o Nukleinovykh Kislotakh, o Dekodirovanii i obo Vsem Prochem. *Agrobiologiya*, Nr.6, 825–833. T/63.

[WITH] J. D. Karkas. Studies on the Stability of Simple Derivatives of Sialic Acid. *J. Biol. Chem. 239:* 949–957.

[WITH] E. D. Gray and A. M. Haywood. Rapidly Labeled Ribonucleic Acids of *Rhodopseudomonas Spheroides* under Varying Conditions of Catalase Synthesis. *Biochim. Biophys. Acta 87:* 397–415.

Aspects of the Nucleotide Sequence in Nucleic Acids, in: *New Perspectives in Biology* (ed. M. Sela), Elsevier Publishing Co., Amsterdam-London-New York, 85–91. **C-S**

[WITH] E. D. Bransome, Jr. Synthesis of Ribonucleic Acids in the Adrenal Cortex: Early Effects of Adrenocorticotropic Hormone. *Biochim. Biophys. Acta 91:* 180–182.

[WITH] H. S. Shapiro. Studies on the Nucleotide Arrangement in Deoxyribonucleic Acids. VIII. A Comparison of Procedures for the Determination of the Frequency of Pyrimidine Nucleotide Runs. *Ibid.*, 262–270.

[WITH] A. Temperli, H. Türler, P. Rüst, and A. Danon. Studies on the Nucleotide Arrangement in Deoxyribonucleic Acids. IX. Selective Degradation of Pyrimidine Deoxyribonucleotides. *Ibid.*, 462–476.

[WITH] H. J. Lin. Metaphase Chromosomes as a Source of DNA. *Ibid.*, 691–694.

[WITH] R. Rudner and B. Prokop-Schneider. Rhythmic Alterations in the Rate of Synthesis and the Composition of Rapidly Labelled Ribonucleic Acid During the Synchronous Growth of Bacteria. *Nature 203:* 479–483.

1965

[WITH] N. Z. Stanacev. Studies on the Chemistry of Mucolipids: Occurrence of the Long-Chain Base Icosisphingosine, Composition of Fatty Acids, Fractionation Attempts. *Biochim. Biophys. Acta 98:* 168–181.

[WITH] H. S. Shapiro, R. Rudner, and K-I. Miura. Inferences from the Distribution of Pyrimidine Isostichs in Deoxyribonucleic Acids. *Nature 205:* 1068–1070.

[WITH] J. Buchowicz, H. Türler, and H. S. Shapiro. A Direct Test of Antiparallelism in Complementary Sequences of Calf Thymus Deoxyribonucleic Acid. *Nature 206:* 145–147.

[WITH] J. D. Karkas and H. Türler. Studies on the Specification of Accessory Biochemical Characters, as Exemplified by the Fatty Acid Patterns of Various Strains of *Escherichia Coli*. *Biochim. Biophys. Acta 111:* 96–109.

On Some of the Biological Consequences of Base-Pairing in the Nucleic Acids, in: *Developmental and Metabolic Control Mechanisms and Neoplasia*, The Williams & Wilkins Company, Baltimore, Maryland, 7–25. **C-G**

[WITH] R. Rudner and E. Rejman. Genetic Implications of Periodic Pulsations of the Rate of Synthesis and the Composition of Rapidly Labeled Bacterial RNA. *Proc. Natl. Acad. Sci. U.S.A. 54:* 904–911.

[WITH] T. Andoh. Formation and Fate of Abnormal Ribosomes of *E. Coli* Cells Treated with 5-Fluorouracil. *Ibid.*, 1181–1189.

1966

[with] H. J. Lin. On the Denaturation of Deoxyribonucleic Acid. *Biochim. Biophys. Acta 123:* 66–75.

[with] R. Rudner and H. S. Shapiro. Studies on the Nucleotide Arrangement in Deoxyribonucleic Acids. X. Frequency and Composition of Pyrimidine Isostichs in Microbial Deoxyribonucleic Acids and in the DNA of *E. Coli* Phage T_3. *Biochim. Biophys. Acta 129:* 85–103.

[with] H. S. Shapiro. Studies on the Nucleotide Arrangement in Deoxyribonucleic Acids. XI. Selective Removal of Cytosine as a Tool for the Study of the Nucleotide Arrangement in Deoxyribonucleic Acid. *Biochem. 5:* 3012–3018.

[with] J. D. Karkas. Template Functions in the Enzymic Formation of Polyribonucleotides, I. Integrity of the DNA Template. *Proc. Natl. Acad. Sci. U.S.A. 56:* 664–671.

[with] H. J. Lin and J. D. Karkas. Template Functions in the Enzymic Formation of Polyribonucleotides, II. Metaphase Chromosomes as Templates in the Enzymic Synthesis of Ribonucleic Acids. *Ibid.*, 954–959.

[with] J. D. Karkas. Template Functions in the Enzymic Formation of Polyribonucleotides, III. Apurinic Acid as Template. *Ibid.*, 1241–1246.

1967

[with] H. J. Lin. On the Denaturation of Deoxyribonucleic Acid, II. Effects of Concentration. *Biochim. Biophys. Acta 145:* 398–409.

[with] R. Rudner, H. J. Lin, and S. E. M. Hoffmann. Studies on the Loss and the Restoration of the Transforming Activity of the Deoxyribonucleic Acid of *Bacillus Subtilis. Biochim. Biophys. Acta 149:* 199–219.

[with] E. F. Brunngraber. Purification and Properties of a Nucleoside Phosphotransferase from Carrot. *J. Biol. Chem. 242:* 4834–4840.

[with] F. E. Farber. Studies on the Specificity of the Enzymic Synthesis of Polyribonucleotides. *European J. Biochem. 2:* 433–441.

[with] J. D. Karkas. Template Functions in the Enzymic Formation of Polyribonucleotides, IV. Denatured DNA as Template. *Proc. Natl. Acad. Sci. U.S.A. 58:* 1645–1651.

Remarks, in: *Reflections on Research and the Future of Medicine* (ed. C.E. Lyght), McGraw-Hill Book Co., 25–26. **C-G**

1968

[with] H. S. Shapiro. Remarks on Sequence Characteristics of the DNA and Transfer RNA of Yeast. *Proc. Natl. Acad. Sci. U.S.A. 59:* 161–163.

What Really Is DNA? Remarks on the Changing Aspects of a Scientific Concept, in: *Progress in Nucleic Acid Research*, Academic Press Inc., New York. Vol. 8, 297–333. **C-R**

A Quick Climb Up Mount Olympus. *Science 159:* 1448–1449. **G**

[WITH] R. Rudner and J. D. Karkas. Separation of *B. Subtilis* DNA Into Complementary Strands. I. Biological Properties. *Proc. Natl. Acad. Sci. U.S.A. 60:* 630–635.

[WITH] J. D. Karkas and R. Rudner. Separation of *B. Subtilis* DNA Into Complementary Strands. II. Template Functions and Composition as Determined by Transcription with RNA Polymerase. *Ibid.*, 915–920.

[WITH] R. Rudner and J. D. Karkas. Separation of *B. Subtilis* DNA Into Complementary Strands. III. Direct Analysis. *Ibid.*, 921–922.

[WITH] S. Morisawa. On the Bias of the Distribution of the 2'-O-Methylribonucleotide Constituents of Yeast Transfer RNA. *Biochim. Biophys. Acta 169:* 285–296.

1969

[WITH] L. C-Y. Cheong. Native and Denatured DNA of Phage T_3 and of *E. Coli* B as Templates for RNA Polymerase. *Nature 221:* 1144–1146.

[WITH] E. Cassuto. Role of Base-Pairing in the Control of an Enzyme Reaction. *Proc. Natl. Acad. Sci. U.S.A. 62:* 808–812.

[WITH] R. Rudner and J. D. Karkas. Separation of Microbial Deoxyribonucleic Acids into Complementary Strands. *Proc. Natl. Acad. Sci. U.S.A. 63:* 152–159.

[WITH] A. F. Wu. *L*-Uridine: Synthesis and Behavior as Enzyme Substrate. *Ibid.*, 1222–1226.

The Paradox of Biochemistry. *Columbia Forum 12:* 15–18. **G**

[WITH] L. C-Y. Cheong. Complementary Fractions of Denatured DNA of Coliphage T3 as Templates for Transcription. *Proc. Natl. Acad. Sci. U.S.A. 64:* 241–246.

[WITH] H. Türler. Studies on the Nucleotide Arrangement in Deoxyribonucleic Acids. XII. Apyrimidinic Acid from Calf-Thymus Deoxyribonucleic Acid: Preparation and Properties. *Biochim. Biophys. Acta 195:* 446–455.

[WITH] H. Türler and J. Buchowicz. Studies on the Nucleotide Arrangement in Deoxyribonucleic Acids. XIII. Frequency and Composition of Purine Isostichs in Calf-Thymus Deoxyribonucleic Acid. *Ibid.*, 456–465.

1970

Vortwort zu einer Grammatik der Biologie. Hundert Jahre Nukleinsäureforschung. *Experientia 26:* 810–816. G

[WITH] J. D. Karkas and R. Rudner. Template Properties of Complementary Fractions of Denatured Microbial Deoxyribonucleic Acids. *Proc. Natl. Acad. Sci. U.S.A. 65:* 1049–1056.

[WITH] E. Cassuto and M. Stein. Complementarity of RNA Produced by Enzymic Transcription of Native and Denatured *B. subtilis* DNA. *Proc. Natl. Acad. Sci. U.S.A. 66:* 197–203.

[WITH] E. Cassuto. Translational Complementarity of RNA Transcripts of Native and Denatured *B. subtilis* DNA. *Ibid.*, 863–868.

[WITH] E. F. Brunngraber. Nucleoside Phosphotransferase from Carrot. Kinetic Studies and Exploration of Active Sites. *J. Biol. Chem. 245:* 4825–4831.

[WITH] E. F. Brunngraber. Transferase from *Escherichia coli* Effecting Low-Energy Phosphate Transfer to Nucleosides and Nucleotides. *Proc. Natl. Acad. Sci. U.S.A. 67:* 107–112.

Nekotorye Zamechaniya o Kontseptsii Matritsy, in: *Funktsional'-naya Biokhimiya Kletochnykh Struktur,* Nauka, Moscow, 232–237. C-S

1971

Preface to a Grammar of Biology, *Science 172:* 637–642. T/70

[WITH] R. B. Goldberg. On the Control of the Induction of β-Galactosidase in Synchronous Cultures of *Escherichia coli. Proc. Natl. Acad. Sci. U.S.A. 68:* 1702–1706.

[WITH] J. G. Stavrianopoulos and J. D. Karkas. Nucleic Acid Polymerases of the Developing Chicken Embryo: A DNA Polymerase Preferring a Hybrid Template. *Ibid.*, 2207–2211.

1972

[WITH] J. D. Karkas and J. G. Stavrianopoulos. Action of DNA Polymerase I of *Escherichia coli* with DNA-RNA Hybrids as Templates. *Proc. Natl. Acad. Sci. USA. 69:* 398–402.

[WITH] J. G. Stavrianopoulos and J. D. Karkas. DNA Polymerase of Chicken Embryo: Purification and Properties. *Ibid.*, 1781–1785.

[WITH] J. G. Stavrianopoulos and J. D. Karkas. Mechanism of DNA Replication by Highly Purified DNA Polymerase of Chicken Embryo. *Ibid.*, 2609–2613.

[WITH] R. Rodgers. Nucleoside Phosphotransferase from Carrot: Chemical Characterization and Investigation of Catalytic Sites. *J. Biol. Chem. 247:* 5448–5455.

1973

Bitter Fruits from the Tree of Knowledge: Remarks on the Current Revulsion from Science. *Persp. Biol. Med. 16:* 486–502. **G**

[WITH] E. F. Brunngraber. A Nucleotide Phosphotransferase from *Escherichia coli*. Purification and Properties. *Biochem. 12:* 3005–3012.

[WITH] E. F. Brunngraber. Nicotinamide Adenine Dinucleotide as Substrate of the Nucleotide Phosphotransferase from *Escherichia coli. Ibid.*, 3012–3016.

[WITH] J. G. Stavrianopoulos. Purification and Properties of Ribonuclease H of Calf Thymus. *Proc. Natl. Acad. Sci. U.S.A. 70:* 1959–1963.

[WITH] R. Milanino. A Purine Polyribonucleotide Synthetase from *Escherichia coli. Ibid.*, 2558–2562.

[WITH] L. Margulies. Survey of DNA Polymerase Activity During the Early Development of *Drosophila melanogaster. Ibid.*, 2946–2950.

1974

Bittere Früchte vom Baume der Erkenntnis: Anmerkungen zur gegenwärtigen Ablehnung der Naturwissenschaften. *Scheidewege 4:* 326–345. **T/73**

Building the Tower of Babble. *Nature 248:* 776–779. **G**

1975

Bemerkungen über Evolution aus der Sicht des Biochemikers. *Nova Acta Leopoldina 42:* 247–252. **C-G**

A Fever of Reason. *Annual Review of Biochemistry 44:* 1–18. **C-L**

[WITH] Jürgen Dahl. Text of an Interview: Die Schrift ist nicht der Text — Genetik und Evolution. *Scheidewege 5:* 56–66. **G**

Variationen über Themen der Naturforschung nach Worten von Pascal und anderen. *Ibid.*, 365–398. **G**

Voices in the Labyrinth: Dialogues Around the Study of Nature. I. Amphisbaena; II. Ouroboros. *Persp. Biol. Med., 18:* 251–285. — III. Chimaera; Epilogue in the Labyrinth. *Ibid.*, 313–330. **L**

[WITH] J. D. Karkas and L. Margulies. A DNA Polymerase from Embryos of *Drosophila melanogaster*. Purification and Properties. *J. Biol. Chem. 250:* 8657–8663.

Profitable Wonders. A Few Thoughts on Nucleic Acid Research. *The Sciences 15:* 21–26. **G**

A Few Remarks on the Impact of Biochemistry on Genetics. *Stadler Genetics Symposium, 7,* University of Missouri, Columbia, Mo., 9–14. **G**

Archaisches Lächeln. *Scheidewege 5:* 227. **L**

Türkenflucht. *Ibid.*, 228. **L**

Bemerkungen. *Ibid.*, 229–234; 487–490. **L**

1976

Acidi nucleici. *Enciclopedia del Novecento*. Vol. 1, 1–18.　**C-R**

Beliberdinskoye Stolpotvorenie, Khimiya i Zhizn', Nr. 1, 45–49.　**T/74**

Initiation of Enzymic Synthesis of Deoxyribonucleic Acid by Ribonucleic Acid Primers. *Progress in Nucleic Acid Research*, Academic Press Inc., New York, *16:* 1–24.　**C-R**

[WITH] J. G. Stavrianopoulos and A. Gambino-Giuffrida. Ribonuclease H of Calf Thymus: Substrate Specificity, Activation, Inhibition. *Proc. Natl. Acad. Sci. U.S.A. 73:* 1087–1091.

[WITH] J. G. Stavrianopoulos. An Assay of Ribonuclease H, Endoribonucleases, and Phosphatases. *Ibid.*. 1556–1558.

Bemerkungen. *Scheidewege 6:* 209–211.　**L**

Nützliche Wunder. *Ibid.*, 309–322.　**T/75**

Review of R. Olby, The Path to the Double Helix. *Persp. Biol. Med. 19:* 289–290.　**G**

Triviality in Science: A Brief Meditation on Fashions. *Ibid.*, 324–333.　**G**

An Informal View of Science Funding in the United States. *Trends Biochem. Sci. 1:* N51–N52.　**G**

Late Evening in Berlin. *Ibid.*, N171–N172.　**L**

On the Dangers of Genetic Meddling. *Science 192:* 938–940.　**G**

1977

Stimmen im Labyrinth. Dialoge über die Erforschung der Natur. *Scheidewege 7:* 83–103.　**T/75**

Kommentar im Proszenium. Einige Bemerkungen über die Grenzen der Naturwissenschaften. *Ibid.*, 131–152.

Trivialität in der Naturwissenschaft: eine kurze Meditation über Moden. *Ibid.*, 327–340.　**T/76**

A Few Remarks Regarding Research on Recombinant DNA. *Man and Medicine 2:* 78–82.　**G**

Experimenta Lucifera. *Nature 266:* 780–781.　**G**

Contribution to Forum on "Recombinant DNA." *Chem. & Eng. News 55* (May 30): 32–35; 41–42.　**G**

[WITH] E. F. Brunngraber. Nucleotide Phosphotransferase of *Escherichia coli:* Purification by Affinity Chromatography. *Proc. Natl. Acad. Sci. U.S.A. 74:* 3226–3229.

[WITH] E. F. Brunngraber. Action of Nucleotide Phosphotransferase of *Excherichia coli* on Nicotinamide Riboside and Nicotinamide Mononucleotide. *Ibid.*, 4160–4162.